PRAISE FOR
AUDREY CARLAN

"FIVE STAR REVIEW! I recommend this book to anyone looking for a sweet, fierce love story. It takes a lot to write an original story that takes twists and turns you won't see coming."
~Abibliophobia Anonymous Book Reviews Blog

"Damn Audrey did it again! Made me smile, made me laugh & made me cry with her beautiful words! I am in love with these books."
~Hooks & Books Book Blog

"I have a new addiction. I count down the days until the next Audrey Carlan's Calendar Girl book releases as soon as I am finished with the current one. I am loving the journey that Mia is on. It's seductive and powerful - captivating."
~Maine Book Mama Book Blog

Sacred Serenity

A LOTUS HOUSE NOVEL: BOOK TWO

This book is an original publication of Audrey Carlan

This is a work of fiction. Names, characters, places, and incidents either are the product of the author's imagination or are used fictitiously, and any resemblance to actual persons, living or dead, business establishments, events, or locales is entirely coincidental. The publisher does not assume any responsibility for third-party websites or their content.

Paperback ISBN: 978-1-943893-11-9
PRINTED IN THE UNITED STATES OF AMERICA

Sacred Serenity

A LOTUS HOUSE NOVEL: BOOK TWO

AUDREY CARLAN

WATERHOUSE PRESS

DEDICATION

Emily Hemmer

*I have chosen to dedicate this book to you,
because there is no other person in my life
who understands the true passion and desire
it takes to create beauty through your words.*

*Thank you for being my book sister.
My love to you in all things.*

Namaste

CHAPTER ONE

SACRAL
C H A K R A

For centuries, the practice of yoga has been paired with many types of yoga disciplines. The act of Tantric yoga, in particular, pairs well with the aligning and opening of each chakra, especially the second, or sacral, chakra. Known as the source for passion and pleasure, this chakra is the wellspring of our feelings, enjoyment, and sensuality. It is located in the pelvic/spleen area on the body.

AMBER

"Tantric sex? You of all people chose Tantric sex as your final project for your human sexuality course?" Genevieve's platinum shoulder-length hair shimmered and bounced when she maneuvered around the yoga studio. Her rounded belly seemed to lead her through the room as she lit candles.

I helped her set up bolsters and yoga blocks that would

assist her prenatal yoga clientele with the myriad positions she'd lead them through during her class.

"Why is that so hard to believe?" I said, not able to avoid a hint of sarcasm in my tone.

My best friend in all the world stopped, rested her hands on her seven-months-pregnant belly, and rubbed in a circular motion. The baby was either kicking or pushing one of his mother's body parts into an uncomfortable position.

Genevieve sighed and pressed on one side of her belly. "I don't know. It seems odd that someone who..." She lowered her voice and glanced around the room. Class hadn't started yet, nor was it supposed to for another twenty minutes. Not a soul in sight.

"Who hasn't had sex?" I said succinctly. My being a virgin was not a secret. It was a choice, a commitment I'd made not just because of my faith in God—although I held Him in the highest regard—but because of my faith in myself and in my will.

She nodded. "Yes." The word came out as a hiss. "It makes sense for you to study the behavior of sex in society or how it pertains to your medical discipline, but the Tantric practice as a whole can be overtly sensual in nature. Physically, spiritually..." She let out a breath. "I mean, how do you plan to truly know what the practice of Tantric sex is without ever experiencing it?"

I set my hands on my hips and glared. "Just because I haven't had sex doesn't mean I haven't studied every facet of the human body. Heck, Vivvie, I'm certain I know more about how to trigger a vaginal orgasm than ninety percent of the population actively experiencing coitus."

Genevieve rolled her eyes and took a deep breath. "Well,

what do you want from me? You usually don't go into detail about your coursework. So why now?"

I grinned. "I need your help."

She leaned her head to the side and locked her dark gaze to mine while she unrolled a yoga mat into position. "How so?"

"Get the Tantric yoga teacher to allow me to sit in on his class and observe."

She blinked as though waiting for me to say something more. "That's it? I mean, he's pretty easy to talk to. Why not ask Dash yourself?"

Dash.

The name so perfectly fit the man it belonged to. He was a dash of everything any woman in her right mind would drool over—tall with an incredible form, dark blond hair, and the most stunning caramel-colored eyes I'd ever seen. Those eyes could have been cast from the very amber stone I was named for. I'd only ever seen him from a distance, which was self-imposed because he had this essence, a unique masculine aura that scrambled my mind and made me feel like a teenage girl again. Not a twenty-two-year-old woman who'd just been accepted into the elite UC Berkeley-UCSF Joint Medical Program on a full scholarship.

I'd had my pick of medical schools—Stanford, Irvine—but I couldn't leave my aging grandparents. They'd taken care of me since my mother died giving birth to me. I owed it to them to be present in their lives through the remainder of their days. And Genevieve was the closest thing to a sibling I'd ever have. My relationship with her was one I cherished and held above all others. She knew *me* and accepted my life choices in a way very few did. I didn't want to leave San Francisco, my grandparents, or Genevieve—especially since her son was due in a couple months.

I cracked my neck to relieve the tension that built at the mere thought of Dash Alexander. "I sent a couple emails and put a note in his staff box here. He returned an email, stating that his classes were private, and he wouldn't want to spook his clientele with an outsider watching them."

Vivvie grinned wide. "I can see that. The course is... pretty *involved*." She settled on those two words as if they were molasses coating a thick slice of Focaccia bread. Sumptuous and divine when paired together.

"That's why I'm here. I need you to talk to him. You have a rapport with him. Besides, haven't you assisted in his class before?"

Genevieve widened her eyes. "I have and don't you *dare* mention it to Trent." She rubbed her belly where said man's child gestated. "He'll lose his mind all over again if he's reminded about my stint with Dash."

My face heated and I clenched my teeth. "Did you have a fling with Dash?" An uncomfortable prickling sensation licked up my spine. Vivvie would notice any subtle change in my demeanor and jump on it like a child on a trampoline. I clenched my molars harder, trying to appear unaffected.

"No. Not really. Definitely not in the way you're thinking." She pushed her hair off her neck and fanned herself. "I mean, when you assist his class there is some heavy petting, but it's not like we had sex. I will say I had to take a cold shower after the class to ward off any latent emotions. That man has a gift. The way he opens chakras as if he's peeling back layers of an onion is intense. He gets right to the spicy part inside of you, and with a quickness I didn't expect." Vivvie fanned herself while a blush stole across her cheeks.

What I wouldn't have given to be the bearer of that blush. Or rather, to experience the man himself causing it.

I brushed my thick hair off my now sweaty neck and leveled my gaze at her. "Please, Vivvie. I need this. It's my last class before I start my medical school coursework in the fall. I've left it to the last possible semester because... Well, you know why. It's the one class I knew I'd have to delve into without experience. I want a perfect grade." Of course I was fibbing a little about my rationale, but she didn't need to know that.

Genevieve stood in front of me. Her belly bumped against mine and we both giggled. "I'll never get used to my size." She groaned.

I placed my hands over her bump to feel my soon-to-be nephew, trying to differentiate his little feet from his head and booty.

"Look, you're my best friend. My sister-from-another-mister. Of course, I'll get him to help you. You have to promise to be open-minded. In this course, the couples involved are there because they want a deeper connection to their mate and their higher selves. I know your own personal beliefs may differ, but try not to let that color your experience."

I ran my hands down to hers and clenched them. "I promise. I'll be open-minded and respectful."

She smirked, one eyebrow lifted in question before she huffed. "All right, I'll talk to him. Use my powers of persuasion to get him to cave."

"Powers of persuasion?" The mere suggestion that those powers involved something innately sexual or personal in nature sent my blood boiling.

"Yeah...guilt." She chuckled.

I snorted, and that boiling shifted to a simmer. *Jesus in heaven, I need to cool my jets.*

"Speaking of guilt...when are you going to put Trent out of his misery and marry the man?" I asked rather pointedly.

Genevieve groaned loudly and lifted her face to the sky. The ceiling was painted in vibrant rainbow swirls. When lying down on the mat in a supine position, I found the colors awe-inspiring, a serene place to let my mind wander while my body relaxed.

"Ugh, don't remind me. You know he asks me to marry him every single day?" She shook her head.

"And, again, why are you denying him and yourself the joy of matrimony? In a couple months, Viv, you're bringing his son into the world. You know how I feel about babies being born out of wedlock, seeing as I was one of them. You, on the other hand, do have a choice. You love Trent. He loves you. You're having his child. Why not prevent your child from going through the stigma of being a bast—"

"Don't you dare say it!" Vivvie cut me off with a pointy finger to the sternum.

Ouch!

"My child will *not* be a bastard. Don't put your holier-than-thou, Bible-thumping opinion on me right now. I know that my son will be raised with God's love whether he's born in or out of wedlock. We've already had this discussion, and I'll not have it again. I want Trent to marry me for *me* and to spend his life by my side because I'm the woman he wants to be with forever, not because I'm carrying his progeny."

This time I grumbled. "Can't you see that he worships the ground you walk on?"

She bit her lip and nodded. "I know he does. But is it

because I'm having his baby?"

I choked on my frustration. "No! Goodness gracious. You are one of the most intelligent, loving, and kind women I know, yet you can be so dim-witted when you don't want to see what's right in front of you! Marry the man already! Please! If not for yourself, do it for him, for the baby you're carrying." My voice rose with my conviction.

Genevieve pointed her red-painted index fingernail at me. "Stop. I already know what you think. And I will marry him. When the time is right." Her lips were pursed and her jaw hardened.

Sorry, God. I tried.

"Sorry," I said and meant it with my entire being. I prayed for her every night to find clarity, to heal from her parents' passing, to be strong for her siblings and those around her. And I prayed every night that she'd marry Trent Fox and save the baby from years of stereotypical garbage. Kids and adults alike could be all too cruel. I knew firsthand.

Genevieve scowled and then laughed. "Thank you. What you should focus on is yourself. Can't wait to hear what the big man upstairs is going think when you want to get freaky with Dash Alexander after one of his classes!" She threw out the statement, and her eyes seemed to twinkle in the track lighting above.

I opened and closed my mouth. "You know?" I gasped.

She snorted. "You have God...I have women's intuition. And my intuition has told me for the last couple years you've been hard-core crushing on Dash from afar. Probably the reason why you've avoided asking for access to his class in person."

Attempting to backtrack wasn't going to work in this

SACRED SERENITY

scenario. Besides, the Bible taught us to be honest and
forthcoming in all things. "Dash is a beautiful man. I won't
deny it." I lifted my chin and waited for her reply.

Genevieve grinned and glanced at something or someone
behind me. "Hey, Dash, you've got impeccable timing. We were
just talking about you." She smirked.

My entire body went stone cold. If someone so much
as touched me, I'd shatter into a thousand pieces and float
away. Inhaling a full breath, I turned around. There he was,
the single man who had inhabited every naughty thought I'd
had since the first time I saw him over two years ago. The one
man I envisioned when I pleasured myself in the wee hours of
the morning under my homemade quilt in my grandparents'
home.

Dash Alexander.

DASH

I grinned at the sinfully sexy brunette, arms crossed over my
chest. She thought I was beautiful. Interesting.

I'd seen Genevieve's best friend roaming around Lotus
House. Watched her in action, taking the classes here. Her
body was long and lean, perfect for the more complex *asanas,*
or yoga poses as the Westerners called them.

While I stood there, her green eyes shined like emeralds
as she assessed me. The catlike shape added to her allure. Only
that wasn't what made my knees quake. The thick, long, dark
chestnut-brown hair that she wore plainly, straight, and parted
down the middle, the length covering her ample breasts, had
all my attention. My guess was she didn't dye it either. The
color hadn't changed in the two years since I'd first seen her.

The natural hue glinted in the sunlight that streamed through an open window Genevieve had yet to close before class. What I wouldn't give to grasp a thick chunk in my fist, wrap it around my wrist, and tug her head back gently to feast on the long exposed column of her neck.

Her simple earthiness appealed to the deepest part of a man. The instinct to hold and protect this woman was a powerful aphrodisiac. Those feelings plowing to the surface were rare for me, but I'd learned long ago, through my Tantric practice, not to deny or hide how I reacted to those around me. In this case, a desire born of aesthetics wasn't the only thing sending a flushed excitement through my veins. Her energy called to me. The magnetic field around her sizzled and threaded with mine in the most sensual of caresses, making me want to wrap my arms around her and keep her close, bathe in her true spirit.

My cock thickened and stirred, awakening after being too long at rest. I let my hands drop into clasped ease in front of my groin. No need to scare off the little bird. As it was, I could see her form fluttering, cowering under the weight of my appreciative gaze, making ready to fly away. I wanted her to do the opposite. Respond to me instead, the way a proud swan would. I wanted to set my gaze upon not only her bare body but also her unhindered soul.

Though the woman stood tall, at least five foot ten, her shoulders curved inward in my presence, as though she was silently submitting to me, or worse, was afraid. I held out my hand and plastered a calming smile over my features.

"Dash Alexander. I don't believe we've been formally introduced."

She looked at my hand and, as if readying for battle,

straightened her shoulders, firmed her spine, and clasped my hand in a steady grip. Grinning, I yanked on her hand and caught her off guard, which was my intent. When she bumbled into my chest, I wrapped my arm around her waist and quickly kissed one cheek and then the other. I allowed myself the barest touch of my lips along the silky skin from her cheek to her temple, where I laid another soft press of lips. She gasped, and that soft intake of air along with the tightening of her fingers spoke volumes to my senses.

This scared little bird wanted me. She didn't just think I was handsome. No, her attraction sparkled along her body like a fine gossamer mist. The scent of strawberries enveloped me. I squeezed her body to me in the smallest of embraces before grudgingly stepping back, putting a more appropriate distance between us.

Her eyes were glassy and unfocused. She shook her head and blinked several times. "Uh... Amber... Amber St. James."

I smiled and cupped her cheek. She leaned in. A wave of male pride rushed through my chest. I caressed one high cheekbone with my thumb, appreciating the blush that pinked them both. Her face was free of makeup, just the way I preferred a woman. Raw beauty.

"Happy to meet you, Amber."

For long moments, we stared at one another, our bodies' energy reaching for one another in a cosmic way I was used to experiencing in my classes, but not privately.

"Dash, glad you're here." Genevieve interrupted our visual seduction of one another. "Amber is premed and needs to learn all she can about the practice of Tantric sex for her human sexuality coursework. As you're our resident guru, I thought you could help her out."

I turned my attention to Genevieve. She pouted and put her hand over her rounded belly, reminding me of the debacle I'd caused between her and her mate half a year ago. Payback could sometimes be a pain in the neck. Then an idea formed. An absolutely brilliant one, and not only would it help Amber with her coursework, it would solve a major issue for me.

I stared at Amber and then at Genevieve, whose hands were clasped in a prayer pose at heart center—only this was no prayer. She was downright begging. Her lips moved in a "Please, please, please," silent request.

"All right. On one condition."

Amber's green gaze brightened exponentially, her lips tipping up into a shy smile. "Name it." Her voice was filled to the brim with gratitude, and I loved it. In fact, I wanted far more of it and looked forward to the time where I'd feel that gratitude surrounding me in a far more primal connection.

Flashes of her in myriad Tantric sexual poses zipped across my mind. Amber in yab-yum position sitting in my lap, face-to-face with me until I tipped her head back, allowing all that hair to dangle and tickle my thighs. I'd worship her breasts, plucking her nipples into tight little berries. Our sacral and root chakras would meld in perfect alignment as I plunged into her, awakening the lioness hiding under the lamb's wool she wore.

"How better to observe the class than through participation?"

Two simultaneous gasps rang through the cavernous room until Genevieve spoke. "Dash...um, there's probably something you should know about..."

"In what manner are you suggesting I participate exactly?" Amber squinted, and she crossed her arms over her chest. Classic defensive posture. I hadn't expected that. This woman, who had just admitted to being attracted to me, who had responded instantly in my arms, didn't seem altogether eager to physically bond. Perhaps she had a significant other? A trail of prickling heat built in my chest and expanded out.

Jealousy. Now that was a new one for me. I couldn't recall the last time I was jealous of a partner—potential, current, or past, much less a woman I didn't even know.

I lowered my voice so as not to sound too forceful or demanding. "My assistant bailed again. It seems I can't keep a single one for more than an eight-week session," I admitted begrudgingly.

Her brows pinched together. "Is that how long a normal Tantra course is? Eight weeks?"

I nodded. "Yes, though some couples like to repeat it and work in detail on specific sections of the workshops."

"Would I have to assist you naked?"

It was impossible not to laugh. Genevieve and I both burst into unbridled laughter at the delicate woman before us. She was beyond the pale. Her innocence positively emanated from every pore.

"Hardly, though I definitely won't deny the concept appeals to me...greatly."

I watched as her breathing became audible, slow inhales and longer exhales. There was a pattern to her breathing, which indicated to me that she'd practiced this technique before. Probably in other more strenuous or uncomfortable situations. And that's when I felt like a heel. There were so many misconceptions about the practice of Tantra on the whole and the workshop was titled *Tantric Sex & Yoga for Couples*—it made sense that she'd have preconceived notions about the content.

Noticing her discomfort, I stepped forward and laid my hand on her shoulder. I wasn't sure if the act was to ground me or her, although touching her definitely made me feel better. "All of the participants wear standard yoga attire, though I recommend some looser clothing in specific areas so that certain parts of the body can be touched or caressed. All in areas not considered overtly sexual, I assure you."

Amber bit down on her plump, pink bottom lip. My dick caught the movement and rose up from its resting place within my loose pants. Once again, I locked my hands at the wrists in front of my groin.

"I'll do it," she declared with complete confidence.

Genevieve's mouth opened and she blinked slowly. "Amber, honey, you do not know what you're committing to."

That's when my gaze shot to my friend. "Are you suggesting that I'd do something inappropriate?"

She groaned and put her hands on her hips. "No, I'm not. But Amber is..." Her dark eyes locked onto what was fast becoming my current obsession. "Amber's sweet."

Now that we both could agree on. So sweet I positively wanted to lick every morsel of her skin and find all the sugary goodness hidden beneath her clothing.

Amber sighed. "Jeez, thanks, Mom. You want to send me to my room for being out of line?" she scoffed.

"Amber, you know I'm just trying to protect you." Genevieve did sound like a mother hen, but what she said rankled.

"From who?" I chimed in. "Me?" Shock tinged with frustration swirled in the air around our threesome.

"No. It's just... Ugh. I'm pregnant. I don't know what I'm

saying. You two can deal with it. Amber, I warned you. Dash, I warned you. Now, can the two of you take the rest of your conversation to the break room? You're messing up my juju." The skin around Genevieve's eyes and cheeks tightened as she pursed and looked away. The natural pearl color of her skin made her bright red lipstick pop even more while she rubbed her belly in large circles.

"Come on, Amber. How about I buy you a cup of coffee?"

Amber tilted her head down and nodded, her shoulders curving inward again. "Sure. Thanks."

I stopped in front of her and tapped at her chin with a single finger until she lifted her gaze. "Don't walk with your head down. The world should bask in your beauty. They can't do that if you're staring at your feet."

CHAPTER TWO

Bound Angle Pose
(Sanskrit: Baddha Konasana)

Sit comfortably with the seat bones touching the mat. Bend the knees and bring the feet toward the pelvis so that the soles of both feet are touching, creating an energy network. You can clasp the feet and then, on an exhale, slowly bend forward, leading with the chest. This classic pose will open the hips and release tension in the lower back.

AMBER

Hand-in-hand, Dash led me through Lotus House and out to the street. He turned to the left and ushered me through the doors of Sunflower Bakery. There was a line of seven people. With Sunflower though, people got used to it. I've never walked into this establishment and not had to wait at least fifteen minutes to order. The place was always packed. I appreciated the cheery glow, sunflower motif, and jaw-dropping smells that dazzled the senses to the point I didn't mind waiting. Standing next to Dash Alexander while waiting was not a hardship, either.

My stomach growled as I glanced at the daily spread. It changed each morning. The Jackson clan who ran the bakery tended to make pastries and baked goods based on their moods. Today, it seemed they were influenced by the Danes. I leaned forward and rested one hand on the glass while I read the little cards next to each pastry: blueberry, peach, strawberry, apple, cinnamon, vanilla cream, chocolate cream, hazelnut cream-filled and more—a veritable cornucopia. I chuckled and decided I'd go with the cinnamon and apple. They'd go amazingly well with a vanilla latte.

I licked my lips and then heard a soft groan as a warm hand settled at the small of my back. "Do you always look at food as though you're going to devour it in one go?"

I looked up and our gazes locked. "I'm sorry?" My belly growled again.

Dash crowded against my side and close to my ear. "Don't be. I love a woman who can appreciate carnal pleasures in such a way. Gives me hope."

I shifted my head to the side and assessed his overconfidence. "Hope? Hope for what?"

He smirked, and the sexiest dimple appeared on the right side of his jaw. I refrained from licking my lips, warring with the desire to kiss that dimple.

"Hope for our future." His eyes positively danced while his strong jaw, messy hair, and the simmering way he looked at me all added to his swoon-factor.

Our future. Good Lord above.

A warm wave rose from my toes up through my body. My face had to be flaming red. He was hitting on me? Dash Alexander. The man who starred in all of my late-night fantasies was flirting. With me. Boring. Homely. OCD student. Girl next door. Amber St. James.

"I'm sorry, Dash. I don't believe I understand. What do you mean?" I had to ask. There was no getting around it. My mind would replay his words ad nauseam if I didn't clarify his intent.

He grinned, and that drop-dead sexy dimple appeared again. I wanted to kiss it. Lift up on my toes and press my lips to the small indentation.

"You will. When the time is right."

Of course, as fate would have it, the line cleared and we stood at the counter.

"What's up, Doc?" Dara Jackson greeted me. Not only was she the daughter of the couple who owned the bakery, but she was also the meditation teacher at Lotus House. I'd taken her course during the dreaded finals weeks in college for my bachelor's. She often helped me relax and find some perspective on my studies.

"Doc?" Dash asked.

I rolled my eyes. "Not yet. Only a few more *years* of medical school."

Dara's brown sugar-colored skin shined right along with her smile. Her piercing blue eyes steadied on me. "Yes, but Genevieve has been going on and on about how you scored a full ride to that awesome medical school. Girl, bring it here!" She held up her hand, and I smacked it five. "Whoop! Now that's what I'm talking about. We need a doctor running around here. With the new AcroYoga class going in, I'm certain we'll need our own on-call doctor."

I laughed heartily. "Not that kind of doctor."

Her brows came together. "Any doctor is better than none. Those padded mats only go so far. And I hear the Italian stallion, Nick Salerno, can't keep up with kissing his clientele's boo-boos." She made a sound best described as a snort and a laugh. On her, it worked. When a woman was God's gift to mankind like Dara and Genevieve, they could make piggy noises and men would still fall at their feet.

"All right, enough gabbing. What do you want to eat and drink so we can discuss the particulars of assisting the course?" Dash nosed his way into our chitchat.

Dara's eyes widened to the size of giant moons. "You're going to assist the Tantric couples' class?" Her smile turned into a knowing smirk. "This will be very interesting. You gonna behave?" She turned her attention to Dash.

He frowned. "Why is it that you're the second woman today that believes I'd dishonor or disrespect any assistant in my class?"

Dara put her hand on Dash's and smiled softly.

Her gesture made the back of my neck prickle and itch.

"Dash, honey, you're one of the most sexual and sexy, *available* teachers we have. Every woman wants you to disrespect them in one of your hot, sweaty, tangled-up-in-one-another's-bodies courses, but I thought you wouldn't allow anyone that's not serious about the practice to participate." She turned to me. "Just surprised you're the one he ended up with, Doc. You know, being a medical-type chick and not a yoga teacher."

I crossed my arms over my chest. Both Dash and Dara clocked the movement. "It's for my human sexuality coursework." Not that I needed to explain, but I didn't want her to get the wrong idea. I especially didn't want Dash to think I had any concerns about assisting. Though it did worry me how many people had left the course. Something I'd definitely need to ask him about.

"Oh, well, that makes sense. I'm sure you'll have a very *enlightening* experience." She grinned and finally took our order.

Dash ordered a couple donuts and a peach Danish with a large Columbian coffee. I ordered an apple and a cinnamon Danish with a latte. He paid and refused repeatedly when I tried to pay for my half. Then he led me over to a table in the far corner where we'd have a bit more privacy.

Dara's words kept running through my mind.

"Can I ask you a question?"

He smiled. "I'd be concerned if you didn't." His butterscotch eyes hinted at mirth.

"Why is it that you can't keep an assistant for more than one course?" I bit into the Danish and fresh, hot apples exploded on my tongue. The sticky substances dribbled onto my lip. Before I could lick it away, Dash used his thumb to sweep the sugary confection across my lips and into my mouth. I sucked on the tip of his thumb, and his nostrils flared as he watched my mouth. Then he slowly put that same thumb into his own mouth and licked it clean.

Holy mother of God. I clenched my thighs as my center became slick. With that one touch, my body was readying for something far more salacious. The scientific principle of cause and effect was definitely working in this female body at the moment.

Dash inhaled and exhaled slowly before wiping his mouth and hand with a napkin. "The course can be intense."

I tilted my head to the side. "How so?"

He bit down on his bottom lip and scooted his chair closer to mine so he could lean even farther into my personal space. More heat flooded between my thighs when I caught a whiff of his unique male scent. Mint and eucalyptus mixed with something darker, richer, headier, and masculine.

His voice, already smooth as dark chocolate, lowered to something more suggestive. "It's better if I show you. That way you can form your own opinions."

"Give me a hint then?"

Dash exhaled audibly, his breath tingled against my cheek. His nearness was warm and created a comfortable cove that was intimate in ways I'd not experienced before with the opposite sex. Then again, I hadn't experienced much with men since my head was always stuck in a textbook.

He took a huge bite of one of his donuts, chewing slowly as he watched me squirm in my seat. Racy images ran through my mind as I thought of the many possible reasons why a person wouldn't want to work with him anymore. He shrugged and looked out the bakery window facing the street.

"Sometimes my assistant felt things that I didn't share. As I said, the course work is deeply personal, and when two physical bodies and minds come together in such a way, feelings can and usually do occur. Those feelings were not reciprocated by me, which caused a bit of dissention between me and my assistant."

I rolled what he said around in my mind.

"So what you're saying is they fell in love with you?" I

asked him point blank. No need to mince words. We were both adults.

He winced and lifted his head. "I won't go so far as to assume that, but they definitely left with stronger feelings than what I was willing to return."

"But not with Genevieve?" I not only wanted confirmation of this fact, I *needed* it in order to continue. Following girl code, I would never, ever, *ever* put myself in a situation to have any type of romantic relationship with a man who used to be with my bestie.

On hearing Genevieve's name, his frown turned upside down. "No, Genevieve and I were strictly friends. She was probably the best assistant I ever had, only..." His words fell off.

This time, I smiled huge. Knowing Trent and his crazy alpha me-Tarzan-you-Jane-type mentality when it came to Genevieve, it made sense that he wouldn't want his woman assisting a class known for having sexual overtones. "Trent."

He nodded. "Yeah, Trent. But seriously, unless you're mated to the person assisting, it's probably better to teach a course with someone you can stay friends with or have new assistants regularly so that those types of feelings don't crop up."

Sitting taller in my chair, I focused on him and crossed my arms over my chest. "Well, you don't have to worry about that with me. I'm focused solely on the scholarly information I'm going to glean from this course so that I can offer my professor an incredible final report."

He grinned. "So you think you're going to be able to separate your mind from your heart?"

"Absolutely." The words came across confident and firm. Exactly as I wanted them to.

On that note, he stood up and grabbed our empty plates and napkins, preparing to take them to the garbage. "We'll see." He winked, leaving me confused and a little off kilter.

DASH

"Dash, my husband and I are so excited to finally get into your class. We've been on the wait list for half a year!" My client exclaimed happily, hands at her chest as if she'd finally received the gift she'd waited all year for. I relished in the fact that people were eager to take my class. When minds were open, so were their abilities to unite with their partner on more than the physical plane. Enlightenment and connection were essentially the purposes of the course as a whole.

I smiled and patted Rose on the shoulder. "Your enthusiasm is fantastic. I hope it's contagious." I caught a whiff of strawberries on the hint of a breeze that tingled against my shoulder. Closing my eyes, I grounded myself once more, turned around, and practically swallowed my tongue. "Excuse me, Rose, my assistant just arrived."

Amber set down her bag and pulled off her scrubs. Then she proceeded to chuck her doctor-in-training garb, which left her in only a pair of tight, black Spandex workout shorts and a teal tank. I stared as she removed her socks and folded everything into a neat pile. Then she pulled her hair out of its ponytail, and I had to physically choke back the groan that climbed its way up my throat when I saw all that thick hair tumble down her back. Christ! The woman had no idea how sensual her natural beauty was to a guy like me. Heck, to any guy. If she removed all her reservations and let the real woman underneath free, she'd have to beat men off with a stick.

She turned around completely, and our eyes met. I couldn't help it. I checked her out. Definitely in that sleazy, you've-got-a-great-body, will-you-hold-it-against-me way. Admittedly, it was a weak moment. Usually, I tamped down those base urges, especially when the object of my physical affection was standing in front of me. She stood with her hand on her lush hips and nipped-in waist, ample bosom heaving as if she'd just run a marathon to get here on time. Stunning.

"Dash?" Amber's head was tilted to the side. She hadn't missed my blatant ogling. Let her see. Dancing around my attraction to her would not serve me in life or in this class. In order for my charges to feel a deeper connection, I couldn't hide my own biological and emotional responses, or I'd be a hypocrite.

I smiled and walked over to Amber, who self-consciously plucked at her knotted fingers. "Am I dressed okay?" she asked nervously. "I came straight from lab, and I didn't want to be late. I'll try to be ready before, but sometimes I might have to just drop my clothes when I arrive." She bit her lip, and her eyes got wide as she realized what she'd said.

Being the type of man not to miss those subtle slips in human response, I jumped on it like a pillow-top California King mattress, taking in her length and curves without hiding my response. "Feel free to drop your clothes for me anytime, little bird. Any time."

That beautiful pink blush I liked colored her cheeks on a wave. Then she shook her head and straightened her spine.

"So what do I do?"

I couldn't help appreciating her lovely form from head to toe. Her body was ripe for the taking, and I wanted nothing more than to put my hands and mouth all over it. "You're already doing it. Have a seat, get comfortable, and I'll start class. Just follow my lead. If something feels uncomfortable, scratch your nose. Then you won't disrupt others, but I'll know to back off of something or to come back to it later so we can discuss. Sound good?"

She nodded and then sat down on one of the yoga mats I had laid out on the raised section of the room at the front of class. She chose the orange mat versus the purple mat I'd picked for her. That single choice was very telling.

A memory flitted into my mind. One where the co-owner of Lotus House Jewel Marigold was teaching a workshop on the chakras.

"Something as simple as the color you wear most or the color you are driven to surround yourself with, can determine what chakra you are most connected with. Even the color of the yoga mat you use can be telling. For example, I always choose a royal-blue mat, wear a lot of royal blue, drive a blue car, and surround myself with the color all the time. Why?" she asked the class.

"Because you are driven by the Vishudha or throat chakra in your daily life?" I answered in front of the room of thirty other aspiring yoga teachers during my training years ago.

Her smile not only lit me from within from pride, but also set the room aglow. "Exactly. I most identify with the throat chakra or Vishudha as it's called in Sanskrit. It suits my role as a teacher, professor, and scholar of the practice. Wouldn't you agree?"

I would and did. I found through her class and further study of the seven chakras and how they coincide with the body, mind, and spirit that I was most driven by the second chakra. The *Svadhisthana* or sacral chakra. Passion fueled me in all things, hence the reason why I now taught Tantric yoga and sex to couples who were interested in expanding their passions in and out of the bedroom.

Amber's choosing the orange mat, the very color of the second chakra, over the purple, which was a far more likely choice for most women, gave me a tiny speck of hope that perhaps once her inner *kundalini* or enlightened self was awakened, she too would be connected to the sacral chakra and driven by passion. There was no way in hell she wasn't blocked. Even the most inexperienced gurus could see the way she avoided touching and speaking out. Her clothing choices were baggy and boxy, an obvious sign that she's not in touch with her more feminine attributes, nor did she actively use those attributes to seek male attention. Something I hoped would change after eight weeks of training with me.

"Welcome, class. You all know me, as I've had personal one-on-one discussions with all of you prior to the start of today's first workshop. However, I want to introduce you to my assistant, Amber St. James. She is currently assisting to observe the practice and the class as her final project for a class at UC Berkeley. Amber will be following along as my partner, aiding me in showing you the finer points of tantra that require a mate. Any concerns?" I waited a full breath to ensure that none of my clients had a problem with her observing. I didn't anticipate any and was glad that no one spoke up.

"Okay then, I'm going to take you through a twenty- to thirty-minute hatha yoga routine to get our bodies in line with our physical selves and our breathing, or *pranayama* as it's called in Sanskrit, all working together."

While I took the class through a series of poses, Amber followed along like a true yogi. Obviously, she'd taken a lot of the classes here because she knew every pose by name and moved into each one fluidly, without the detailed directions I gave the rest of the class.

I ended the asana portion of the workshop with them in bound angle pose. I had the fifteen couples facing one another, their legs out in front of them with the soles of their feet touching. I instructed them to grasp their ankles and bend forward close enough so that their foreheads rested against one another.

Amber and I faced each other and paired off. The moment my forehead met hers, I closed my eyes. A spark of electricity buzzed against our skin where we touched. Then I told each couple to place their right hand on their partner's heart and hold their mate's hand over where they were being touched. It was a grounding technique. However, the instant I placed my hand just above Amber's heart, on the patch of slick skin above her breasts, her heart beat double time, sending my own into a rapid pace.

I whispered to her, "Look at me."

Her eyes shot open, and her breathing became erratic.

"Relax. Breathe with me. In for four beats through the nose and then out for four beats through the mouth."

She nodded and we breathed together. I could feel the heavy thud of her heart turn into an even thump after a few rounds of guided, measured breaths. Through breathing, she relaxed, closing her eyes once more.

Then the craziest thing happened. Something that had never happened—not once, not ever before with another partner—our heartbeats began to synchronize spontaneously.

Not only were we breathing evenly, our heartbeats matched.

The simple, extraordinary occurrence speared ribbons of heat down my arms and into my hand where it rested over her heart. My hand became fiery hot, the chakras in my palms swirling in dizzying circles. I blinked a few times and watched in awe as her eyes opened, and those green orbs blasted straight into my soul.

One thought flared in my mind as simple as flicking on a light switch.

Soul mate.

Spooked, I released our connection. Her head bobbed drowsily and her eyes opened, half-lidded while she blinked rapidly. I hopped up and walked through the room, pretending to assist the couples. Usually, I didn't need to assist through a simple breathing exercise, but I needed a moment to put my head together, and distance from the ethereal being waiting on the riser was priority. What the hell was that?

The zap of connection I'd had with Amber was far beyond anything I'd ever experienced with another human being. And I was including partners, friends, and past lovers. The ghost of her heartbeat still called to mine as I stood in the back of the class watching her take in each couple and write something down in a notebook she kept close enough to reach but hadn't yet used since we'd started class.

Cringing, I assessed her. She was relaxed, perfectly at peace as she sat on the stage writing in her notebook, whereas I was a maelstrom of doubt and insecurity, completely unusual responses from me. On the whole, confidence and the ability to center myself were traits I was proud of. But with this woman, the surprising jolt of a deeper union prevented me from being capable of centering my reactions.

How could I have felt something so unique and she not be affected? Perhaps I mistook the experience for something that wasn't there. Maybe I wanted something more to be there?

Exhaling all the air out of my lungs, I vowed to find those answers and soon.

CHAPTER THREE

SACRAL
CHAKRA

The sacral chakra is where you will find a spiritual energy center that is directly connected to happiness and self-confidence. With every good attribute there are negative ones. The second chakra can also be linked to greed, fear, and an uncontrollable desire for self-preservation.

AMBER

Dash barely looked at me as he instructed the class through the final points and gave them each a homework assignment over the next two days to practice synchronized breathing techniques. When the last person left, I grabbed my notebook and found him rolling up a mat in the farthest corner of the room.

"Hey, what's the point of synchronized breathing?" I

tapped my pen on the paper, waiting for his response.

He lifted his shoulders dramatically, as if he was taking an extra large breath. I watched in fascination as the muscles in his back bunched and shifted delectably. It almost made me sigh. After another breath, he tossed the mat he'd rolled into the woven basket where the others were stored.

"Why don't you tell me what your experience was?" he asked and then turned around to face me.

I thought back to when we sat facing one another. A sense of togetherness had come over me. "I didn't feel alone."

He smiled, rolled another mat, and placed it next to the others. "What else? What did you hear?"

Again, I scoured the experience with a mental toothbrush, moving over the finer, grittier points. "Your breathing and mine. It had an oceanic echo to it."

He nodded.

"And I felt warmth. Your body was so warm." While I spoke, my skin heated.

"As was yours. You carry a lot of energy within you. When you were letting it out, I could feel it tingling around us. Could you sense it?"

"Is that what that was? I had a moment where it felt as though a warm blanket had been placed over my shoulders."

His corresponding grin was huge. "Exactly. Now you're getting it."

I grinned and scribbled down what we'd talked about, noting the finer points with bullets.

- Unity
- Warmth
- Energy
- Breath = Life

"This is really great stuff, Dash. I can't wait for Friday's class." I scribbled more notes, trying to remember how the couple who'd sat in front of me moved through their practice. It was hard because, a lot of the time, I was solely focused on Dash. The practice demanded it, which, I guess, was the point—unite with a partner or, in my case, his assistant. He wasn't doing it to connect with me specifically, and I'd do well to remember that.

"About Friday's class, wear a sports bra, leaving your abdomen bare." He said this nonchalantly, the same way a stranger asks how you are, and the corresponding reply is always, "Fine."

A chill swept up my spine. "Why?"

He waggled his eyebrows, which confused me more. Was he playing with me or being serious? "Because I'll be touching your bare skin."

That I did not expect. I swallowed, my throat so dry it would give the California desert a run for its money. "Can you be more specific?" My voice cracked, and I cleared my throat of the tumbleweeds.

Dash licked his lips, and one blond eyebrow rose up into his hairline. "I'd rather you experience it organically, the same way the class will. It's more powerful if you are not anticipating my movements. Then your response will be honest."

"Honest response? Um, okay. But you're not gonna touch me in my...you know." I did a quick hand gesture to my breasts and lower half.

He crossed his muscled arms over his chest, his eyes flashed a startling sienna, and his bearing clearly screamed offended.

Shoot. Not what I was going for.

"We do a lot of touching in this class, but I will never, ever lay my hand on a woman anywhere she isn't comfortable. That's why we have the itchy nose signal."

Right. The nose signal. It never dawned on me to use it in today's class. Then again, I was more comfortable sitting with Dash, foreheads pressed together and hands touching, than I was curled up in a snuggly blanket on my grandparents' couch watching a game show. And I'd been doing that my entire life.

"Was touching your breastbone over your heart too much?" His head was cocked at an angle, waiting for my response.

I wanted to say I'd rather he'd cupped my breasts, but that would be the sexy dream vixen Amber St. James—the one I pretended to be alone in my bed, not the real-life me. In the daylight hours, I held strong to my conviction to save myself for marriage. For me, more so than for God. Because it's something I wanted. Most men, after a handful of dates and light petting, lost interest when I refused more. People didn't want to find their forever mate. They just wanted to bring their bodies together in the most intimate way as a means to an end. I wanted the end to be *forever,* and I planned to give that final boundary to the one man who loved me in every way possible. It would be my gift to my husband. Only he would ever have all of me, and that included my virginity.

Eventually, I shook my head. "No, it wasn't."

"And I never plan to push you too far." He stepped forward and cupped my cheek, his thumb tracing my cheekbone the same way he had yesterday. A thrill of heat whispered against my lower back. "There are so many ways I want to touch you, Amber, each with a promise of a deeply profound experience." He leaned closer, resting his forehead against mine. The act was more intimate than any gesture I'd expected. "Promise you'll trust me to take care of you."

I closed my eyes and focused on his minty breath, the scent of essential oils filling the air, but most importantly, his energy curling around me like a hug. "I'll try."

"That's all any man can ask. Now, I'm starving. You up for a sandwich at Rainy Day?" He pushed back, putting a good foot between our heads, but he wove his hand through the thick hair at my nape. I found myself nodding dumbly, not really hearing anything other than the whooshing sound in my ears that started the second he cinched his fingers at the roots of my hair. Even now, he was rhythmically tugging and releasing, massaging and tantalizing, an ounce of pain coupled with a tingle of pleasure. Sublime. A spiral of excitement zipped down my spine to settle hotly between my thighs. My center became heavy, and my clit throbbed.

Is this what women feel before they're ready to have sex?

I coughed and backed out of his hold quickly, my mind scrambled.

His brow tightened. "You okay?"

"Uh yeah, just hungry. Shall we go?" I asked, my throat going dry while other parts of me, more private parts, slickened.

"Lead the way." He held his hand out in front of me.

"No, that's okay. You go ahead," I offered, needing the distance.

He shook his head and got close once more. "If you don't walk ahead, I can't check out your fine ass. And that, little bird, would be a travesty."

Dash put his hands on my shoulders, turned me, and guided me ahead of him with a light nudge.

"Smokin' hot," he growled as I shimmied ahead of him

down the hall, my legs eating up the distance between our door and the one that led us to exit the building.

A sense of feminine pride filled my chest at his outburst, and I added a touch of sway to my hips. If he was going to look, I might as well give him a show.

"Jesus Christ," he muttered.

I frowned and stopped, firing him a pointed look over my shoulder. People hated being preached to, but I'd been raised not to take the Lord's name in vain. It rankled my nerves. Still, I needed to remember that everyone was different. Besides, his outburst was a direct reflection of his feelings about me. Well, about my body at least. He choked out a laugh. "What?" He smirked, and his square jaw tightened. Looking at him should be a crime. The exact temptation a girl like me shouldn't want.

"Enjoying the view?" I said with as much conviction as I could muster and waited for his reply. A burst of feminine pride caressed my skin and made my heart thump hard in my chest. This insanely hot man found me attractive. Me. Boring, book nerd, med student Amber St. James.

Dash slung an arm over my tense shoulders. "There's my proud swan." He nuzzled my cheek, and I almost fell to the floor.

My entire body was alight in sensation, awash with not only his scent but also his masculine essence. It practically caressed me. The feeling was overwhelming, the same way it had been when we'd touched one another's breastbone and synchronized our breathing with our heads pressed together... only *that* times about a thousand.

"I was wondering when she was going to surface. Interesting to see your feisty side come out."

"You were gawking at my bum and took the Lord's name

in vain. I was fighting my good and bad angels."

"Sounds like our first topic of conversation at lunch. Good and bad angels." He winked. "Come on, little bird, let's fly. Or in this case, let's walk." He slid his hand down my arm to my hand where he curled his fingers around mine and held tight... again.

He held my hand firmly with intent and purpose. The same way he'd led me to the bakery yesterday. This time, we walked out of Lotus House hand-in-hand down the street to the Rainy Day café like any normal couple.

I had no idea when I'd requested to observe his class that I'd be holding hands with my ultimate crush about to go on a lunch date.

Lord, help me not make a fool out of myself.

DASH

Coree, the strawberry-blond owner, took our order. She grinned when we entered holding hands. Instead of letting Amber go, I held on. I don't know what had come over me, but I didn't want to let her go. The more I touched her, the more I wanted to be near her and have her energy wash over mine.

Most of the time, I felt drained after a Tantric couples' class. Probably because when I'm working with an assistant, it's a one hundred percent hands off situation. Typically, I try my best to discourage any potential romantic feelings, even though that's what often happens. It's the nature of the subject matter. Tantra, in general, embodies coming together, being closer in all things. Breathing, physical form, mental connection... everything a person wants with their mate. Only with Amber, I wasn't pushing back against my natural inclination toward unity, I found myself moving toward it...with her. Her energy radiated like a soft glow around her body, giving off an almost supernatural resource that, in turn, energized and baffled me in equal measure. I'd not had this type of response to any assistant or other woman before.

"Hiya, Dash. You're looking spunky as usual." Coree smiled. The freckles across the bridge of her nose seemed sharper today.

I grinned and leaned against the edge of the counter. When I got closer to Coree, Amber's hand tightened infinitesimally as if she was pulling me back. I chanced a glance at my little bird. She was biting her lip and doing her best to look nonchalant, but I knew better. Jealousy was not a hard emotion to recognize. A man only had to look at the object of his affection while he talked up another lovely woman to see it. A carnal burst of excitement zipped through my chest and squeezed around my heart. I liked seeing Amber jealous. It gave me hope. Hope for more.

Intending to put Amber back into the comfortable place we'd been, I lifted up our clasped hands, brought hers close to my face, and kissed the inside of her wrist. She gasped the moment my lips touched her pale wrist, and gooseflesh rose across the skin of her arm. Just as I'd suspected. As much bravado as Ms. Doctor herself tried to put off, she was not unaffected by my touch.

"Just taking my assistant out to lunch after the start of a new workshop. Amber, this is Coree, one of the owners of Rainy Day." I didn't mention it, but I'd actually dated Coree for a few months last year. Aside from great sex, we had zero in common, which led to a mutual breakup. Now we were good friends.

Coree pursed her lips. "Uh-huh," she said and then furrowed her brows. "Don't I know you?" she asked Amber.

Amber nodded. "I've been in here a few times with my best friend, Genevieve. She works at Lotus House with Dash."

Coree scratched her head and tugged at her high ponytail. "Right, right. Well, it's good to see you looking so happy, Dash. I want that for you," Coree said in a tone that left absolutely no doubt as to the nature of our previous relationship. Then she placed one of her hands over the one I had on the counter and squeezed.

On that note, Amber yanked her hand back and held them in front of her. "Can we order?" she said, her tone more prickly than a porcupine.

Coree's eyes widened. "Of course. Sorry. Here I was chattering away when you probably have a date to get back to. Sorry, D. You want your favorite? My ham and Swiss on rye?"

I winced. Of course she'd know my favorite because I'd told her many times when we dated that it was incredible. I couldn't get enough of it. "Sure. Thanks, Coree. Amber?"

She glanced up at the board with the day's specials. Her jaw was hard, and her normally full pink lips were plastered into a flat line. "I'll have a half turkey and Swiss with a cup of potato soup. Thank you."

I found it interesting that she was responding the way a jealous lover would. I thought that beyond anything else proved she had stronger feelings for me than what she let on.

"A half?" I looped an arm around her shoulders and leaned into her space. "Is that going to be enough? I know from experience that the food here is special. You're going to want more of it."

Her entire body seemed to bristle, but I didn't let go.

"I'm sure you've had plenty in the past." Amber's gaze shot to Coree's.

My friend shivered. "Whew. That was cold. Positively frosty. I'll leave you two to get a table. I'll have Bethany bring the food out if it's all the same to you."

I let go of Amber and put both of my hands on the counter. "Coree...sweetie," I said, trying to smooth her ruffled feathers.

She shook her head and lifted a hand. "It's all good, D. Carry on with your date."

When I turned back to Amber, she was already across the room sitting in the farthest corner possible. Her legs were crossed, and her arms were folded over her chest. If I had a book on defensive postures, that image would be on the cover.

I made my way over to Amber, pulled out the chair, and sat heavily. "That was interesting."

Amber lifted her chin. "You take your dates here often then?"

"Is this a date?"

Her shoulders seemed to sag, and she let her arms fall to her lap. "I'm sorry. I thought this was something else. Why did you ask me to lunch?"

I grinned, ready to turn the tables on her. "We had our first class. I wanted to get your thoughts on the experience. Answer any more questions. And besides, why would I go to lunch alone when I can sit across from a beautiful woman and share a meal?"

Amber sat back and pushed her hair behind her ear before she leaned an elbow on the table. "So this is a working lunch?"

"Do you work for me?"

I'd have sworn it was like watching a balloon deflate. Amber's sparkling green eyes dulled, and her face went pale.

"Not really."

"Amber, I'm just joshing with you. This is most certainly a lunch date. I wanted to learn more about you. Plus, we're going to be working together for the next several weeks. We need to be able to communicate openly and honestly. Starting with why you were so flustered about Coree." I laid my hand over hers where it lay on the table. "I didn't expect that."

She jerked her hand away and sat as far back as she could, obviously preferring more distance between us. "I'm sorry. I don't know what you're talking about."

At that, I let my head fall backward and laughed. Loud. "Are you kidding? If you had been any more stone cold to my friend Coree you'd have been an iceberg!" I chuckled and propped both elbows on the table. "You obviously picked up that I had a relationship with her in the past. I'm just trying to figure out why that bothers you."

"It doesn't!" she countered instantly, her voice sharp as a knife edge.

I huffed. "Really? I thought with your religious nature, you'd be less likely to lie or blow smoke up my ass."

"Excuse me? I can't even believe you said that. Look, just because I'm faithful and live my life according to much of the scripture that *He* set forth doesn't mean I have a weird complex about it. Besides, you were all over that woman, leaning in, letting her touch you. It was embarrassing," she huffed.

Again, another bout of laughter ripped through me. I hadn't had this much fun bickering with a woman in ages. Damn, Amber was refreshing.

"Fine. Let's start over. Can we do that? I brought you here to share a meal. To learn more about you. I thought, perhaps, you'd like to learn more about me. Am I wrong?" I slanted my head and gave her my best puppy dog eyes. I'd been told by women all my life that my eyes were the way to their hearts. If it would help get me back in Amber's good graces, I'd work with what I had.

She inhaled deeply, licked her lips, and nodded. If she were mine, I'd have leaned over and kissed away any concerns or confusion. But since she wasn't, I could only imagine what it would be like to tunnel my fingers into her thick hair, cup both of her cheeks, and kiss her until she'd succumbed to the power flowing between us. It would be beautiful. Wild. Untamed. Exactly the type of relationship I'd been searching half a decade for. The one private takeaway from all my studies in the art of Tantra was to never settle. Be respectful of the women I'd allowed in my life or taken to bed, but never commit to anyone with my whole heart and soul who didn't feel like the one. My other half.

I didn't know if the woman who sat before me with her stiff upper lip, her quickness to assess a situation, a zealous relationship with God, and her sharp tongue was that woman, but I had a desire to find out.

CHAPTER FOUR

Warrior 2

(Sanskrit: Virabhadrasana II)

Warrior 2 is an "asana" or pose that encourages power. In this position, the yogi feels strong and balanced. Place your feet leg width apart on the mat. Make sure that the knee facing the top of the mat is at a ninety-degree angle. Attempt to rip the mat apart with your feet, spreading them wide. Expand the arms out in a "T" and focus your gaze intently over your fingertips. You are mighty. You are power. You are a warrior.

AMBER

A brunette woman with similar features to Coree's brought our lunch, setting down the food and a stack of napkins. I promptly grabbed one, unfolded it, and placed it in my lap, smoothing the creases over and over. My nerves were shot. Fear and anxiety crawled up my throat like a spider looking for an exit. I took a deep breath, grabbed my water, and chugged down half of it in several long gulps. The chilly liquid slid down my throat, bringing a sense of calm and serenity with it. That was until Dash set his hand on my knee. The simple gesture burned like a white-hot brand.

"So Amber, tell me about you. What do you do for fun?" Dash bit into his sandwich and waited patiently for me to gather my thoughts. His hand didn't leave my knee.

I lifted the soup spoon, blew on the creamy concoction before eating it, and tried not to focus on the press of his warm palm to my bare skin. The moment the potato and bay leaf hit my tongue, I had a small reprieve. Scrumptious heaven. I moaned around the spoon as I removed it from my mouth and went for more, still not sure how to respond to his question or find a way to politely move his hand from my knee. Dash didn't make a sound until I looked up.

"Amazing." He shook his head and leaned back in his chair. Finally, the hand went with him.

I looked away, feeling uncertain. "What's amazing? The food? I agree. They really make a stellar homemade soup."

Dash's amber eyes deepened into a rich caramel. I could stare into those eyes for days on end.

He smirked and blinked slowly as he seemed to catalog my entire face in one look. "No...you."

I slurped down another bite of velvety goodness. Briefly, I wondered if they would give out the recipe. Probably not. Trade secret or something. Wait... "Huh?"

"You really have absolutely no idea how beautiful you are." He rubbed his chin with one hand. "Even the simplest things you do with a grace beyond your years. For instance, the way you delicately hold your hair back as you lean forward over your bowl to eat." His eyes zeroed in on my mouth. "How succulent your lips look when you blow on your spoon. Makes me want to clasp your neck and do sinful things to that mouth."

I gasped and dropped my spoon into the soup, proving to be the very opposite of his flattering comment. The spoon splashed into the liquid, plopping generous blobs onto the tablecloth.

Dash didn't seem to care. His eyes were focused solely on me. It looked like he had given up on his plate altogether to gorge on what I feared had become his new obsession...namely me. With an ease and self-confidence built by years of what I imagined was a whole lot of experience, Dash leaned forward and set his elbows on the table, bringing his face closer to mine.

His voice took on a gravelly, box-of-rocks-rumbling-around quality when he responded. Lifting a hand to my hair, he caressed a lock, rubbing it between his fingertips. The sound of the strands moving against one another was mesmerizing.

"Amber, I'm going to show you how desirable you are. Mark my words, little bird. One day you, too, will see the siren hiding just under the surface. And I want to be the man who brings her out."

Dash's scent hovered around me as I breathed him in. Man and musk after a long class, but on him, it was divine. His face was so close to mine, all I'd have to do was close the few inches between us and our lips would meet. But I wouldn't. I'd never make the first move. Rejection and I were BFFs, and I wouldn't be able to handle my crush denying me something I'd dreamed of almost every night for the past two years.

Slowly, I backed away, putting distance between us. He

grinned and did the same.

"So, back to my question. What do you do for fun?"

"Fun?" I huffed. "This?" I looked around at the environment, watching the people come in and out, checking out what the other patrons ordered for their lunch, avoiding Dash's gaze.

Dash chuckled, and I swear the sound trickled from my ears and flowed down my chest to knock at the door of my throbbing clit to say, "Anyone home?"

I crossed my legs and sat up straighter, trying to fend off my body's response to the handsome yoga teacher.

"No really. What do you do? I know you hang out with Viv," he coaxed.

I shrugged. "Kind of. Mostly, I help her out, spend time with her siblings. Now that she's pregnant and Trent's in and out for away games, I mostly just try to keep her busy so she doesn't worry about him. Ever since she lost her parents, she's been überprotective of her siblings and now her boyfriend, Trent."

Dash nodded and finally picked up his sandwich and took another big bite. I liked watching him chew. His jaw working and the muscles flexing in his neck while he ate were heart-pounding and panty-melting. I figured Dash could be sleeping, and I'd be happy just watching him sleep. Everything about him roared masculinity and called out to my most primitive feminine side.

He shook his head and tilted his chin. "That's not really fun. What do you do for you? How does Amber St. James let loose?" His eyes twinkled.

I smiled and rested my head on my hand. "Honestly, not much. I'm a professional student. I live with my grandparents

and go to school full-time." I huffed. "More than full-t
Usually, I take around sixteen units, but now that I've l
accepted into the joint medical program between UC Berk
and UC San Francisco, it will undoubtedly be more of my
than I'm used to."

"Whoa, whoa, whoa." Dash held his hands up in a
gesture before shaking them. "Seriously, you got into
program? I've heard about it. They only pick the elite. The
of the best from the surrounding universities."

Heat flashed through my cheeks and crept down my r
I shrugged. "I don't know. I worked hard. Did well."

He chuckled. "Uh, I'd say so, Amber. That's trul
accomplishment. I'll bet your parents are proud."

My parents. I attempted a smile that wouldn't have fo
anyone. "I wouldn't know," I finally admitted. "Never
them."

Dash put down his sandwich, placed his elbows on
table, and leaned his chin on his clasped hands. "Were
adopted?"

I shook my head. "No. My mother died in childbirtl
grandparents raised me."

His eyelids narrowed, leaving only a sliver o
mesmerizing eyes visible. "And your father? Where's he
all this?"

Again I shrugged. "Don't know. No one does, tho
have a sneaking suspicion my grandparents do but pla
taking the information to their graves."

Dash clenched his teeth. "That's really not for the
decide." His words came out short and curt.

Without even realizing it, I reached across the tabl
grabbed his hand. He held mine instantly. "It's not a big

me.
een
eley
ime

stop
that
best

eck.

an

oled
met

the
you

My

his
at in

gh I
on

m to

and
deal.

hat you've never had, right?"

my hand closer to his face, leaned forward, and ainst the back of it. "In my experience, it's the l that we miss the most. The same can be said ons." His eyes were laser-focused on mine. "I s them because they are a part of what makes ne way the soul calls out for its missing half. l women go through so many relationships, ching for what they're missing."

wn the urge to laugh. "You're referring to soul e in that?"

 across his face, one I could feel against the hand.

One of his eyebrows quirked up into a point. yes and inhaled slowly. "If it's true, I haven't

interesting. I feel the exact opposite. I may met mine."

I tugged my hand out of his grasp and sat ays this forward?"

g words is for people trying to hide who ating, telling people what they want to hear. hat you really want to say is exhausting. I nest."

estly believe we are soul mates?" I coughed y water. My throat suddenly felt as though it on.

his arms, leaned back, and pulled one knee on the opposite leg. "I can't answer that yet, ng here I'm eager to explore."

★ ★ ★

After Dash's rather profound statement, his phone rang. Within moments of the call, he'd apologized and taken his leave, claiming it was his publisher, and there was some type of issue with his manuscript. I hadn't even known he was a writer. Something else I'd have to ask the overly forward Tantric teacher the next time I saw him, which wouldn't be until Friday's class. That would be the workshop where I'd have to wear shorts and a sports bra, and Dash's hands would be all over my bare skin. I could barely stand the heat of his hand on my knee today.

I sighed and pushed open the door to the only home I've ever known. My nana calls it a cottage, but I didn't think a four-thousand-square-foot three-story home, in the heart of Berkeley, walking distance of the university, could be considered a cottage. We were surrounded by thick, luscious trees that had been alive longer than I had. My grandparents had built this house from the ground up back in the day when it didn't cost an arm and a leg to live in the Bay Area. Now it was worth millions, but they'd never sell. They told me they planned on dying here and leaving me the home in their will. I, in turn, told Nana and Papa to sell it and live like kings in their golden years. They wouldn't have it.

To this day, my grandfather drove a school bus. That was fun when I was in kindergarten. Not so much when I was in high school. At least Papa was cool to the few friends I had. Mostly, I hung out with Genevieve, the girl next door. We're only three years apart in age, and since I skipped a grade in elementary school, we had two solid years together in high school. Freshman and sophomore years were my best. After that I hit the books hard, making sure that I was valedictorian and the head of every club that mattered to the Berkeley board of admissions. It had paid off now that I'd been accepted to the joint program.

The joint medical program between UC Berkeley and UC San Francisco allowed medical students to earn their doctorate after five years of hard-core schooling and on-site learning. I didn't technically need to take the human sexuality course like I'd told Genevieve. To be perfectly honest, I *wanted* to take it. Choosing to remain a virgin didn't mean I wasn't curious. I'd never let a boy go beyond kissing in my teen years. When I turned twenty, my hormones were worse, almost as if I needed sexual intercourse or something close to take the edge off. That was when I went out and bought a small clitoral stimulator. A few seconds of that and I soared into the stratosphere on a blissful cloud. Now, though, at twenty-two, I wanted more than sexual satisfaction. I was aching for...companionship. A man I could love, who loved me back. A person who wanted to spend the rest of his life growing old with me and vice versa.

And perhaps yes, like Dash suggested, to find my very own soul mate. Though I didn't think I'd be finding such a person through a lusty crush on the Tantric yoga teacher. Just thinking about how many women he's probably been with gave me the heebie-jeebies. He was a Tantric teacher. I imagined they had sex all the time. Probably every day. The woman in the café today seemed pretty familiar with him, and he said he'd "dated" her. Translation: he spent a lot of time under the sheets with her. Heck, Vivvie mentioned many times over the years how desired Dash was by the clientele and the other teachers at the studio. Who was I? A student and a virgin. I didn't know jack crap about the spiritual Tantric world. I could do yoga with the best of them. Not in a teaching capacity, but wanting to hang out with Viv, I'd spent some free time in her classes. I learned a lot about the practice and the spiritual side. I funneled all that through the good Lord above. While I practiced my poses, I prayed. Worshiping silently in a room full of people has always been a beautiful meditative practice for me.

I blew out a loud breath and dropped my yoga mat on the kitchen counter. My nana came into the room from the backyard, her gardening gloves still on her hands and a wide-brimmed, white thatch hat covering her head.

"Hey, poppet. How was assisting that yoga class? Was Vivvie there?"

"No, Nana. I'm helping out in a couples' yoga class. The teacher is a friend of hers named Dash Alexander. Cool guy. Very nice." The moment I felt my cheeks heat, I turned around, heading to the fridge for some water.

My grandmother laughed and started to heat the kettle on the stove. "Is this Dash a handsome man?" she asked with nonchalance.

Oh no. Nana was fishing, and she normally caught what she wanted.

"Sure, he's nice looking. A few years older than me. He's really gifted at yoga and has a way of connecting with his clients. I think I'll learn a lot from his class." I grabbed a glass from the cabinet and filled it to the top from the pitcher.

Nana hummed while preparing her afternoon tea. Teatime, a habit my grandparents picked up while living abroad. Even though the St. James clan came over from England long ago, my grandparents lived there while my grandfather served in the Air Force. During that time, Nana taught at the local church. To this day, she still taught Sunday school to the little ones at St. Joseph's.

"Oh, speaking of class. You received a call from a Professor Liam O'Brien's office. Well, technically it was his teacher's aide. Someone named Landen. Anyhoo, they're doing a meet and greet of the new program residents Thursday at the lecture hall at UCSF. The information is on the notepad over there, darling."

"Thanks, Nana. This is so exciting. I can't wait to meet the other fifteen students in the program." I shook my head and shuffled my bare feet. My neon pink painted toes looked bright against my skin. "Do you think my mom would have been proud?"

Nana put her arm around my shoulders and hugged me to her side. "Poppet, she would have cried until her tear ducts dried out. You're doing everything your mother wanted to do. You know she was premed too when she got pregnant. And even though pregnant and only twenty years old, she told me she was going to make sure you had everything the world could offer. Sadly, the good Lord took my sweet angel and left us with another gift. When the nurse put you into my Kate's arms, she looked down, kissed every inch of your pink face and said, 'You are a gift from God, Amber, and I'll love you even beyond this world.' And well, you know the rest." Nana sniffed and kissed my temple several times.

I did know the rest. The placenta didn't separate properly from the uterine wall and my mother hemorrhaged, losing more blood than the doctors could pump into her. She bled to death minutes after I was born, taking with her the secret of who my real father was.

"Thanks, Nana. I wish I could have known her."

My grandmother pushed a lock of hair behind my ear and

stared deeply into my eyes. "Just look in the mirror, poppet. I see her in you each and every day. In the way you walk, talk, and your beaming smile. The unbelievable intellect, your tenacity with your studies, and your humble faith in our Lord and Savior. Those are all gifts given to you by my Kate. She's always with you, honey. I believe she's your guardian angel, leading you through your life and watching over you. She'd be so very proud. As proud as your grandfather and I are."

I nodded and pushed back my hair and dabbed at my eyes. I may have attempted to put on a front with Dash when it came to my parents and never having known them, but my grandmother made sure I knew as much about my mother as possible. Pictures of her were all over the house, including a large eight-by-ten of her pregnant with me. We did look a lot alike.

God, please tell my mother I love her and miss her. That I didn't mean what I said to Dash before. He was right. You can miss something you've never had.

I cleared my throat and waved at my wet eyes, trying to dry them. "Nana, you always get to me!"

She chuckled sweetly as the back door opened and my grandfather entered.

"Hi, Papa, did you have good day?" I asked.

He came over to give me a hug, his rounded belly bumping me the same way Vivvie's did, but his was all grandma's cooking and too many late-night cookies. Nana always joked that he'd eat his weight in cookies if the stash was available. What she didn't know was Papa bought his own stash and hid them. I found his hiding spot by accident one night when I was a kid. We'd made a promise that night that he'd always share with me if I didn't tattle on him to grandma. I knew I'd struck gold, and ever since, we'd share cookies and milk in the wee hours of the morning—mostly when I was still up and studying for finals through college. During those times, he'd set a plate of cookies and a tall glass of milk on the table and pet my hair in passing on his way to his easy chair in his den.

"Hey, pumpkin. I did. A rowdy bunch of teens today. Woo boy. They can be a handful."

Nana shook her head. "You need to retire, Harold. The house is paid off, the cars are paid, Amber's school is on a full scholarship now. You've got your government and school pensions. Take a load off."

Papa groaned. "Woman, would you stop pestering an old man? I'll quit when I'm dead. You see, pumpkin, an old man like me can't just retire. That's when you die."

"Oh pishposh! Such dramatics," Nana tsk-tsked.

I shrugged. "I don't know, Nana. I read a study recently that shows that blue-collar workers have a higher mortality rate. Basically, the study showed that for every year of early retirement, those people on average lost two months of life expectancy. I believe the end of the study gave some suggestions for retiring but still working in a smaller capacity."

Papa hooked me around the waist and hauled me over to his side and kissed my cheek. "Thanks, pumpkin. See, Sandy, even the doctor said so!"

Nana sighed. "Amber, I really wish you wouldn't back his neuroses with scientific studies." She shook her head and placed her hands on her hips.

"Sorry, Nana, but it's true. There are a lot of statistics about it..." I tried to continue, but Papa put a hand over my mouth.

"That's enough. Let your nana pout in peace. Come on

into the den and tell your grandpa about your day."

I followed Papa into his den, one of my favorite places in the entire world. Almost every inch of it was filled from floor to ceiling with dark mahogany bookcases, all loaded with books. My grandfather was a voracious reader and passed down the trait to me. He liked it all. Fiction, nonfiction, biographies, historicals, periodicals. You name it. If it was in the written word, he'd read it. He always said to me, "Knowledge is power, pumpkin. Be smarter than you need to be to get by, and you'll do well in life." I took it to heart, and it's been sound advice.

"So, I ran into Vivvie outside. She looked as pretty and as plump as can be." He chuckled, sat in his recliner, and then propped the footrest up.

I sat down on the squishy chaise opposite his and curled up into a ball. "Don't tell her she's plump. She'll end up crying for days."

He nodded. "Pregnancy hormones. I remember those but would rather forget 'em, if you know what I mean."

I grinned. "Got you."

"Funny thing. She mentioned you're helping the instructor for the Tantric yoga class. Gotta say, pumpkin, I was a bit surprised by that." He furrowed his eyebrows, and two lines appeared between them, a sure sign of his tension regarding the subject.

If there was a way to beam myself up into my room and away from this conversation, I would have. "Papa, it's not what you think."

His hair had whitened long before he hit his late sixties but shone a startling white that looked distinguished on him. My grandmother, on the other hand, kept up her dark hair by way of bimonthly visits to Genevieve's in-home salon.

He opened his eyes wide, adjusted his glasses on his face, and with a quickness I didn't expect, hooked the footrest back down and propelled up and out of his chair like a man on a mission. He went over to one of the bookshelves and skimmed the titles with a finger. "Ah, there it is." He pulled out a book and started flipping through it. "Whelp, pumpkin, if you're going to assist in this class, you should probably read up on it. A man who claimed to be a healer gave me this book when I was doing a tour in Asia. It was so long ago I don't remember all the ins and outs, but Tantra is a very sacred practice and largely based on uniting with your partner. As you know, that's not what we've taught you in this house or in the eyes of the Church, but you know what I always say..."

"Knowledge is power...I know, I know. Don't worry. I'm a big girl. I can handle myself."

"Now that trait you got from me."

CHAPTER FIVE

SACRAL
C H A K R A

The inner state of the sacral chakra is tears. If this is your chakra and it is well balanced, tears may come easy for you. It is likely you are an emotionally-driven person who searches out intimacy, connection, and a mate that matches your intense passionate desires in all things.

AMBER

The auditorium was huge for such a small number of people. At least two hundred chairs were available, yet the sixteen students in the program huddled in the center seats. Eager minds with a thirst for knowledge. The room smelled of old parchment paper, like walking through the aisles of the county library—a tad musty, yet intriguing. I made my way down the steps to the middle section and sat next to a dark-haired guy furiously tapping on a tablet. Trying not to bother Mr. Tappy, I laid my backpack on the floor and dug out a notepad. The boy glanced over, down at his gadget, and then back to me.

"You're going to take notes on that?" He grinned while looking at my standard issue yellow legal pad.

I glanced around the room and shifted in my chair. "Uh, yeah. What's the problem?"

The guy sat up and held out his hand. "Landen, second year and the teacher's aide. You are?"

I shook his hand. "Amber St. James. First year."

"Top of your class, I assume?" He smirked and started tapping on his tablet again.

"Yeah, so what's the problem with my notepad?"

His eyebrows rose as he smiled. "Nothing. Just a little old school." He waved a hand around, indicating the other students. Some had laptops primed and ready on the long wooden beam that acted as the desks. Other students carried handheld devices, and here was little ol' me with a notepad.

Blowing out a slow breath, I straightened my spine and set my perfectly sharpened pencil to rest above my pad. "Yeah, well, I like to do things the old-fashioned way. The act of writing something down helps me remember more information."

"Kind of like the art of repetition." He chuckled.

I jerked my head side to side and cracked my neck. "I guess. So, how's the teacher?"

He grinned and looked at me askance. His eyes burned a sparkling green and his corresponding smile, while pleasant, seemed almost too big for his face. He had a dimple in his right cheek that I could swear winked when he spoke. I found dimples an attractive feature on a man. This guy was no exception.

"He's a piece of work for sure. I love him, though." He

shrugged and went back to multitasking on his device.

Love. Hmm. Not often you hear a guy toss out the term love so casually, especially when referring to a teacher.

"I'm excited about being here," I said, chatting him up. The nervous bubbles in my belly popped and gurgled with anticipation of my first day.

He laughed that time. "The first-year med students always are. See that dude over there?" He pointed to an Asian man who looked about our age, typing furiously into a laptop. He kept pulling on his hair and finally banged his head down on the desk in front of him. "That's Hai. He's a fifth year about to get his MD. See how stressed out he is? I am not looking forward to that!"

I watched as Hai continued to pull at his hair, tug at his tie, and twist his fingers together. This program was unusual to say the least. Merging first years with fifth years for cross-training sounded like a great idea when I reviewed the course material. Seeing how wound up Hai was put an X in the con column for this untraditional format. When I chose it, I appreciated the severity in the differences between standard medical school and the joint program. The knowledge that students further along in their studies would be leading sections of the coursework alongside credentialed professionals, as well as the intense overlap in the training, would allow earlier advancement and more hands on support than the average program is what sold me on this course. Alas, seeing Hai, I no longer felt certain in my choice.

"Yikes. I hope I'm not like that," I whispered, feeling really bad for Hai.

"Depends on what your specialty is. He's going to be a brain surgeon. That comes with some serious emotional, mental, and physical pressure that a lot of us who just want to be GPs don't have to suffer through."

Brain surgeon. Yeah, that's nowhere near where I want to go with my studies. "I'm focused primarily on pediatrics and gynecology. I figure I'll determine which specialty I prefer once we start our residency."

Landen nodded. "Makes sense. I think I'm shooting for the general practitioner route. Maybe emergency medicine. Haven't decided yet. What you'll find in this program, though, is there are usually only a couple in each year of the program, except the newbies. There are two fifth, fourth, third, second, and the remaining eight are first-year students like you. It's good to partner with someone further along in the program. Maybe we can pair up."

Landen set his hand on top of mine and squeezed. At first touch, I thought it was a simple gesture of solidarity, but the longer he held my hand and didn't let it go, the more anxious I became. Was he interested in me? I smiled softly and tugged on my hand but not too hard. The last thing I wanted to do was upset him or put him off. I needed a partner, and Landen was not only a year ahead of me, but he was also the teacher's assistant. That had to mean he was talented or the instructor wouldn't have chosen him.

I faced him. "That would be great, Landen. Thank you."

"Awesome. Ah, there's the old man now."

In the center of the front of the class was a wooden desk and beside that, a podium with a mic. Since the class was small and we hadn't spread out too much, the teacher likely wouldn't need the mic. Professor O'Brien shuffled to the desk and dropped his shoulder bag on the solid oak surface with a heavy thud. Whatever he had inside must have been heavy because the noise echoed off the walls of the mostly empty room.

My instructor was much younger than I expected. He couldn't have been more than in his late forties, which was strange, since the information I'd found out on him stated he'd been teaching for over twenty years. Either he looked good for his age, or the timeline was off. He was very tall, easily a few inches over six feet, had a bit of weight around the middle but wore it well. His hair was curly, dark brown, shaggy around the sides in that cool, older gentleman way that attracted women of all ages. He had on a pair of silver-rimmed glasses that magnified his light eyes.

The professor walked around his desk and leaned on the front, his hands bracing on the edge as he crossed his legs. On his feet were a well-worn pair of burgundy Vans. I almost snickered. The man wore a white lab coat that spoke of his stature in the medical community, not to mention the UCSF Medical Center badge dangling from the coat pocket that demanded respect. Yet, he wore a shoe the local teen skaters would wear. I enjoyed unique oddities from others as I typically felt a little out of the norm myself.

Dr. O'Brien gripped the desk's edge and glanced at each member of the team. When his gaze hit me, he jerked back, took off his glasses, wiped them with a handkerchief he'd pulled from his pocket, and put them back on. Again, his eyes met mine. He frowned, opened his mouth, and shook his head as if he were shaking off a memory or something he didn't want to think about.

"Welcome to the Joint UC Berkeley-UC San Francisco Medical Program. You have been chosen because you are the best in your fields of study. This five-year program is intense. There will be many nights where you will find your ass sitting in the very chair you're in now, only for a full twenty-four hours. Some days you will be helping at the hospital in an assistant capacity to the doctors. They may have you run to the supply room, take blood pressures, set up IVs, listen to heartbeats, check pulses, etc. Right now, most of you are peons. In five years, you will be doctors."

He scanned the crowd again looking at every student one at a time. By the time he got to me, his eyes were hard, cold, and sharp. I shivered trying to shake the sense of unease.

"This program is going to set you up for the rest of your career. Consider it medical boot camp because, some days and nights, that's how it's going to feel. If you cannot keep up or handle the level of commitment this program entails"— he lifted his hand and pointed at the double doors with the shining red "EXIT" sign glowing above it—"there's the door. Use it. You have five minutes to make your decision."

I'd never heard a room so quiet. A raindrop landing on the roof would have sounded like an atomic blast. Not a single person spoke, shifted, or made a sound. I'm pretty sure I spent five straight minutes holding my breath with only a scant, shallow intake of air when absolutely necessary.

"All right then, let's get started. We're going to connect as a team, introduce ourselves one at a time, and give your anticipated field of study." His eyes came back to mine when he finished his statement. "At the end of this evening, we're going to pair you off and set you each up with white lab coats. I expect your lab coat to be clean and pressed for every class. The first thing every patient looks at when you enter a room is your coat. Show them, and me, that you have respect and put your best self forward." The professor pointed at Hai. "Introduce yourself."

Hai stood up and fisted his hands. "Hello, I'm Hai Cheng. This is my last year in the program. I'm going to be a neurosurgeon. My father died of a brain tumor when I was a boy, and I want to help save the lives of people suffering from neurological conditions. Thank you." He offered a curt chin dip and then sat back down abruptly.

Lord, please bless Hai and his family and help him achieve his dreams. In you I trust. Amen.

Each person stood up and delivered their information. I said a silent prayer for each member of the team as they finished their introduction. So far, there wasn't another person who wanted to go into pediatrics. The one running theme was that each student had chosen their field of medicine for a deeply personal reason.

Finally, the instructor came to Landen. "Hello, I'm Landen O'Brien, and the professor is my father." Dead silence met his admission. He glanced around at his peers. "And no, he does not give special treatment. I promise he's harder on me than he will ever be on you." The entire class laughed, breaking the ice once more.

I stared in shock and shook my head. What a phony. He totally played me in the beginning of class acting like a regular Joe, making it sound as though he didn't know the instructor so personally. Well, I'd have to think of a way to get him back. At least the love comment now made a whole lot of sense. Landen looked down and winked at me. I felt that wink zip through my heart, but it wasn't the same as when Dash winked at me. Those winks went straight between my legs and sucked all ability to speak from my throat. In this case, there definitely wouldn't be a love connection with Landen, though he looked the part and had a bright future.

"I'm probably the most boring of the entire crew here. I just want to be a doctor. An everyday man who goes to work and helps those from all walks of life, the young to the old and everything in between, much to my father's disappointment."

I shifted my gaze to the head of the class. He huffed and scowled.

"After I get my MD, I plan to set up a practice, marry a beautiful woman..." This time Landen's eyes were laser-focused on me as he smiled huge.

Oh dear Lord, I think he likes me.

"...and come home to my family. I guess you could say I'm shooting for the American dream."

"That's quite enough, Landen." Professor O'Brien took a deep breath and lifted a glass water bottle to his lips, the kind environmentally crazed people bought. "Next?" He tipped his head toward me before taking a sip.

I looked around and realized I was the last person to answer. Slowly, I eased out of my chair and stood. My five feet ten inches seemed overly large when standing on an elevated platform. "My name is Amber St. James. I graduated from UC Berkeley right where I was born and raised by my grandparents."

A deafening crash pierced the air. The instructor cursed and crouched down to where he'd dropped the glass bottle to the concrete floor.

"Jesus!" he said as he scrambled to toss the big chunks into the waste bin near his desk. I cringed at the outburst.

The professor stood up and walked closer to me, the mess forgotten after he'd trashed the bigger pieces. "I apologize, Ms. St. James. Please continue. You stated you live in Berkeley with your grandparents. Are your parents not from around here?"

He caught me off guard with his question. He hadn't asked anyone else a direct personal question. "My mother's dead. Anyway, I want to practice pediatrics or gynecology." I moved to sit down, but his quick response stopped me.

"Any particular reason why pediatrics or gynecology?" He took off his glasses, and his expression softened. His curt speech and cool demeanor when he entered the class were now gone. In its place, a kinder tone, one that spoke of hugs and pats on the head. It was probably the tone he used to connect to his patients. I'd heard that a lot of doctors did that. Lower the voice, get on the patient's level, and look them in the eye. All of it was part of earning the patient's trust and respect so they'd feel confident in their doctor's care and diagnosis.

I licked my lips and compressed them. His eyes seemed to follow the movement, and for a split second, a flash of pain rippled across his face. The expression came and went so fast I couldn't have catalogued it if I'd tried. He definitely did not want me or anyone to see so deeply into his psyche.

"Well, just like a lot of my classmates I also lost someone. My mother died in childbirth. She was only twenty. I'd like to prevent complications such as the ones my mother experienced, if I can."

"Childbirth," he practically gasped. "Twenty years old. Such a catastrophic loss."

I offered a small smile. "Yes, well. Such is life, I guess."

"Yes, Ms. St. James. I do believe you're right. We never know what challenges life is going to put in front of us until the moment occurs."

He took a slow breath, looked at me, and then at Landen, and turned on a heel, moving back to his desk.

"All right. Now that introductions have been made, and we know why you want to be physicians, let's try to help you look the part."

DASH

"That's him, getting on stage now." I pointed to my longtime friend, Atlas Powers. His dark brown, curly hair hung down to his chin in loose waves. He had on denim jeans with a hole splitting the knee as he sat down on the lone barstool under the track lighting. The black, shiny stage was worn and scuffed, putting breaks in the light shining on it. Atlas hooked a booted foot on the bottom rung of the stool, rested an acoustic guitar on his lap, and smiled at the audience. The purple scarf around his neck popped against the black background, sharing space with the single key necklace he had dangling against his shirt. The key sparkled like a camera flash when he shifted. I never did find out what the key was for, and every time I asked, he avoided an answer and changed the subject.

"And this is the guy you wanted us to see?" Jewel Marigold raised her pointed chin toward the stage. "Why, Dash? This is a bar not a yoga studio," she declared, removing her coat and scooting into the booth next to Crystal.

I'd asked both of my co-owners from Lotus House to come tonight to see Atlas in action before he approached them about working in the studio. His music was such a huge part of his being. Before they chatted about employment opportunities, I wanted them to see his inner light. I believed it would make the case for bringing him on board far easier.

"What better way to get to know a person than to see them broken wide open? Anyone with a credential could technically teach yoga at Lotus House as you've mentioned. If my memory serves, the two of you hire instructors who have more to offer than a simple lesson, right? They need to have that something special that makes them unique to the center. Atlas has that. In spades."

Crystal nodded. "This is true. We want the clients in our house to experience more than a typical class."

I grinned. "Not only have I personally taken several of his heated Vinyasa Flow classes but also he has an idea for a brand-new class that would set Lotus House apart from all the rest."

Jewel smiled and leaned forward. Her fiery red hair bounced around her pretty pixie face in heavy waves. "We're already different. When our clients come to us, they receive spiritual and physical health beyond what money can buy alone. How can this friend of yours do that?"

Before I could answer, Atlas strummed his guitar. The volume in the crowded bar eased as the sound from his instrument began to filter through the space. I closed my eyes and waited for the words to come. Words I knew would settle within the minds and hearts of both Crystal and Jewel in a far more ethereal journey that traversed time.

Open your heart to me...
In there you will see...
I have come to protect and save...
Don't push me away...
What we have will never again be...
If you don't open your heart and see me...

Atlas's voice rolled and crested, a wave with power built

of a thousand tsunamis, each one hitting stronger and more devastating than the last. He continued his song, and I opened my eyes. A tear dripped down Crystal's face. Her ice-blue eyes filled with more unshed tears. She was riveted to the man on the stage. Jewel sniffed and pushed her hair back.

"I want to know more about the new class concept he has," Jewel said when Atlas sang his last words.

"Absolutely. This friend of yours is beyond gifted. Why is he teaching yoga when he should be in the recording studio?" Crystal asked.

"He'd love to be in the studio, only he hasn't met the right people. He does these amateur nights every week hoping a scout will find him."

Jewel nodded and put her hand up for the waitress. "Hot tea, please," she said.

"Oh, me too!" Crystal jumped in.

The waitress's expression was a mixture of disbelief and surprise. "You want hot tea? In a bar?"

"Do you not have it?" Crystal asked.

The waitress chuckled. "Yeah, I guess we do. I've just never had anyone order tea before. I'll see what I can pull together. And for you?"

"Beer. Imported IPA. Whatever's on tap." I thanked the waitress and winked.

She grinned and swayed her hips delightfully. Man, I loved the female form. Long legs, narrow waists, curvy hips, and voluptuous breasts. Instantly, my mind went back to Amber walking away from me earlier in the week. She had an athletic body from all the yoga but with enough curves that a man would have a little bit of something to hold onto when he made love to her.

"Oooh and fresh honey if you have it. I don't do sugar or aspartame," Jewel called out.

The waitress held up a hand and waved. "You got it."

"So, no liquor?" I asked.

"Nope," both women said simultaneously.

"Yet you agreed to meet me in a bar on a Thursday night?"

Crystal put her hand on my shoulder. Jewel canted her head and pressed her lips together. Both of them looked at me the same way my stepmother who raised me did. Like I was the best thing that ever happened to them.

"Dash, honey, you asked us to come and hear your friend play. You are important to us. Been with us for years. You're part of our yoga family. Of course we'd accept the invitation."

I laughed and sat back farther in the booth. "But you don't drink. Why is that?"

Jewel clasped her hands together on the table. "For me, it's part of my enlightened path. You know I'm a vegan. In order for me to find my truth, I need to protect my body and only put things into it that are good for me. Alcohol, my young friend, does nothing but alter your perceptions and dull the richness of life around you."

I swayed my head from side to side, thinking about what she'd said. "I don't know if it dulls life. Some would say it magnifies it." I grinned.

Crystal pushed a long lock of golden-blond hair behind her ear. For a woman just hitting her sixties, she could easily bed a man half her age if she wanted. Though I knew her husband, Rick, doted on her and worshipped the ground she walked on, and rightly so. Crystal Nightingale was a knockout. Jewel was no beggar, either. Her slight body and pixie-like features would capture the eye of any man who enjoyed a petite woman.

"To each his own," Crystal said when the waitress set an entire teakettle and two coffee mugs on the table and then set my pint on a coaster.

"Apparently there is honey in a few cocktails," the waitress remarked.

"Life is full of surprises wouldn't you say?" Jewel replied.

Once the waitress left, Crystal nudged my arm. "How did class go with the new assistant? It's Genevieve's neighbor Amber, right?"

"They're neighbors?" I was soaking up any bit of information on the woman that had so recently captured my attention.

Crystal nodded. "Amber lives next door. They grew up together. Smart as a whip, that girl. She's going to be a doctor."

"I know. Only twenty-two and already has her sights set and her future laid out."

"She'll do it, too. I must say that I caught the two of you talking after class. Seemed a bit friendlier than you usually are with your assistants."

"Don't you normally avoid your assistants after class? Something about them all falling in love with you?" Jewel batted her eyelashes playfully.

I groaned. "Am I that predictable?"

They both nodded and waited for me to dish about the tall brunette who very recently had become my favorite morning fantasy. Imagining her naked and sudsy each morning while I stroked myself to release in the shower worked wonders for easing the tension.

"Amber is working out great. I'm helping her out as a favor to Genevieve. I owed her one."

Crystal sipped her tea. "What did you owe her?"

"She helped me out assisting for a while until her man came along. He doesn't like the idea of her assisting a Tantric class."

"I can see that. It's a very personal experience, and you teach the class so well. Rick loved the course when we took it last year. We were actually thinking about discussing you doing a couples' Tantric weekend up at Lake Tahoe. A yoga retreat for couples only. The pay would be consistent with what other yogis make at these types of events. What do you think?"

I grinned. "What is that saying?" I tapped the edge of my bottom lip. "Cash is king?"

Jewel and Crystal both balked. "That's not funny, Dash."

I full-belly laughed as the two mother types frowned and chastised me. Then they lectured me for the next thirty minutes on the benefits of why money shouldn't be worshipped, nor should a lot of time be spent on making it. The women believed that if a company provided a service or a product and offered kindness, honesty, and good will toward mankind, the money would simply make its way to the facility.

I believe in a lot of things that could be considered modern, or inlaid in spirituality, karma, and other alternate forms of thought, but that isn't one of them. Money is money. We use it to get what we need and some of what we want in life. The trick for me has always been to make enough to obtain what I want and want what I have. So far I've been successful.

After we finished watching the show, I introduced Crystal and Jewel to Atlas Powers. We spent the night chatting about his ideas for a unique offering that would set Lotus House apart and put it on the cusp of edginess in our chosen field. When we said our goodbyes, the owners offered Atlas two classes a week for heated Vinyasa flow and one spot for his new idea. I couldn't wait to see what the other female teachers were going to think about Atlas. From what I understood, he's considered a good-looking guy, and the ladies all swooned for him. That would definitely help him book clients initially. Keeping them, on the other hand, was where the hard work and talent would come in.

CHAPTER SIX

Boat Pose
(Sanskrit: Navasana)

This pose can help fire up your sacral chakra. Designed to provide the body with a solid core and abdominal workout, when you sit with your spine straight, and extend your legs and arms out, you are working almost every major muscle group in perfect harmony. Holding this position for thirty to sixty seconds will give any yogi a sense of pride and accomplishment.

AMBER

Today I entered the yoga room with anxiety and fear as my companions. The lighting was dimmed even more than the last session I'd assisted. On every available sturdy surface was a single red candle. My guess would be fifteen in all. The candlelight gave just enough of a glow that the couples setting up their mats could see the other patrons but not discern every texture or detail. A minty scent wafted across my senses. As if on autopilot, I inhaled a huge breath, appreciating the air expanding my lungs. The crispness that followed exhalation brought with it a sense of peace, calming the ravaged nerves I'd yet to shake.

I felt rooted to the floor. Mentally, I forced myself to put one foot in front of the other as I walked over to the dais. I'd worn a tracksuit over my sports bra and barely-there biking shorts. When I hit the riser, Dash turned around.

Good Lord. Did You have to make the male form so tempting?

I gobbled up his massive bare chest from the top of his clavicle down to the square firm pecs I wanted to feel pressed against my cheek. Each one of his abdominal muscles was a rectangular brick of finely-toned magnificence, leading down to distinct indentations where his hip bones were. He had a trail of hair that started a couple inches above his navel and ran below the loose, white drawstring pants he wore.

I cleared my throat and forced my gaze back up to focus on his eyes. The irises were yellow gold today and marked me in a way that could have lassoed me to his side. My feet seemed heavy, laden with weights as I inched closer. He smiled and then regarded me from head to toe in a quick glance.

"I thought I requested you wear...a little less clothing." His voice was a sexy rumble.

Without saying a word, I lifted my hand, wrapped my fingers around the zipper-pull, and tugged down. I don't know what in me called to do so at a leisurely pace, but I did it all the same. Dash watched, his jaw clenched and one eyebrow lifting into a point. Time and space around us slowed as I let each tooth release oh-so slowly, revealing a pale pink sports bra that in this light probably looked nonexistent.

Dash swallowed, his eyes riveted to my body as I let the jacket fall open, revealing my bare abdomen. Then I shrugged, the swish of the fabric the only sound between us. I held my breath but Dash did not. His chest moved powerfully up and down with each labored breath. He licked his lips just as I held the jacket loosely in my right hand before letting the thin material sink to the ground. Then once more, without speaking, I pulled at the drawstring and shimmied my hips left to right ever so slowly as the pants inched down, revealing the tiniest cotton shorts known to mankind. Lord knew I didn't do that on purpose, but if the carnal way Dash looked at me was any indication, I might have to buy another pair.

Once the pants hit my ankles I kicked them off, standing practically naked in front of the man I'd crushed on for two years. I felt bare. Bare of my misgivings. Bare of my need to hide. Bare of my control.

"My own angel," he said, awe tingeing each breathy word.

I smiled and felt a heat so intense race up my chest it set my cheeks aflame.

"Have you come to save me?" he teased.

The tone in his voice rumbled around my body, making my knees feel weak and shaky.

Taking from every seductive movie I'd ever watched each time Vivvie told me to let loose, as well as somehow finding the inner vixen in me and setting her free, I responded, "Do you need to be saved?"

His lips twitched as he put one foot in front of the other. I glanced down at his feet. Large, squared-off toes, just a smidgen of hair along the tops. Nice as far as male feet went. I'd bet that hair on top was incredibly soft, too. Not realizing how long I stared at his metatarsals, I shivered when a single finger touched my chin and lifted my head up.

"Would you if you could? Save me, that is?"

I licked my lips and bit down on the flesh. The only answer I could muster lifted me on gossamer wings of honesty. "Yes, I would."

"Do I deserve saving, little bird?" He pushed a lock of hair behind my ear.

I closed my eyes against the onslaught of emotions that battered against my heart. He was too close. Too warm. Too everything.

"All of God's creatures deserve redemption."

Dash got really close. So close I could no longer discern the presence of air between our bodies. He put one hand on my shoulder and trailed two fingers down my arm. I didn't move. Couldn't. I didn't want to, either. Near him, I felt safe. Safe in the way I did when attending Sunday mass.

"I guess we'll see about that after today's class. Go ahead and have a seat on the mat facing my mat. And remember, you always have the itchy nose signal to use. I won't judge you."

I huffed and rolled my eyes. "Whatever you say."

He smiled huge. Again, that weak feeling hit my knees, and I scrambled to the mat. I took in the dim room and noticed that all the couples were just about finished getting ready and were facing the front of the class.

"Everyone, we're not going to start with hatha yoga. Today, I want the full ninety minutes to be about your partner. Equally. In Tantra, so much of the connection to our mate depends on our five senses. We're going to work on two of them. Sound and touch. Let's start by facing one another."

Dash came over to his mat and sat in front of me. "Make sure that your knees are touching your partner's. Then I want you to place your hands on just the outer thighs of the other's legs. Ground into the Earth together. Close your eyes and start your pranayama breathing technique you learned last week."

I closed my eyes and started breathing in full and deep. In through the nose, out through the mouth.

"Now, connect your foreheads and keep breathing. Synchronize your breathing."

Dash's forehead was warm when it touched mine. The hairs on the back of my neck stood at attention, like the flapping of butterfly's wings tingling down my spine. I jolted until Dash's hand cupped the side of my neck holding us together.

"Breathe with me, Amber. In...and out. Slow it down. Do what comes naturally."

His voice had deepened when he continued speaking to the class again.

"Once your breathing is paired, I want you to slow it down and then alter your breathing pattern. Reciprocate your inhalations so that you are breathing in your partner's air and vice versa. Do this for a few minutes. If you need to, touch your partner's face or neck, letting them know you're there for them. Holding one another, you are in the safest place possible. Together, allow yourselves to be vulnerable. Trust your mate to breathe life into you."

I sucked in a fast breath, suddenly uncertain. Both of Dash's hands came up and cupped my neck. He rubbed his forehead back and forth. Every time I'd take a breath, he'd exhale and when he'd exhale, I'd inhale. For long minutes, we shared life, breathing in one another's breath. My body became weightless, practically floating on the yoga mat as if it were on a magic carpet. The room didn't matter. The people taking the class were gone. It was just Dash and Amber. Two souls, living one for the other.

"Now that we've activated the third eye chakra through breathing, I want you stay where you are and for five minutes, with your eyes closed and breathing reciprocally, share something you love and adore about your partner. Whisper it quietly to only them."

I waited, holding my breath, as the warmth from Dash's head settled against mine. I swear it was like a puzzle piece notching itself home. I shook off the thought and tried to let it disappear, but Dash would have none of it, instead, wooing me with his sultry voice.

"Amber, I see your beauty even when you don't. Everyone does. It is only you who is blind to it," Dash whispered. I could feel his breath against my face.

Were we doing this? Really doing this? "We barely know each other," I returned.

He chuckled so low I had to strain to hear him. "The heart knows its mate instinctively."

"Are you suggesting I'm your mate?"

Dash inhaled as I exhaled, breathing in life-sustaining air. A breath of air I gave him. One that came from my life source. Something incredibly intimate could be found in that single act. One I most assuredly would not feel with another human being again.

"I believe anything is possible. I also know that I'm drawn to you."

"You're drawn to anything with legs. I've been told you love all women."

He rubbed his forehead back and forth against mine so that I had no choice but to feel the intention behind the act. "Not true. Women are beautiful, as are men. I'm attracted to those unique qualities in a person. Like you. When you entered today, you were frightened, anxious. Am I right?"

I didn't answer. He knew too much already from the way I tensed up. This time, he responded by using both hands on my shoulders and massaging my neck, relaxing me physically as an emotional bomb was about to explode internally.

"You don't have to answer. I know the truth. Yet you took off your clothes as if presenting me with my wildest fantasy come to life."

With that statement, I attempted to rise, but he held me down. "You were so powerful. With the simple touch of your hands to your clothing, you had me wrapped around your little finger. You could have asked for anything, and I would have given it to you. Absolutely intoxicating."

"Dash..." I warned, squirming in my seat. My entire body started to tremble.

He stroked my cheeks with his thumbs, never releasing our physical connection. "I watched you shimmy off your clothes as if you were leaving behind an outer layer of skin and baring your soul to me for the taking."

I didn't know how to respond. Denying the truth in his statement would be a sin. Not that I didn't sin regularly. Father McDowell could attest to that, but on average, I attempted to fib as little as possible. Dash made me want to lie. Want to pretend this unholy connection to him was just physical. Did I want to physically be near him? Yes. Lord, yes, a million times over. But doing so would end everything I'd worked for. The true essence of who I wanted to be for the man I would one day wed, bear children for, spend the rest of my days with. I didn't think it likely that this yoga teacher, a Tantric professor, was that man, but oh, did he tempt me.

DASH

"My soul will be gifted to the man who is destined to be my mate." Her words were even and succinct, conviction breathing confidence.

I grinned. "And why are you so sure that man isn't me?" I said before I removed our connection and spoke to the class.

"All right, now I want the women to lie longways on the mat. Men, I have set out a basket full of tactile items you can use. First, blindfold your mate. Ladies, if you are uncomfortable with this practice, you can close your eyes, but remember trust doesn't come easy. It's a gift. This is a good time to practice that trust."

Amber lay down on the mat. I held up the blindfold. "Do you trust me?"

Her eyes looked panicked, but her bravado stopped her from giving into it. With a stiff upper lip, she responded. "Not particularly, but I'm not afraid of you. Just give me the blindfold."

I handed it to her, and she looped it over her head. The red satin was a rich contrast against her pale white skin and dark brown waves. She pursed her lips and then sucked in a breath.

"Now, class, I want you to use whatever items you like from the basket to tease and entice your partner. Only do not speak, and for this round only touch with the item. Let's keep it PG for now. Ladies, lie back and enjoy the pampering."

Amber was stiff as a board. I'd definitely need to loosen

her up. The girl was wound so damn tight. Before I started in on my victim, I turned on some music. Indian songs were ideal and expected in a yoga setting, but I wanted something that would soothe and entice my clients. Get them outside of their comfort zone and into one far more hypnotic. I pressed play and allowed the flowing strains of Atlas Powers' guitar to echo through the room. He'd paired his acoustic guitar with a tentative tapping against the wood of the instrument and dubbed it over itself. The result was a mesmerizing forty-five minutes of music for seduction.

Going back to Amber, I sat close enough that she'd feel my heat but not know exactly where I was. She'd have to use her senses and focus on the moment instead of the finicky side of her intellectual mind. Tantra was not about academics or scholarly facts. It was about what a person felt—that meditative space within each of us being tapped and coalescing with the universe and, when in perfect harmony, coexisting with our mate. I wanted that so badly with a woman. Not just any woman. The *One*.

I had no idea if Amber St. James was my One, but every time I was in her presence, I couldn't shut down the urge to make her mine, an uncontrollable desire, a lust so pure, it burned like white-hot fire through my veins. That had to be my sign, one impossible to ignore. Whether ordained by the Great One, Mother Earth, the Universe, or God Himself, she was put in my path for a reason. One I rejoiced in finding out.

Sitting quietly, I picked up a long feather from the basket of trinkets. Starting at her forehead, I tickled her third eye chakra, known in Sanskrit as the *Ajna*. She smiled and her chest puffed several times in silent laughter. I'd take laughter over irritation any day. Definitely a good start to this practice.

With a light caress, I ran the feather down the side of her face and over her clavicle. She sighed. Another pleasant response. In my peripheral vision, I could see her fingers tightening as I ran the tip of the silky feather between her breasts, never straying or disrespecting her trust. Once the touch met her abdomen, I twirled it around the spherical indention of her navel. Her mouth opened on a soft gasp. That reaction was key. I had her.

As the guitar strings were plucked, I moved with the highs and lows, running the feather up and down each arm until I could see gooseflesh rise up. I'd made sure the room was set at a comfortable seventy-four degrees. For a moment, I stopped and watched her breathe. With every rise of her diaphragm, I counted her breaths and paired mine with hers so that we were connected through pranayama, as well as through the tip of the feather.

Speaking barely above a whisper, I addressed the class. "Good. Next, I want you to follow the same path of the instrument, but use just your fingertips."

Amber shivered, and her hands tightened into fists. I started there, hoping to ease her. Breaking my own rules, I hovered near her head and brought my lips to her ear. "Itchy nose if it becomes too much. Trust me." I covered one of her fists with my hands. I uncurled each finger and brushed each one with a single stroke of the tip of my index finger until she relaxed. Then I moved from her hand up her arm. When I got to the crease in her elbow, she inhaled. I used that reaction as my guide, wanting more of those little gasps and unexpected breaths. Every new spot I uncovered was like opening the locks hiding a precious treasure.

Being careful not to startle her, I pressed my entire palm

over her heart, allowing the warmth of my hand chakra to meld with her heart's energy. I could have sworn a delicate thread of pure turquoise blue weaved from her heart chakra into my hand, infusing my own senses with pure love. The sensation careened through my hand, up my arm, and straight into my own heart where it squeezed tight. It sounded so ridiculous even as I thought it, but it seemed as if her heart's energy was embracing my own.

I became overwhelmed with a pride so strong it filled every single one of my senses down to the tips of my toes. I leaned forward and replaced my hands with my lips. Slowly, I nuzzled the space between her breasts and pressed my lips over her heartbeat. She gasped and wrapped her hands around my head and held me to her.

As quickly as the need came, it went. Whispered words around us brought me out of the meditative state. This woman completely tore away any restraint I had and renewed me with a simple heart-to-heart connection.

I cleared my throat and pulled off Amber's blindfold, needing to see her eyes. I had to know if she regretted what I'd done. I hadn't planned it, but it had happened, and I needed to know if she felt it too. When she opened her eyes, they were filled with love. She'd felt it. Taking a deep breath, and without speaking, I closed my eyes and handed her the blindfold. She put it back on.

"Okay, men, now you have carte blanche. The goal of this last exercise is to kiss every bit of skin you touched. Remember, respect your mate and don't take it too far. This is a test of your will and control as much as it is for you to feel as one with each other."

I turned back to Amber and saw her now in a completely

different light. Whatever had happened between us through our heart chakra was real and intense, and I'd never experienced it with another woman before. A first for me, which told me exactly what I needed to know.

"Amber, if you don't want to do this, I won't." I had to be sure. With all the other assistants, I wouldn't continue with the kissing. Usually we'd just sit quietly and mediate while the others performed the act on their mate. Now though, touching her was like a siren's call. I wanted nothing more than to put my lips all over her beautiful body and glowing skin. I salivated at the mere thought.

And then Amber floored me. I don't know if it was the aphrodisiac of the breathing, the touching, the feather, or more, but whatever it was, I would worship this moment later, reliving it a hundred times over.

"I trust you, Dash."

Those four words gripped my heart and squeezed like before. I'd never forget the moment I'd finally earned this woman's trust. All I knew was that I would die before I betrayed it.

Leaning forward, I started at her forehead, placing a dry kiss. Silently, I sent her joy, peace, and love. Being this close, the scent of strawberries warred with the peppermint diffuser. I wanted to rub my face all over her hair and neck, imprinting the fruity smell so I'd smell like her later. Not being able to contain myself, I laid a row of kisses down her temple, cheek, and along the silky column of her neck. When I reached the tender patch behind her ear, I nipped the flesh. Her mouth opened in a soft "O" that made my dick stand at attention.

Moving along her clavicle, I bit into the bony protrusions, losing myself in the exotic taste of her skin. After I'd kissed down each arm, nibbling on every finger, her legs were shifting restlessly and a musky scent overwhelmed both the strawberry and mint of the room. Oh sweet mother, she was turned on. Her arousal was soaking her panties right here on the stage in front of a roomful of people. The woman was a gift from God. Absolutely perfect.

I wrapped my fingers around her hips and held her steady. I glanced around the room, making sure everyone was in their zone. They were. Not one couple was paying attention to us, all lost in one another. Man, I loved my job.

Back to Amber, I straddled her legs and squeezed. Her body went rubber band tight until I circled her waist with both hands. Then I did exactly what I'd wanted to do when I saw her bare midriff exposed. I kissed and then dragged my tongue around her navel.

She mumbled a sleepy, "Dash."

I sighed, resting my forehead against her abdomen. The musky smell was intense this close to her center, making my mind dizzy with a lusty haze. My cock was thick, long, and so hard I could have pounded a nail into wood with it. This close to her sex, I could so easily imagine pulling down her shorts and burying my mouth in her slick heat. I didn't need to be a sorcerer to know it would be the sweetest pussy I'd ever have the honor of tasting.

Breathing shallowly, I lifted my head away from the temptress's sweet spot and focused my gaze on something far less likely to get me slapped, punched, or thrown in jail for misconduct—Amber's pretty, plump lips. She'd licked, pouted, pursed, and bitten down on the tender bits of flesh so much throughout this session that they held a raspberry hue.

Easing up her abdomen with firmer, more staccato kisses,

I went over her sports bra along her neck where I was gifted another sensual sigh. I traced her jawline and kissed just the corner of her lips.

"Is your nose itching?" I asked, kissing the other side of her jaw up toward her lips.

"Not even a little." Her voice shook.

I smiled. My brave little bird. She wanted this as much as I did, but she didn't want to take it herself. If I gave it to her, she'd have no choice. Well, less so than if she'd instigated it.

Breathing close, I rubbed my nose along hers and allowed just the tip of my lips to barely touch hers. "How about now? Do you need to scratch anything?"

She moved her head from left to right.

My lips got so close I could inhale her breath directly. I was only centimeters from kissing her. "I'm going to kiss you."

"Oh my," she said against my lips.

"Unless you suddenly have a need to scratch, my lips are going to take yours in a kiss that will change everything. All you have to do is touch your nose."

For long moments, I held myself above Amber, waiting for her to move away, to do something, anything.

Our breath mingled until she closed the distance and touched her nose to mine in a simple Eskimo kiss. That was it. I had the ability to hold back but no will. No longer caring about the circumstances, I covered her lips with mine.

She moaned, my mouth masking any sound outside of the cavern of our joined lips. She tasted of bubble gum and walks through the park, innocence and warmth wrapped in one package. I ate it up, delving my tongue in farther to taste, devour, and mark as my own. I wanted the kiss to go on forever. Amber responded with long licks of her tongue into my mouth and nibbles against my bottom lip while I tended to her top one. I lost all track of time and space, beginning to understand that Amber narrowed everything down to one simple thing. Us.

Kissing her, laying my body over hers, was one of the single most pleasurable moments of my entire life, and I'd had some wild experiences. Maybe that's the reason it was so special. It couldn't be duplicated. Nothing had ever been this perfect in my twenty-eight years of life. No woman had broken me down to my base self where the core of my being rested. She woke me up, made me see, and with every swipe of my tongue against hers, she brought me to a higher plane of existence where alone was a thing of the past. Not something I'd ever wish for again. With her under me, wrapped around me, inside me, I was whole.

CHAPTER SEVEN

SACRAL
C H A K R A

Strongly connected to issues around sexuality, relationships, and sensuality, a woman whose sacral chakra is closed will find herself having trouble in her relationships, connecting with her mate, and lack pleasure in the act of having intercourse. It could mean she is not with the right person, or the person she is with is not seeing to her needs intimately, physically, and spiritually.

AMBER

A distant clapping noise filtered into my subconscious mind. Dash's lips kept at mine. I had no intention of stopping our kiss, save for the sound...roaring, cresting, getting louder by the second, prodding at my concentration on the finest lips I'd ever touched. Eventually, the cheering poked and pierced the little bubble of heaven we'd created around us until all I could hear were twittering birds. No, not birds, laugher. Chatter rising in volume until it could no longer be ignored. Dash pulled back first. I lifted my head, my mouth chasing his lips in the dark. He plucked the blindfold off my eyes with a flourish. Speckles of light flickered and colorful starbursts flared against my vision before I could see his face clearly. His eyes were black as night. He grinned and then oddly, looked to his left.

"Sorry, class. Looks like Amber and I got a little swept away in the exercise."

Class.

We were on stage.

In front of a roomful of people.

Oh. No.

Dash held my hand as I sat up and rubbed at my eyes. A wave of heat not connected to my lady bits resurfaced and spread up my chest and over my neck to blister my cheeks. I looked down at our joined hands and focused on his words.

"Homework for the next three days is to practice what you learned in class today on each other. Take turns. Once you get to the kissing step, give it enough time before you ramp up and employ what you've learned to a more corporeal, united activity."

He waggled his eyebrows, and the couples around us laughed. Me, I was mortified. Humiliated beyond reasonable comprehension. I'd lost my mind and made out with my yoga instructor in front of an entire class full of people. A person couldn't return from that. Pretend like it never existed. Walk away with a twinkle in your eye and a smile.

No, Dash would want to discuss it. A sense of pure dread made every hair on my body stand at attention. What was I thinking? The truth? I wasn't. Plain and simple. I felt like the second I put the blindfold on, I was lost to him. He'd taken me to a place in my mind that was light, love, and pure...heaven. Of course, I knew spiritually and cerebrally that I wasn't in *the* heaven. Though I couldn't deny that I'd never felt the way I did when Dash touched me. Each caress of the feather he'd used on my skin brought with it a tingle that skimmed every nerve ending, lighting them on fire. I burned with it. Longed for each new scrap of his essence over mine.

Regardless, none of that compared to the moment when his lips touched my bare skin. My head and heart pounded a jungle-like rhythm. Each new expanse of skin anticipated his next movement. Yearned to be found, conquered. I'd tried to repeat the quadratic formula in my head, count and name all two hundred and six bones in the human body, if only to distract me from the sheer bliss he'd bestowed. Dash overpowered and overwhelmed the smallest body part. He drowned me in a sea of sensations so acute I'd have died and gone to heaven just to experience them again.

The couples in the class moved around, rolling up their mats, whispering to one another as they prepared to leave. *Leave.* Yes! That's it. I needed to be on that train.

No. You're not a child, Amber. Put on your big girl panties and address this like a mature adult.

I could do that. I'm certain Dash could do that being six years my senior. Easy. I'd tell him we got carried away, he'd agree, and then we'd commit to it not happening again. Perfect.

Once I'd gotten my swishy track pants back on to cover some of the nakedness I felt, I sucked in a huge breath and planned to lay it out for him.

"Dash..."

That was the only word I got out before he curled a hand

around my nape and the other looped around my waist. We slammed chest to chest only seconds before his lips were on mine. He didn't work up to seduction like he'd done when I was blindfolded. No, he went straight for the gusto. I told my fingers to push against his chest, break the seal, but somewhere, lust and pleasure clouded and deadened each synapse that fired. Instead, I dug into his chest, circled my arms around his waist, and did the exact opposite of what I should have done. I held on. Tight.

My fingertips pressed into the sinewy, muscular texture of his back, clinging when I should have let go. Dash did the same, adding a vise lock around my waist as his hand moved to my cheek where he could slant my head left and right, getting just the right angle to delve deep...so deep. He consumed me from the inside out. I couldn't get enough. He tasted so good. Like honey and spearmint. I moaned, pressing closer until I could feel the hardened ridge of his erection against my belly.

That was the jolting wake-up call that finally penetrated my moral psyche. I pushed with all my might, breaking our connection and sucking in a gasp of air so large I had to bend over to get control. I rested my hands on my thighs, digging into my quads. The pinch of pain did nothing to calm the roaring train of lust chugging through my system.

Lord, help me.

Dash wiped off his mouth as if he'd just taken a huge gulp of water instead of having kissed the sanity right out of me. "Amber...why did you stop?"

Why did I stop? Was he for real?

"I know you enjoyed it. Held me tighter even." He stepped closer, his face a mask of desire, ready to partake the fruit he so obviously craved. "Your body sealed to mine..." He closed his eyes, and his nostrils flared on a sharp inhale. "Didn't you feel it?"

I licked my lips, the remnants of his taste still there as I backed up a step. He advanced a step closer.

Dash grinned. "Are you afraid of me, little bird?"

I shook my head but didn't respond. Honesty clogged my throat and stole my nerve.

He bent his neck and progressed another step. If I moved back one more foot, I'd be off the riser, and he'd know I was attempting to escape. What I was running from, I didn't yet know.

"Hmm. You're not afraid of me. If you were, you wouldn't have kissed me like that. Possessed my heart and body with one press of your lips to mine." He squinted. "Admit it. I bring out a side of you that you're afraid of. A piece of your soul no one has ever seen, perhaps not even yourself."

"Dash..." I swallowed, trying to think of what to say, how to deny it. Still, I came up empty. He was right. I'd never felt like this before, not with anyone, not ever, and it scared the living hell out of me.

He finally stepped close enough to cup both of my cheeks. His palms were warm and soft. Instinctively, I closed my eyes, letting the connection soak into my skin. He leaned forward, so close that our breath mingled, and I thought he'd kiss me again. Unfortunately, that wasn't his intent. Surprisingly, he rubbed his nose against mine and then pressed his forehead to mine. A current of heat rippled through me, like skipping rocks on a serene lake, the instant waves breaking the serenity and calm.

Dash's voice was strong, confident, and genuine when he spoke. "I would *never* hurt you. Never betray your trust. Your innocence is safe with me, Amber."

My innocence is safe with him.

I pushed my head back so that I could look directly in his eyes. "What do you mean my 'innocence'?" I'd not told him I was a virgin, and Genevieve would never break the best friend code.

He chuckled and sifted his fingers into my hair, massaging the back of my head with strong, blunt pressure. I briefly succumbed to the modest pleasure and sighed.

"Amber, I know a lot about a person the moment I meet them. I've always been that way. People speak to me with their body language, the words they speak, the way they dress, even a simple gesture can say a lot about a person."

I didn't mind backing up and stepping off the riser then. Space was necessary for some reason.

Not wanting to give attitude, but still uncertain where he was going with his innocence comment, I stiffened my spine and placed my hands on my hips. "So you think you're what? Telepathic?"

Dash smiled huge and rubbed at his chin. The prickly hair on his chin grated against his palm as he did. For all intents and purposes, that could have been a mating call with the way my body reacted. I clenched my thighs against the flow of arousal coursing through me to land heavily there. Throbbing. Aching.

"No, no. You misunderstand. I'm merely stating that I'm observant. Not only have you told me that you are religious, but also you've been very concerned about how much or how little I'd be touching you. Then, of course, when I did touch you, there was your reaction." He smirked.

That dirty devil. "My reaction? This ought to be good. Please, enlighten me."

Dash pursed his lips. "You acted as if every touch was the first one you'd ever received. As if each kiss to your flesh was a new one. A brand-new beginning."

I frowned and tightened my hold over my chest. "A new beginning. To what?"

Dash smiled wide and rested his hands on his hips. He'd left his shirt off and was displaying his golden body to me like a bronzed god bathing under the sun's rays. Only it was actually track lighting that created the effervescent hue surrounding him, though it definitely fit the mood.

"Haven't you figured it out?" He grinned.

I cringed and sucked in an irritated breath. "Figured out what?"

"That this is the beginning of us."

DASH

How can she not see and feel what's happening? My mind seized with the fear that I'd misinterpreted the connection between us. For me it was a live wire, filled with energy like a wild electrical current. Never ending, only getting stronger.

"Us? What *us*? There is no *us*, Dash." Her brown hair hid her face.

I wanted nothing more than to push it back and gaze upon the canvas in its entirety. "Amber, there is."

She shook her head. "What planet do you live on?" Her voice cracked with the strain of her denial.

"What rock do you live under?" I shot back with a heaping dose of mirth.

The corresponding glare I received was priceless and so pretty I wanted to kiss it away. If I'd been certain she wouldn't sock me, I'd have done so.

Amber sighed. God, each sigh she blessed me with was a direct shot to my dick. Every single one made me harder than the last. For all the money in the world, I couldn't describe what her little sounds did to me, or why such a deluge of need was attached to her presence. It's as if it always was. Kismet, fate, whatever you wanted to call it. And now, it was my duty, my *pleasure*, to get her to see the light, of what we were meant to be.

"Dash, I... We kissed, and it was good."

I cringed. Good. When referring to a kiss, good sounds bad, especially the way she was circling around what she really wanted to say.

"Great even." Another sigh and a slump of her shoulders said it all, until she put the nail right into the coffin.

"I'm not the girl for you. We need to stop whatever this is between us right now. Cut our losses and just be friends and partners for this class. Nothing more."

"To hell with that!" The words left my mouth so harshly she practically jumped back a foot. "Amber, I have never in my life experienced what I did today. When I'm touching you, everything disappears. I've studied the Tantric arts and have put them to the test many times in my sex life, but nothing, absolutely *nothing* holds a candle to the simple act of putting my lips on your skin. Taking your mouth with mine. Holding you. I can't explain, but I know enough that when the universe hands you a gift, you do not thrust it back in its face. You treasure it." I stopped and strengthened my resolve. "Unless, of course, you can look me in the eye and tell me right here and now that you feel nothing. That this, whatever it is...is completely one-sided?"

I held my hands in fists at my sides, waiting, dreading what lie she'd spew. I knew with my entire being that Amber St. James was meant for me. Ludicrous as it might sound after having known one another for such a short time, the facts were there, laid out in black and white on the floor of a yoga studio in Berkeley, California. Each touch shared, each of her gasps, our mouths melding like perfect liquid sunshine. No matter what she said next, I vowed then and there that I'd prove it to her or die trying.

She inhaled sharply and pulled at her elbows where her arms were folded over one another. Like she was trying to hide how affected she was by me, more than her exposed flesh in the flimsy sports bra. I saw her puckered tips, wanted to wrap my mouth against each peak and warm them until graced with a needy sigh. If she'd just let me, I could take her to places she'd never even heard of before.

Amber pursed her lips. "I'm not going to lie to you. Not only is lying a sin, it's ridiculous. Obviously, I reacted rather..."

"Pleasurably, excitedly, sinfully."

She glanced to the side, blew out a puff of air, and tapped her foot. "You are determined to make this more than it is, aren't you?"

I laughed. "No, little bird. I only want you to see exactly what this is. Me and you. Now let's get to the good part. I want to take you out to dinner. When are you free?"

Her mouth opened and closed, and she shook her head. "You're not hearing me."

I smiled, went over to my stuff, and pulled my T-shirt out of my bag and over my head. She watched every movement. *Yeah, she's not affected by me at all.* I rolled my eyes. "I am. I'm just not willing to allow you to step away from what is meant to be before we've even had a chance to experience it."

She dropped her hands and slapped the sides of her legs before balling both hands into fists. I couldn't help but chuckle under the weight of her obvious frustration. What can I say? She was so damned cute. Made me wonder what other layers would peel back the more time we spent together. I sure looked forward to finding out.

"Dash, we cannot date. We are colleagues. It would be a conflict."

I huffed. "Just because you're assisting in my class does not make you my colleague. Last I recalled, you were a medical student and going to be a doctor. How does that in any way pose a conflict of interest toward a yoga instructor and author?"

She scrunched up her nose. Yep, cute as a button.

"You're an author? What have you written?"

Like a dog to a bone. "In order to find out, you'll have to ask me that question again when we go on our date. Now, I know you have a busy school schedule. Besides my classes here, I'm flexible and can work with your timelines."

"Um..." She blew out a breath. "I don't know."

"What day?"

Amber rolled her head and pressed her hand to the back of her neck. That gesture alone spoke volumes. She was going to try to come up with another excuse.

"Amber...I'm waiting. Don't make me come over there and coerce it out of you."

The skin around her eyes tightened as she glared. "You wouldn't dare."

I snickered. "Oh, little bird, there are a lot of things I would do that you would find ab-so-lute-ly sinful."

Her mouth dropped open.

"You're getting it now. So just answer me, because I'm not going to stop pursuing this. When. Are. You. Free?"

Without a second's more thought, she spat out her next words on a testy eye roll. "I have class on Monday and a study date on Tuesday, so it will have to be Wednesday."

This time I grimaced. The green-eyed monster blinked its eyes open and slithered up from the base of my spine to tighten around my chest. Its claws dug into my flesh to the point I had no control over my knee-jerk response.

"Study date?" I growled.

She smirked, grabbed her jacket, and slipped it on. I watched as her breasts arched with the movement. If only I was standing before her. I could feel those erect tips brush against my chest, cooling the beast growling for attention.

"Yep. Each student gets paired off. Lucky me, I got the professor's son. He's a second-year student and is going to show me the ropes."

I snarled, even though I tried my damndest to hold it back. "Does this study buddy have a name?"

She smiled and zipped up her jacket. "Landen. Why?"

Landen. Of course. Perfect poster boy for Mr. Doctor *GQ*. Well, he wasn't going to get his hands on my woman.

My woman. Oh, hell.

I had no right to claim her...yet. That didn't stop every nerve, pore, and thought within me from screaming otherwise.

"Does he have a girlfriend?"

She shrugged. "Don't know, don't care." Amber looked away quickly as if plotting her escape.

Nuh-uh. A woman only did that if she was uncomfortable, hiding something.

"Did he already make an advance toward you?" I inhaled

slowly so as not to frighten her with how hot my anger was with just hearing about her planning to meet up with another man. A medical student, someone who was probably exactly like her. Had the same goals, the same dreams. I'd never had to compete for a woman's attention in my life, but I'd start now. For her.

Amber sighed long and loud. "Dash, we are not having this conversation. You've cornered me into dinner on Wednesday. It's none of your business what I do with my life, or who I do it with. So unless you want me to stand you up on Wednesday, you'll drop this...now."

I held my hands behind my back so tight the muscles in my shoulders protested painfully. "Fine. Enjoy your study date. I'll pick you up at seven, if that suits you."

"Since I get off school at five, that will be fine. I'll text you my address."

Without anything more I could do, I nodded curtly. She hefted her mat and bag over her shoulder and tilted her head. She pushed an obstinate lock of hair behind her ear and smiled sweetly.

"I, uh, did feel what you felt today." Her words were hurried and uncertain.

The wave of relief washed over me like aloe to a prickling itch. I watched her walk to the exit before I called out, "Thank you."

Amber stopped, turned around, and rested a hand to a hip. "Why?"

"For admitting our truth."

She huffed. "Which is?"

I grinned and ruffled my fingers through my hair, trying to find the right words. If anything, she needed something to remember today by. A bit of hope to last through the weekend and Tuesday's class and subsequent date with Landen.

The time was now or never. "That something, the universe, or perhaps your God brought us together."

"My God?"

I nodded.

"Does that mean you're not a believer?" Her face paled, and her eyes glistened. A slight tremble marred her moistened lips.

Instinctively, I knew that my answer to this question would mean more than any other she'd ever ask.

"I don't know," I finally admitted, not at all certain where my answer would stand. I wasn't raised in a religious home and never went to church. I knew as much about God and religion as I could find in my theology texts. Didn't mean I was a believer. At least not right now.

While I waited, I could count the ticks on the clock, the room was that silent. My breath sounded loud, like when you put your ear up to a conch shell and hear the ocean. Unusually, I was using *Ujjayi* breath—a form of breathing that's done by inhaling and exhaling strictly through the nose. When done correctly, it created an ocean sound as the throat narrowed and air was pushed through. Once the air was released, the result was an open root and sacral chakra. Together, the breath created a rushing sound that could help center and focus your attention internally. Dara, the meditation teacher, taught it to me when I was having trouble meditating last year.

I waited for what felt like an hour for her to respond, but was probably only a few seconds. Then, she smiled and her entire face lit up into the most beatific smile I'd seen on her yet. She was unearthly gorgeous when she smiled.

"Then I shall enlighten you." She waved a hand over her head and called out, "See you Wednesday."

Her footsteps echoed down the hall. I strained to hear every one before I crouched down and balanced, flat-footed, ass almost touching the ground. I continued the *Ujjayi*, breathing for a solid ten minutes until a sense of calm replaced the nervous energy and jealousy I'd been plagued with.

I stood up, pressed my hands to the center of my chest, palms touching, and thanked the universe for all that it had given me today. I could only imagine what was in store for me next. With a majestic little bird like Amber, the only thing I could count on was that it would be unique.

CHAPTER EIGHT

Garland Pose
(Sanskrit: Malasana)

A great pose for opening the sacral chakra and the hips. Many yoga practitioners use this pose to center and root the body down to Earth. The closer you are to the ground, the more of the Earth's energy you feel. To get into this asana, shift your weight into a wide-legged squat so that the bum comes close to the floor but does not touch it. Press your elbows into your inner thighs and place your hands into heart center to aid with balance. Stay in this position for as long as it feels good.

AMBER

"My father was such an ass today!" Landen groaned and tossed his backpack onto the long oak dining table in his family's home.

With slow steps, I followed him into the mini-mansion. My grandparents' home was worth a couple million, and this one had to be worth double, possibly even triple, that. Set into the San Francisco hillside, I could see the Golden Gate Bridge, the heart of the city, its skyscrapers, and the choppy waters of the Bay out every window. Dr. O'Brien had done very well for himself indeed. I guess when a person was responsible for teaching the brightest minds the complexities of modern medicine in a hard-core program such as the one I'd been accepted into, he likely got paid a pretty penny.

I set my bag on the rectangular solid oak table. The thing had twelve chairs, but could have fit twenty chairs squeezed around it. On the walls surrounding the table were family photos. Pictures of Landen as a baby, of his father holding him—the same stuff my nana had all over her home. Landen definitely took after his father based on the pictures because his mother had flat, shiny blond hair.

"Iced tea?" He handed me a full glass.

I smiled. "Sure. Thank you."

Landen shook his head and paced in front of the table. "I can't believe how much of a jerk Dad was. To ask you personal questions like that...I don't get it."

Sipping the tea was as good a distraction as any, so I went with it.

"It's just not like him. He never gets personal with his students. He's always been strictly professional. I'm sorry he asked about your mom like that today." Landen's eyes were a mix of sadness and something else, the little lines around them starkly visible.

Without agreeing with him, I just nodded. I wished I could have rubbed a reassuring hand down his back, but that would have been too forward and possibly given an impression I didn't want him to have. Although he had an excellent point. The last thing a new student wanted to do was get on her professor's bad side. I reached out and placed my hand on Landen's bicep instead, figuring that was a safe friendly area. Like Dash did the first time we met, Landen flexed his arm instantly.

Do not respond. Do not respond. I coached myself and failed when I felt myself smile.

It was too funny. To have a guy automatically flex his muscle like that. Silly. Though it proved once again that he was very likely interested in me in more than a school study buddy type way. It would be wise for me to remember not to stroke his ego in that manner or I'd have to backpedal big time. Besides, Dash would positively lose his cool if he found out Landen was flirting with me.

Dash. I cringed. Seriously, there was nothing official going on between Dash and me. Regardless of what he might think, I couldn't possibly be his type. Of course, the date tomorrow said otherwise. Once he found out that I wasn't willing to bed him, he'd lose what little interest he seemed to have. So technically, I was a free agent to do whatever I pleased with whomever I pleased—including the boy looking down at me with soft green eyes and a winking dimple in his right cheek. Yet I felt a zap of guilt rippling through my veins that chilled my blood.

I pulled back and frowned. "Sorry."

Landen smirked. "Why? I like it when you touch me. It's nice." He shifted his feet and rubbed the back of his neck. "I mean, it feels like I know you already. Isn't that weird?"

That time, I did laugh. He could be right. "I will admit to feeling an odd sense of déjà vu in your presence. Are you sure we haven't taken a class together?"

He shook his head before centering his focus on me. Like a slow caress, he checked me out from top to toe and back up. "Believe me. I'd remember you."

I sighed and pushed at his chest. "Shut up. I'll bet we were at a seminar at the same time and sat near each other or something. Maybe that's what's up with your dad asking personal questions. He thinks he knows me."

The excuse was as good as any. More unusual was that several times throughout the class, I'd caught him staring at me. Not the way some people gazed into space in the general direction of something, but like he was staring right at me. As though he were cataloguing all of my features for a scientific study. Frankly, I found the entire day unsettling.

"Well, I'm sorry about Dad. Then again, if he was staring at you all day and asking personal questions, at least he has good taste." He waggled his eyebrows.

"Eew, gross! Are you suggesting that your dad has the hots for me?"

Landen laughed out loud, pulled out a chair at the table, and finally hefted his tall body into one. A twenty-three-year-old man, he had a nice body. Leaner than Dash in muscle and bulk, Landen didn't have a lot of meat on him, but he definitely wasn't skinny. I think with his studies and his bicycling hobby, the guy probably had a hard time keeping extra weight on. He wore his shape well, and I definitely found him attractive, I just wasn't *personally* attracted to him. I didn't feel that yearning deep down inside the way I did with Dash. Stupid hot yogi.

"I wouldn't say he's into you. Dating a student is not his style. Besides, Mom would kill him."

"What does your mom do?"

"Runs a successful advertising agency here downtown.

Represents a lot of big market products. As you can see"—he lifted his hands and gestured around the room—"they do well for themselves."

I giggled and sat down in the chair next to him. "That I can see."

Landen put his hand over mine on top of the table. "What else can you see?"

Before I could answer, a door opened and closed, and Professor O'Brien strode in, carrying a handful of textbooks. His eyes went to his son, to me, and then to our clasped hands. He scowled and tossed all of his books on the table.

"What are you doing here?" His tone was harsh, cold, and directed right at me.

"I was invited," I scrambled to answer.

"Dad. What the hell is wrong with you? You've been acting weird all week. And now you're being rude to Amber."

The pained expression I saw in his father's eyes once before glowed as bright as the moon on a cloudless evening.

Clearly, something was going on with Landen's father, and I didn't want to be in the middle of it. I stood up, looped my shoulder bag over my arm, and scuttled backward. "I'm sorry, I didn't mean to intrude. Obviously, you two need some time alone," I said.

Landen stood up and grabbed my hand. "Amber, no...stay."

I shook my head and glanced at his dad. His eyebrows were pulled tight, his lips pinched together into a grimace. The little lines around his eyes were so pronounced I could have traced them from two feet away.

"No, I'll go. Let you two talk."

Landen's shoulders dropped a couple inches, his head following right behind. "Fine. I'll walk you out."

AUDREY CARLAN

Just as I was about to pass by the professor, he grabbed my wrist. "I'm sorry. You just look so much like her. It's uncanny."

"Like who?" I asked, searching his eyes for a glimmer of recognition about whom he might be referring.

"My Kate," he whispered, the same pained expression I'd seen several times before when I caught him glancing my way, spilled across his face.

A giant bowl of ice water could have been poured over my body, and I wouldn't have felt a thing. Stone. I'd turned completely to stone. Unmoving, unfeeling.

"Amber?" Landen shook me, one hand warming my shoulder where he held on.

I didn't take my eyes off him when I opened my mouth and spoke, "My mother's name was Kate."

His hand came up to his mouth to hold in what I could only assume was a silent cry. Tears filled his eyes but didn't fall. "My God..."

★ ★ ★

"And then what happened? Don't leave anything out!" Genevieve shifted her big belly to a more comfortable position on her bed.

Right after I left Landen's house, I jetted home and went straight to my best friend's place. I sat crossed-legged on her mattress while she rested her ginormous baby-filled belly on a body pillow.

I pressed my fingers against my temples. "What do you think I did? You know me!"

She snickered. "You ran." Her eyes widened. "Like *literally* this time?"

I nodded frantically and then lifted the glass of red wine to my lips. I didn't drink often, mostly a glass with my grandparents when we were having a celebratory dinner. This time, I wanted to wash away the tension and anxiety crawling all over my skin.

"Wow. So you're tweaked because he obviously knew your mother?" she asked.

I nodded.

"That's deep, girl. *Really* deep. Have you ever known anyone aside from your grandparents who knew her?"

Inhaling fully, making sure my lungs were filled to bursting before letting the breath go, I thought about it and couldn't come up with a single name. "No. Even the priest at church has only been around for the past decade." I felt my shoulders drop as if a two-ton weight held them down.

"I'm sorry. That must have been hard on you. What are you going to do?" Genevieve asked.

"Not sure." I traced the rim of the wine glass methodically.

Genevieve pinched her brow with two pale tipped fingers. "But you're going to ask him how he knew your mom, right?"

I shrugged. It should be such a simple question with an easy answer, but it didn't feel easy. My heart thumped in my chest, my head ached, and a sour taste filled my mouth.

Genevieve laid a hand over mine where it rested on my knee. "Babe, this is your chance to learn something new about your mom. This guy probably went to school with her or taught her in a class back in the day. You're not going to get a chance like this again."

Slowly, I rolled my head around to the left and then to the right. A satisfying pop split the air.

"Oh, honey, you are too tense." Her tone was edged with

worry and concern, two rather regular friends of mine as of late.

I huffed. "Viv, you don't know the half of it."

Her coal-black eyes seemed to zero in on mine. "Sharing is caring. I've got nothing but time on my hands." She rubbed a few swirls around her belly.

While I watched her, I could see a small mound pressing her skin outward. I set my glass down on the end table, flopped onto my stomach, and laid my hand over the spot. The baby pushed against my hand, and for a few moments, we played our little game of push and press with one another. I rubbed my cheek against her belly, and Viv put her hand into my hair and started to massage my scalp.

"Amber, I've been your best friend as long as you can remember. Heck, as long as I can remember, and I'm older..."

I snickered. "A whole three years. And not even that. More like two and three quarters. Big whoop!"

She kept running her fingers through my hair, scratching softly against my scalp, rubbing a spot she felt needed it. I practically purred, enjoying every relaxing second.

"Viv, the past few days have been a lot to take in," I admitted.

"Tell me..." she prompted, continuing her heavenly massage.

I licked my lips and pressed back against what I imagined was the baby's foot or elbow. It seemed a little bony but large enough that it moved in time with the pressure I applied.

"I kissed Dash." The words fell from my lips like a secret revealed.

She briefly stopped her ministrations on my head. I pressed my lips together and waited for her to chastise me.

"And how did it feel?"

I pressed my cheek harder against her belly, listening to the whoosh whoosh of baby and mother, one already like family to me and the other soon to be part of my life. I already loved her baby with my whole heart, and knew I'd do anything to be a great auntie. With Genevieve's lack of family ties, aside from Trent's parents that is, I'd always be there for her and her little one and vice versa.

"Good. Nice. Scary."

She stopped her movements again. "Scary? How so?"

I blinked a few times and thought back to when we kissed. While blindfolded, everything was so acute. "Surreal. As though it wasn't really happening. But also, I liked it so much that I..."

"You what?"

Tears filled my eyes as I sighed against her belly. "Viv, he's temptation incarnate."

Genevieve burst out laughing, her stomach shaking along with her boisterous guffaws.

I turned onto my side and rested my head on my hand and bent elbow. "You think that's funny?"

She nodded, still laughing. "Seriously...oh my...yes. He is definitely tempting."

Okay, at least she agreed with me there. "I just feel things when I'm near him that I've not felt before. Things that I've specifically avoided with other men." I glanced down, waiting to hear what she thought.

"That's understandable. Dash is very sexy, but more than that, I think there's a sensual nature to him. The guy exudes eroticism. I mean, he teaches it for goodness sake."

I pursed my lips and rolled my eyes. "So what do I do

about it?"

Genevieve smiled.

I swear on all things holy, when she smiles, the world smiles back. It's pure sunshine. Who needs Hawaii? Come hang out with the Earth's most kind and beautiful woman and find your own bit of paradise.

"Honey, what do you want to do?" Her tone was soft, that of a mother speaking to her child. Guess she was already in nesting mode.

I choked out my first thought. "Take off all my clothes and make love to him."

My admission shocked not only me but also my best friend by the way her cheeks became rosy and her mouth opened and closed like a hand puppet.

"Amber, you've never—"

"I know. See what I mean. Scary!"

She nodded. "Yeah, I'll say. What are you going to do?"

I shook my head. "We have a date tomorrow night."

Genevieve tilted her head and fluffed her hair. "You have a date with him. Did he ask you out?"

I nodded.

"Interesting. Dash hasn't dated in a long time. Not since the Rainy Day gal." Her lips compressed into a thin line. "From what I understood, he is spending time finding himself and has been for the better part of a year. I'm surprised he asked you out."

I cringed with irritation and jealousy when she mentioned the pretty strawberry blonde. Coree, if I remembered right. Boo.

"Why? Because I'm not in his league?"

Genevieve squirmed around to sit up. "Honey, goodness,

no. Not even." She put her hand on my cheek. "You are the most beautiful woman I know, inside and out. What I meant was he confided something in me a while back."

Confided. That sounded ominous and, on the opposite side of the scale, downright delicious.

Eager for any shred of information about the hot yogi, I sat up quick and grabbed both of her hands. "I'm your best friend in the world. This guy could break my heart into a million pieces. Plus, juicy stuff has to be shared. Who better than me?" I prompted.

She giggled and sighed, her bright pink lips shining in the daylight. "He'd kill me if I told you," she whispered and looked down at our clasped hands.

"I'll preach Bible verses all month if you don't!"

With that comment, she laughed heartily, her belly bouncing along with her. "Ouch!" She winced, pressing her palm to the side of her rounded belly. "All right, you. Mama will eat soon. Quit kicking. I swear he's going to end up being a star soccer player, much to Trent's dismay." Her eyes sparkled.

Yeah, I'd bet a hundred to one this kid comes out with a baseball bat and a glove since his dad is a star hitter for the Oakland Ports, but I let my friend believe what she wanted.

"Uh, Viv, I'm dying here!" I clenched my jaw and held my breath for any scrap of detail about Dash Alexander.

She moved her head from side to side, as if she was warring with her decision to tell me or not. Finally, she closed her eyes and nodded. "Okay. When I asked why he'd had a dry spell in the dating department..."

"Yeah?"

"Well, he said he was done playing the field. The next person he officially dated was going to be someone he felt had the potential to be more. The guy is twenty-eight. He's been around the block a time or two and never lacked for female companionship."

I gritted my teeth. "Yeah, I figured as much. Are you telling me he's a man-slut?"

Genevieve lifted a hand to her mouth and giggled behind her palm. "Yes and no. I imagine he's had a past. I mean he does teach Tantric yoga, and I know he has quite the background in the practice himself from what he's mentioned to me, but... I guess what I'm trying to say is if he asked you out, it's not because you're the next notch in his bedpost. You know what I mean?"

A relief so enormous danced over me like a fine mist on a foggy San Francisco day by the Bay. I closed my eyes and let the tumultuous feelings of hope, joy, and faith fill my every pore. It bathed my spirit in the hope that maybe, just maybe, Dash and I could be something more. If he wasn't out to get into my pants, then I wouldn't be tempted to break my private vow of chastity until marriage. We might very well have a real chance at a healthy relationship.

"Amber, honey, are you okay?" A frown marred Genevieve's doll-like complexion.

"I'm great. Better than great. I'm perfect."

CHAPTER NINE

SACRAL
CHAKRA

The second chakra is located in the sacrum, spleen area and corresponds to the organs that produce the various sex hormones and reproductive needs such as the testes and ovaries. The key concerns that this chakra manages pertain in large part to relationships, violence, pleasure, and the everyday emotional needs of humankind. Mentally, it governs joy, enthusiasm, and desire among others.

AMBER

Dash held the large wooden door open for me and placed his hand at the base of my spine. I tried not to react to the instant spark that sizzled at his touch.

"After you." He smiled.

The shoebox-size restaurant was in a building hidden away in a small section of Berkeley that I'd not spent a lot of time in. As a professional student, most of my jaunts were within walking distance of the college or home to save on parking fees.

A tall, thin man in a suit with slicked-back, dark hair greeted Dash the second we entered. *"Bonjour, Monsieur* Alexander. Your table is ready for you and your *belle femme."*

"Thank you, kind sir," Dash responded.

He placed his hand back on my lower spine and led me toward a small outdoor courtyard. Wistcria climbed the brick walls and along the black wrought iron fencing. The view beyond the small seating area was spectacular. I hadn't realized we'd gone up this high. I wondered if we were technically still in Berkeley or just outside the city based on the view. I stopped midstep and stared at the beauty before me. The panorama of San Francisco and the ocean from this distance was breathtaking.

Dash pulled out a cushioned metal chair, its iron legs grating on the brick foundation. I preened under his gentlemanly manners. Ever since he'd picked mc up, he had been on his best behavior. He hadn't so much as touched me in anything other than a proper way, which I appreciated and despised in equal measures. With him being naturally tactile, the lack of his hands on me was worrisome—quite possibly the most unsettling feature of being in his presence. Worse, I knew I couldn't ask about it without admitting my own desire to put my hands all over him.

Gah! I mentally chastised myself for having such impure thoughts. Sitting across from him in such a romantic setting, the candlelight from the table centerpiece making his face glow like warm honey, his bedroom eyes searching mine and finding all the answers to questions he'd not even asked me yet, tore at my defenses. Not to mention the suit he wore was ridiculously sexy. The suit was dark gray, and he wore a teal dress shirt with the first two buttons left undone so that I could admire a swath of his bronzed skin. The hue of the shirt made his eyes burst a bright yellow amber just like the stone.

"What do you think of the place?" Dash asked, lifting his water glass and taking a sip.

I inhaled the floral scent and shook my head. "It's unbelievable. I didn't even know this place existed and the view... Dash, it's incredible."

His corresponding smile sent a jolt of heat straight through my chest to settle between my thighs.

Lord, please help me, for this man is going to be my downfall.

Dash grinned. "I'm glad you like it. The owner is a good friend of my dad and stepmother. I may have pulled a few strings to get us in."

I put my hand over his on the table. "Thank you. It means a lot to me that you want to show me somewhere special to you."

He squeezed my hand and curled his fingers around mine when the waiter arrived. I pulled against his hold, but he didn't let go, seemingly happy to just hold my hand while the waiter spoke with us.

"*Monsieur*, may I go over the specials?" He handed us two leather-bound menus.

I held the menu against my chest while Dash responded with a French *oui*.

"Today's specials include the chef's pan-seared salmon, dressed with a wine vinegar sauce, rice pilaf, and seasoned vegetables. Also, is his special recipe of steak *au poivre*. It features a New York strip encrusted with crushed peppercorns and seared in a Cognac-mustard sauce. Would you like something to drink while you consider your options?"

Dash glanced at me. "Do you drink, little bird?"

I smiled at his chosen nickname. At least it was unique. "I like wine but don't drink it often. Usually too busy studying."

"I've got the perfect wine for this evening, if you'd let me order for us?"

He asked for my approval. Asked. A lot of men would just order whatever they wanted. I was finding not all books should be based on their covers. The same was true for this man. Just because Dash had a handsome face and a body that women and men alike swooned over, it didn't mean his beauty was all he had to give the world. I made a mental note to pray about my initial prejudices over what type of man he was, based solely on his looks. I'd not make that mistake again.

"I'd love for you to order on my behalf. I'm afraid I know very little about wine other than it's usually pretty tasty!"

He smirked and gave his attention to the waiter. "We'll have a bottle of your *Alphonse Mellot Sancerre Rouge Génération XIX. Merci.*"

"Now that was a mouthful! Do you speak French?" The way he used specific phrases and how his words rolled with the language seemed more familiar than not.

Dash sat back, letting my hand go. "Very perceptive. I did a couple years in Europe when I was studying Tantric practices. So many cultures view it differently. I wanted to gain as much of a full worldview as possible. In answer to your question, though, I learned a bit of the language in each country where I stayed—France, Germany, Italy, Spain—basically, enough to get me into trouble." He chuckled. "How about you? Have you lived anywhere else besides California?"

I tilted my head and leaned my elbow on the table. "Would it blow you away to learn I've never lived anywhere other than Berkeley?"

His eyes widened.

"Haven't even left the very house where I grew up."

Dash rested his cheek on his palm, elbow on the table, mimicking my position. "Yet you come across as far more worldly. Do you want to travel?"

"Very much. I want to go everywhere, but medical school is not conducive to time away. I'm trying to get my education under my belt so I can open up my own practice sooner rather than later."

"Have you chosen an area of practice?"

I plucked at the napkin and thought about the conversation I'd had with Landen regarding general practice, gynecology, and pediatrics. "Not sure just yet. I'm mostly leaning toward pediatrics or obstetrics."

"Do a lot of women go that route?"

Not meaning to, I pressed back in my chair a little harder than was polite. "Is that a jab toward my gender?" I gritted through my teeth.

He shifted his weight and waved his hands in a gesture of surrender. "No, not at all. I just wondered if women are more likely to go into the medical roles that could be considered more nurturing. I would think it would suit the profession."

I closed my eyes. "Sorry. I didn't mean to react so poorly. It's been a really strange week. I don't feel like myself."

Right then, the sommelier delivered our wine and served only enough for Dash to taste. I watched as he swirled the crimson liquid around and then sniffed from the bulbous glass before taking a sip. "*Magnifique!*" he said.

The sommelier poured a couple ounces into each of our glasses and set the bottle down on the table.

"Okay, first you need to swirl the wine around like this," Dash instructed, moving his hand in a quick circular pattern. "Now sniff the notes through your nose, inhaling the sensation the wine gives you."

I followed his instructions to the letter.

"Now sip just a little, but don't swallow it. Let it sit on your tongue and infiltrate your taste buds fully."

We sipped and savored together. I closed my eyes as I swallowed the loveliest wine I'd ever tasted. Before I opened my eyes, I felt a pressure against my cheek. The scent of mint and eucalyptus hinted that Dash had moved closer. I gasped when the tiniest warmth spread along my nose. He was rubbing his nose along mine slowly, tenderly.

"What did you taste?" he asked, threading his fingers through the hair at my nape.

"Berry...uh plum..." I answered, my breath starting to come quicker now that I knew he was so close.

"And?"

"Spice." I breathed out, taking in his air. He'd synchronized his breathing to mine so that we were breathing in one another's life-force the same way we had in class. My entire body lit up like a firecracker, all nerve endings snapping at his nearness.

He touched his lips against mine, giving the slightest pressure. "Very good, little bird."

I brushed my lips along his just enough to feel a touch of moisture when he licked my bottom lip. I couldn't help it. I sighed. Right into his mouth. Such a desperate girl move, but I couldn't help it.

For a few blessed moments, time stopped. The air warmed,

the candle on the table flickered as a spark of familiarity and timelessness covered the two of us like a soft blanket. In that span of space, I didn't want to be anywhere but lost within Dash's essence. His body called to mine on a visceral, carnal level, but it was so much more than that. Almost as if our souls were mingling, dancing in the moonlight, without a care in the world. As soon as the visual entered my mind's eye, I gasped and jolted back.

Dash opened his eyes, and I knew, I just *knew* I wanted to look into those eyes for the rest of my life. Every Catholic believed that God had a plan, and through his wisdom and love, he brought us together. Dash had been right. We were meant to be.

I opened my mouth to tell him, to say...anything. Maybe that I understood what he'd felt earlier, that I now agreed, but I didn't know how to say the words. They were so far out of the realm of what I understood spiritually and scientifically.

"It's okay. I know." His words were filled with confidence and commitment.

I shook my head and rubbed at my temples. "But how?"

He shrugged. "I just do."

I sat back, forcing some distance between us. Dash didn't move his chair back to the opposite side of the table where he'd been before. Instead, he wrapped his hand around mine. "We'll figure it out together."

"Is everything so black and white to you?"

He chuckled and rested his chin in his palm. "No, I find that most things are full of color and painted with a mixture of broad strokes with endless starts and finishes. But the end result is always a masterpiece to the creator."

The creator.

"What if we don't believe in the same creator?" I choked down a golf ball-sized lump of emotion.

Dash hummed. "I think everyone has a sense of the creator or a higher power. We may call that entity by a different name. Isn't it interesting how in every faith there is one primary source that holds the power to all things? For Christians, it's God and Jesus. For Muslims, it's Allah. Buddhism was founded on one man's teachings, a man by the name of Siddhartha Gautama. Even the Pagans worship Mother Earth."

"And your point is?" I asked, afraid to hear his answer.

If he didn't believe in the God above, any relationship between us would not work. I was a devoted believer in the Father, Son, and the Holy Spirit. I'd be accepting if he didn't believe in one specific denomination, but having no faith at all...that would be a deal breaker.

"My point, little bird, is that I believe we all have faith in a higher power but call it by a different name."

Oh, thank you, God in heaven above. He's a believer. Amen to that.

"So you believe in God?" I asked, more for my own sanity than anything else. I should have had faith that God would never put me in a position to feel such intense romantic feelings for a nonbeliever.

"As much as I consider myself a spiritual person, I do believe in the God you love and worship. However, I am not religious in mainstream ways such as attending mass or going to Sunday worship at the local church."

I nodded and sipped my wine, letting the berry notes calm my anxiety over this subject. Probably because I wanted him to have a similar belief system. Needed it in order to continue seeing him. Regardless, religion was a heavy subject to get into on a first real date. Well, technically the second if I counted our lunch at Rainy Day last week. And the third if I included pastries and coffee when we first officially met.

While I was thinking about his response, the waiter came back and took our order. We both ordered the gourmet French steak. Dash promised it would taste amazing with the wine, and I took his word for it.

"So, you mentioned earlier that you had a really strange week. Tell me about it?" Dash asked.

I groaned and leaned back heavily in the cushioned chair. The waiter had turned on the heat lamp near our table, which provided a comforting environment to relax and snuggle into the squishy pillow. I held my wine near my chest so that I could enjoy the aroma while we waited for our meals.

Dash sat patiently while I gathered my thoughts. I appreciated a man who could enjoy the silence between us, not fill the air with useless chatter when a moment of silence would do.

Finally, I took a breath and decided if I was going to have this man be more than just someone I lusted over, I needed to share my life with him. See if we were truly compatible.

"This past week I started the medical program. The one I told you about?"

"Okay, and why is that strange? Is the course work unusual?" He rested his hands on the table and focused his amber gaze strictly on me.

I sipped a bit of wine and let it roll around my tongue, trying to decide how to word the experience. "No, but you know how I told you that my study partner was my instructor's son?"

Dash's gaze turned cold and hardened to stone. "Yes," he

growled.

I giggled, enjoying the bit of jealously. At least I knew he was as affected as I was by this thing between us. "Well, his father has been acting weird around me. All week he'd stare at me, and he made a point to ask me the oddest questions, most of them personal."

Dash reached a hand out and settled it on my knee. "Do I need to talk to this guy? Put him in his place? Did he do anything inappropriate?" His words were rushed and laced with acid.

I shook my head. "No, no. Nothing like that. It's just it was odd. Then I went over there yesterday, and Landen and I hadn't even opened our books when the professor came home. He admitted that I looked like someone from his past. Someone named Kate."

Dash rubbed his warm palm along my thigh, still keeping a proper distance away from my private parts, although I wouldn't admit, even under duress, how much his simple touch was affecting me. I could feel my temperature rise, which made the heat lamps' fiery air a tad stifling. My palms were moist where I gripped the wine glass with both hands.

"Okay. Well, at least he was honest. So what's the problem then?"

I licked my lips and blew out a breath. "The problem is that my mother's name was Kate."

His eyes were soft and welcoming when he spoke. "You said she passed when you were born, right?"

I gripped the glass even tighter, hoping in my anxiety I wouldn't break the fragile goblet. "Yes, she died giving birth to me."

Dash reached over and relieved me of my glass and set it

down on the table before he leaned over and gripped both of my hands. It was as if he knew this conversation was hard on me. I adored that his instinct was to soothe and comfort me.

Oh, Lord. I could fall in love with him so easily. Please guide me to Your will.

"So this professor may have known your mother before she died then?"

I nodded but didn't say a word.

Dash continued, "And this is unsettling. Why?"

"Because I've never met anyone who knew my mother outside of my grandparents. She was only twenty when she died. All of her friends are long gone by now. I wouldn't even know how to contact them, and my grandparents had more to deal with than worrying about keeping connections with my mother's old friends. They had to take care of me."

"Are you going to talk to him?" Dash asked.

I glanced down and watched his thumbs sweep over the tops of my hands. Such a small comfort that carried with it an enormous amount of meaning.

My shoulders felt heavy as I shrugged. "I can't *not* talk to him. But it's more than that. When he saw me, it wasn't simple recognition. It was as though he was cataloguing me, taking in each one of my features as if he needed to memorize them."

That remark made a little muscle in Dash's jaw tick. He leaned forward, getting closer to me. "Is he scaring you? I have no problem ensuring no man ever makes you feel fear."

I lifted my hand and caressed his cheek. "Not really, no. It's more unsettling. I get this feeling there's something he knows or remembers about my mom that he's not bringing up. I owe it to her and myself to find out what it is. Don't you think?"

Dash blew out what could only be a frustrated breath.

"Can I be there when you ask him?"

He squeezed my hand and right then, right there, it was clear that I didn't have to go through this alone. Sure, I had Genevieve, who I knew would be with me if I needed her, but she had her own problems to deal with. Besides, Trent was coming home for a couple weeks, and I didn't want to bother her with my silly little investigation.

"You would do that for me?" I asked Dash, peering into his caramel eyes for the millionth time this evening, knowing I'd never tire of them.

"Amber, haven't you figured out that I'd do just about anything for you?"

"Dash..." My throat clogged, and I reached for my glass, chugging back a few gulps to clear the emotional tickle that had risen at his statement.

"No, listen. I'm all in. Whatever you need. I'm here for you as I hope you'll be for me. I meant what I said. There's something special between us, and I for one want to give it the time it needs to flourish and blossom into whatever it's supposed to be. I had planned on spending this evening convincing you that I wanted to be an *us*. Exclusively."

I set my glass back down. "Like going steady?" I laughed, and he followed suit.

"In so many words, yes. I want to be with you, Amber. Whatever that means. Let's give what we are starting a fair shot. Part of doing so is being there for one another. If this man knows something about your mother that has you feeling out of sorts, I want to be the hand you hold to get you through it."

"Thank you. I want that, too," I admitted.

"So you're going to give us a try?" he asked with a huge smile.

I smiled so big my cheeks hurt. "Yeah, I am."

"You won't regret it. Come here." He curled one hand around my nape and the other cupped my cheek.

Before I could suggest that public displays of affection in fancy French restaurants were not ideal, his lips slanted over mine. He licked into my mouth, tasting of wine and his own brand of spice. He intoxicated me with his kiss, moving my head from side to side. I pulled back to gulp a few rushed breaths before he pulled me back, coming on so strong and delving for more.

Dash took everything I had to give, his body language promising me more than I'd ever dreamed. And I kissed him back with a fervor I didn't know I had. I tugged at his bottom lip then soothed it with my tongue. He groaned and retaliated by sucking on my tongue and nibbling the tip delectably. His hand massaged my nape while his other hand held me close, our chests pressed together. He exhaled, and I inhaled, sharing breath so we could kiss longer, go deeper, until I was lost in him once more. No...in us.

After dinner, Dash took me for a walk near the water's edge. We kissed in the moonlight with the water crashing against the rocks below, serenading the most perfect date in my life. When it got late, Dash drove me home and walked me to my grandparents' door.

"See you on Friday for class?"

I grinned against his lips, enjoying the press of his body against mine as he held me against the wall of my childhood home.

"I'll be there with bells on," I said and then plucked his lips for another tasty morsel.

He moaned against my mouth. "Can I call you tomorrow?"

"I'd love that." I kissed him, gently pressing my lips to his in small pecks.

"Are you going to talk to the doc? Remember, I'll be there if you do."

I pulled back so I could look him in the eye. "I'll ask for a time that I can meet him privately. Maybe this weekend?"

"This weekend works perfectly but not in the evening." His eyebrows rose as he whispered, "I have a date."

Cold, hard dread slithered down my spine. "A date." I winced under the strain of the simple statement. I'm pretty certain that my face paled because my stomach twisted into unbearable knots.

"Yeah." He leaned even closer. "With you. All my weekends are booked from here on out." He kissed my mouth hard. "For my girlfriend."

His girlfriend. We were absolutely the silliest couple on this side of the coast. When I told this story to Genevieve tomorrow, I was going to leave this part out. She'd think I'd gone mad.

"I've never really had a boyfriend. Not in any official capacity," I admitted, smiling coyly. I just barely stopped myself from twirling a lock of hair around my finger like a starry-eyed teenager who'd just been asked to go steady by the coolest boy in class.

He grinned and then gave me another peck on the lips. "Good. Then I'll be your first and your last," he said before turning on his heel and jogging down the steps, my heart his eager companion as he hopped into his car and drove away, waving until I couldn't see him anymore.

Thank You, Lord, for bringing him to me. I cannot wait to see what the future holds.

CHAPTER TEN

Half Lotus
(Padmasana)

Half Lotus pose opens the hips and stretches the ankles and knees. Once you get into a cross-legged position as shown in the image, pull one ankle up to rest on the inner thigh, tucking the other ankle deeper under your alternate thigh. Make sure to switch legs in order to keep your center balanced. To move into full lotus, cross both legs and rest the feet and/or ankle onto the inner thighs simultaneously.

AMBER

Two weeks had passed since I'd seen Professor O'Brien in Landen's house. The plan was to approach him right away about the awkward exchange and find out what, if anything, he knew of my mother. Mostly, I wanted to know if it was truly my mother he thought he knew and, if so, how. Alas, he'd left that weekend for a two-week-long vacation with his wife, Susan. Landen had stayed behind to attend class. We'd spent the time following the doctors we'd been assigned to at UCSF. I got Emergency Medicine. Needless to say, the ER was not where I wanted to be long-term. Too much death and gore for my tastes.

The best part of the last two weeks was that Dash and I'd been seeing one another most days. He'd taken me to the movies and on long walks through the city. We'd spend nights making out at his home or pressed up against the wall of my grandparents' home, petting hot and heavy. I'd been lucky because he hadn't pushed me for more. If he had been a man attending my church, committed to Catholicism, more wouldn't be an issue. Unfortunately for me, I had to fall for the guy that was arguably an expert in sex. I wouldn't be able to hold him off for long. I could already feel the tender fibers of my hold on my vow shredding at the edges.

I looked over at Dash addressing the class, lost in his sheer beauty. He was bare-chested, wearing only a pair of his standard loose, white yoga pants. Any woman in her right mind would want to gobble him up.

"Class, today's lesson is going to be very personal and explicit. You not only have to use the power of your mind to ignore all the other couples around you, but you also have to trust that your partner is focused solely on you and your experience with one another." Dash looked around the class, making sure to lock his gaze with each participant. Silently, each member nodded their agreement to his request.

I had no idea what was in store for class today, only that Dash warned me it was going to be more physical than what we'd done before. Now that we were a couple, I didn't mind him touching or kissing me because he'd not crossed any lines. Besides, I loved touching him in return.

"Remember that Tantra is designed to help you achieve liberation or enlightenment. In Sanskrit, the word Tantra means 'to weave or extend,' which is what we are going to learn today. Do not be afraid if you have an overtly physical response. Today's practice should bring you to the height of orgasm without actually tipping over. That is something you can take with you and practice on one another at home." He smirked devilishly.

Um, what? He couldn't be serious. He was going to bring me close to orgasm? Here, where everyone could see me? I clenched my hands together tightly in my lap. Dash noticed and brought both up to his lips and kissed each finger until I fully unclenched them. He turned his head and mouthed, "Trust me."

I closed my eyes and took a deep breath. I did trust him. He'd given me no reason not to. Besides, we'd played around over the past couple weeks and spent some time rubbing against one another sensually while making out. The most he'd done was stimulate my nipples. Even that was more than I'd done with other men. I wanted to take things further, but so far, he hadn't asked, and I was grateful I didn't have to address my vow, although I knew it would come up sooner rather than later at the rate our relationship was progressing.

Technically, I didn't see anything wrong with touching one another or even orgasming for that matter. My sole requirement, the parameter I personally was unwilling to go past was that he not take my virginity. Over the past couple weeks, I'd thought about nothing else but having his fingers inside me, stroking me, making me come without the aid of my clitoral vibrator.

Dash's instruction filtered back into my mind, bringing me back from my mental jaunt.

"The practice I'm going to teach you today was founded by Charles and Caroline Muir. They crafted the concept of the sacred spot massage. Not only can doing this practice provide intense vaginal orgasms that may be followed by female ejaculation, but more than that, it's designed to build trust between you and your partner. When you attempt this practice tonight on your mate, do not be frightened if either of you experience a deeply emotional connection. One or both of you may cry, which is not uncommon when you are opening the second chakra so passionately."

An intense heat rushed up my chest, scalding my cheeks. I set my hands over the inflamed areas.

"Just like blood flows through our veins, so does our body's energy. In order to tap into a woman's sexual psyche, you must first gain her trust. Putting your fingers inside a woman and expecting her to just open her heart, mind, and body to you would be asinine. First, you need to start with your words. Tell her what her giving herself to you means to you. Women tend to be natural givers. In this context, you need to wash that away and allow, as well as encourage, her to *receive* your attentions."

Most of the members of today's class were holding hands and caressing one another with small touches of the hands, arms, neck, and legs. Watching them interact with each other was a true gift. The couples were here for their own reasons, whether it be a deeper connection, a fun new thing to try, maybe they were even at risk for a dissolution, but right then, they were all one hundred percent focused and committed to the study. It not only showed that couples should spend more alone time connecting, but it also proved to me that the work Dash did in this class was genuinely helping people stay in love. He was doing a service that couldn't be matched for these families. And the best part was that he enjoyed sharing his knowledge and spreading love more than anyone I'd ever known. Regardless of his past experiences, sexual or otherwise, his soul and his intentions were pure.

Dash got up on his knees, turned to the side of the yoga mat, and requested I stand. I followed his instructions, as did the rest of the women in class.

"Now men, cross your legs comfortably. Ladies, straddle your mate and sit in his lap with your feet locked tight to his buttocks."

I straddled Dash, balanced myself on his shoulders, and, with the aid of his hands on my hips, sat softly on his lap. He adjusted me to where we were chest to chest. His was bare and on golden display. I reminded myself with a mental lashing not to drool over my man in front of the class. The same one I'd given myself when he removed his shirt earlier. I bit down on my lip as he smiled and waggled his eyebrows.

Stinky jokester. He loved this, putting our relationship on display. I swear, every chance he got when we were walking the streets or having dinner, he'd make a show of looping his arm over my shoulder, nuzzling my cheek, kissing my neck, playing with my hair. All the romantic things you see in movies, Dash actually did, and he did them regularly.

"All right, Cosmo, where is this going?" I grinned, playfully using the nickname I'd given him. He pretended he hated it, but he was always talking about the moon and stars, pointing out constellations, sharing his thoughts on the universe and how the energies interact with one another, hence how he'd scored this endearment.

Dash gripped my hips and pressed his pelvis against mine. I gasped and held on to his shoulders more tightly.

"Oh little bird, we're about to take this to a whole new level. Before I address the class about what to do next, I want you to know, I'm planning on touching you here." He ran his open hands over my breasts quickly enough that it wouldn't seem too explicit but enough to have my nipples puckering up for attention. "Here." He rounded his hands over my ass and ground me against his hardening length. I bit my lip hard and hummed at the contact. He brought his lips to my ear. "And I plan on touching your center over your shorts if you will allow it."

I let out a slow exhale, knowing my breath tickled against his ear. He shivered, and his penis went from semihard to stone in a second flat. It pressed so delectably against my core. I closed my eyes and ground against him.

His fingers dug into my bum.

"Amber, don't play with me unless you want to experience everything the women in the class are going to experience. We can just sit in one another's laps and limit the touching while I instruct. Frankly, that's probably a good idea." His voice was strained and reed thin when he spoke.

Out of nowhere, the thought of him not touching me hit me like a lightning bolt of pain, starting in my heart and sizzling through my body. I locked my legs and arms around him and shook my head. And without even thinking about it, I said the words I knew in my heart he needed to hear to continue. "I trust you."

Dash inhaled so fully his chest and upper body rose and

my arms with it. He let the breath out through his mouth and then pecked me on the lips. "Okay."

He blinked a few times and smiled. "Class, I want you to spend time face-to-face telling one another how much you love them. What you like about them emotionally and physically. Whatever comes up, tell your partner. While you do that, touch them any way you like, but please keep your hands over the clothing. We are not having sex today, though it may feel like it for some of you." He grinned while several members of the class chuckled.

"Feel free to kiss and show your lover what they mean to you physically within reason. We're all adults. You know what that means. I'll let you know when we're going to take it up a notch."

Take it up a notch? Oh sweet heaven above! I swallowed and tried to relax my shoulders, arms, and legs, melting into Dash. He trailed his hands up my back. When he reached the spot where neck met body, he smoothed his palms down my bare arms.

"You're so beautiful, Amber. Has anyone ever told you that?"

I blinked and made direct eye contact. "You have told me more in the past three weeks than anyone in my whole life. Well, aside from my grandparents."

His lips pulled together in a sexy pout. He didn't say anything, and while the silence sat between us, I realized it was my turn. This was not about him pleasing me. It was about us pleasing one another.

Using just my fingertips, I caressed his head, running my fingers through his hair. The strands were so fine they trickled through my fingers like water rushing down a hillside over smooth rocks and stones. I massaged his entire head, focusing on the pressure points before moving down to his neck, landing at his broad muscled shoulders. I curled my hands over them, expanding my reach fully and not even coming close to covering the breadth of his size. "You're so strong, sculpted. Your body is a fine machine..."

"One that is meant for pleasuring you. The only woman I want to kiss." He moved his head so that our noses touched before he laid his lips over mine and cupped my cheeks with both hands. When my lips were nicely swollen and bruised from repeated, blistering kisses, he pulled back, still holding my face in the palm of each hand. "The only woman I want to touch."

With his eyes locked on mine, he slid his hands down my neck, over each heaving mound where he stopped to swipe his thumbs against the erect nipples poking through the thin fabric of my sports bra. Just as I was getting into it, he moved his hands, skating them along my ribs and abdomen until I inadvertently began a circular motion with my hips.

"The only woman I want to show love to." He set his face next to mine as his hands slipped down to my ass. He gripped both cheeks in his large hands and shifted his hips in sync with my movements so that his penis slid along my clit over and over again.

Intense pleasure rippled through my body like fiery ribbons of need and desire, all settling hotly between my thighs as we gave to one another. My body called to him, and based on the sizeable erection he was sporting, his responded with equal want. My heart cried out, and his instantly curled around mine to soothe and protect. My soul spoke. His answered with honesty.

Words I hadn't meant to say just then slipped from my parted lips. "Oh Dash...I'm so in love with you."

When I realized what I'd said, I held him so tight, my legs and arms locked around his form, not allowing him to move me back so he could look into my eyes. It was too soon. Who fell in love with a man after only three weeks together?

And then none of it mattered, because Dash responded to my proclamation of love in a way that made it all okay.

"I know." Simple, as if he'd always known.

He moved his body so that he could manipulate my limbs and loosen my hold. I closed my eyes, afraid and embarrassed of what I might see when I looked into his.

"Look at me, little bird. Don't fly away. Not now. Be the proud swan because I'm so proud of you."

I lifted my head so fast I worried I'd get whiplash. "P-proud?" My voice shook with unease.

He nodded and cupped my cheek with one hand, the other wrapped around my back, keeping me pressed against him in every way possible.

"Proud of you for admitting it. For taking the chance on me and opening your heart to what we have."

A shaky breath worked its way out my mouth along with a broken, "Do...uh...y-you love me?" I asked even though I was absolutely terrified of his reply. It was ludicrous to think he could fall in love with a woman he'd never even had a sexual relationship with.

"Oh, Amber, I fell in love the moment you allowed me to blindfold you."

DASH

Amber's head shot back as her eyes glowed with interest and surprise.

I pressed a finger over her lips. "Hold that thought."

She grimaced enough that I surmised she wasn't thrilled with the pause in our discussion, but as much as I would have liked to scream from the rooftops that we were in love, I still had a class to teach. While gritting my teeth, I addressed the class.

"Don't look at me. Keep your eyes focused on your partner's." I shifted my gaze so that I was looking straight into Amber's eyes.

Christ, she was a goddess on high. She epitomized everything I'd ever wanted in a woman. Intelligent, strong, loving, but most of all, loyal to the core. I'd not have to worry about my little bird straying to another suitor. I had the utmost confidence in us. The same way I knew the Earth was round, I recognized that, as long as I treated her well and didn't betray her trust, she'd be mine forever.

The best part—we wouldn't need the legal paperwork to prove our bond like so many did and failed. My love and I would not become another statistic like my mother and father. And I planned to ensure that by never getting married. My word and my blood would be our bond. For her, when the time was right, I'd make the ultimate sacrifice. I'd mar my temple by tattooing a ring on the finger that stereotypically held a wedding ring. All for love, faith, and commitment. Just the thought of the needle piercing my flesh with intent to mark me as this woman's forever sent a bolt of lust roaring through my sternum to settle stiffly in my cock. She moaned low and deep in her throat, which made me think about using that mouth and throat for activities far more devious.

With Amber though, I'd held back from pressuring her into more sexual activities. Something about the way she backed off when things got a bit hot and heavy made me leery to press on. I wanted her to be ready to go there physically with me. It was definitely something we needed to talk about, especially since we'd both admitted our feelings. I wanted nothing more than to seal our commitment to this relationship with an act of physical love, and I planned on going there tonight.

Fisting her hair and tipping back her head, I laid a line of kisses against the pale, slender column of her neck. I spoke against her lips loud enough for the class to hear the next steps. "In the yab-yum Tantric position where you face your partner, the pair of you can start rocking against one another, rubbing your genitals more firmly to stimulate arousal. When ready, the female would lift up and insert the penis, moving into intercourse. While rocking against each other, this position allows for a deep physical and mental connection, as well as the ability to work toward mutual orgasms. Looking into one another's eyes while you mate is a powerful aphrodisiac and essential to long lasting unity."

I shifted my hands to her hips and helped rock her lower body against my cock. Her eyes were half-open and her face held a dopey loose expression. I'd seen that before when we'd had our serious make out sessions at my house while sitting on my couch.

"Tonight, you're going to practice giving your woman a G-spot massage as described in the material I distributed at the beginning of class. In the G-spot massage, you'll insert fingers into her vagina and search for the bumpy patch of tissue on the front wall. She'll let you know when you've found it."

I took a slow breath while my woman rubbed and rolled her hips, keeping up the friction I'd set. Pure nirvana. I could only think of one thing that would be better, and that was being inside her.

"Since we can't do that in class, feel free to touch your partner's genitals over their clothes. When your mate gets close to orgasm, back off. Kiss for a while, talk quietly about how you feel, what you are feeling for one another. Then start back up again. Part of the beauty of Tantra and a healthy sexual relationship is the buildup, the anticipation. There are moments when you're mutually pleasuring the other that are so completely...selfless. Find that within the experience today. Give that gift to your mate."

Amber dug her heels into my ass and ground down on my cock. A breath I hadn't realized I was holding shot out as I slammed her mouth over mine. I took her mouth with an intensity I'd not felt for another woman. Long sweeps of her tongue made my balls rise up, and I wanted to plunge my dick into her heat. Needing to turn the tables, I ran my hands down the front of her chest, pinching her nipples until she arched into my touch. I leaned forward and kissed, licked, and sucked on every inch of her neck, whispering things to her, the things I wanted to do to her.

I found it hard to get a good hold on her perky nips. I'd have much preferred bare tits, but her sports bra was made of flimsy Lycra that left nothing to the imagination. It took everything I had not to bite her ample bosom through the small top. However, control was the cornerstone of Tantra, and I'd had years to perfect mine under duress. Though I had to admit, with Amber, the challenge was formidable. She made me *want* to lose control in every way. Perhaps that's what love does to people? It was quite possibly the one aspect of Tantra I'd been missing. A partner I loved who loved me in return. I couldn't wait to test every Tantric theory, practice every position physically, and experience it all with new eyes. Through the eyes of a man in love.

"Are you wet for me, little bird?" I asked while tweaking both tight peaks.

"God...yes," she moaned.

That moan went straight to my groin. I jackknifed up and pressed her down so she could feel every steely inch. Then I held her aloft as I dragged the surface against her sex so that the wide-knobbed ridge at the top of my cock would press perfectly on her hot button. I was rewarded with the loveliest sigh and a clench of her thighs against my waist. The power of her quads as she rubbed against me was the sweetest torture.

"You want me to touch you, relieve some of that ache?" I nibbled on her earlobe as her breathing became labored.

She kissed my neck and ran her tongue down it. I curled a hand up her back and over her shoulder to anchor her to me.

"Please...please touch me," she begged before biting into the ball of my shoulder.

That tiny prick of pain snared the sexual beast I'd been holding back. Locking her close, I slid one hand in between our bodies and cupped her sex possessively. Her entire body went rigid as if that single touch had made her come, but I knew it hadn't. I considered myself quite the expert when it came to making women climax. I'd had countless hours of Tantric training. And in an extraordinary Tantric relationship where two people have invested their entire beings, your partner's body can be conditioned to orgasm on command alone. I'd not experienced that in previous relationships, but I planned on getting to that place with Amber one day. For now, though, I cupped the heart of her, and she squirmed like she had ants in her pants.

I kept our bodies smashed together and paired my breathing to hers. When we were completely in sync, I kissed along her neck, dragging my lips down to where her strawberry scent was most potent. "Close your eyes. Savor me touching you. Trust me to make you feel honored. Worshiped. Loved."

"I love you. I trust you." Amber burrowed her face in the crook of my neck, her heated breath feeding the fire already building within.

And that's when I went to town seducing the woman I loved. I rubbed my hand back and forth across her center, using my thumb to press against her clit. I feasted on every sigh. Each breath gave me life, enriched my soul, and strengthened the feelings I had for her. Soon after I began massaging the space between her thighs, she started to roll her hips, getting into it. When she did that, I backed off and instead caressed her thighs and back and massaged her scalp. She was jelly in my arms and under my complete control.

When her breathing evened out once more, I tunneled my hand into her hair and tugged at the nape until she lifted her head. Her facial expression was dreamy and loaded with pure lust, my very favorite look on her to date. Lost in love. Taking my cues, she wrapped her hands around my neck and leaned forward to kiss me. I let her, giving her the lead, wanting her to feel the power of being in charge. She relished it, and soon her hips started moving again, seeking the hardness only I could give her.

I moved my hand back over her center and cupped her

with intent. She gasped and pulled back from our kiss.

"Are you going to give me this?" I asked, swallowing down the emotional fire that went with the question. My nostrils flared as I searched her face, waiting for her reply. I needed to hear her say the words. I had plans for the evening, and all of them included getting inside her.

"I...I...don't know what you mean."

Those words hit me like a wet towel to the ass, startling and coming out of left field.

Her eyes shone a bright emerald green as I picked up the sensual massage of her most private place. She pressed into my hand, showing me she wanted what I was giving, but her words... They didn't add up. Confused, I circled her clit with my thumb.

"Are you going to give me this pussy? Let me inside. Be with me in all things?"

I focused my gaze on hers and pressed hard on her clit, giving her endless circles. Her breath caught. She was close, so close to coming. I could have written a book just on the different facial expressions women make when they are going to orgasm. I kept up the pressure, my hand jerking back and forth roughly, wanting to see her face as she gave herself over to me.

"Dash, I can't..." She moaned and lifted her head back.

Needing to see her eyes, I tugged on her hair until she winced and brought her face to mine. Our noses were now touching, our lips a scant few centimeters apart. Every time I tugged on her pussy, pressing two fingers against the shorts, dipping into her core through the fabric, panties and all, she'd scowl and bite down on her lip. A scowl when someone was going to orgasm was not uncommon, but there was something else in play.

"You can't give me this pussy?" I frowned and rubbed four fingers back and forth in maddening strokes.

"I can't." She choked on a moan and her body tightened. She was going to come. I should have stopped, brought her back from the precipice like I'd instructed the class, but right then, I didn't care. She was mine and I hers. I wanted to see it. See her face when she gave it to me.

"Do you feel my love for you? Every touch, every caress, it's me showing you. My proof."

Amber closed her eyes, and her mouth opened. "Dash, I can't give you what you want," she said, her words featherlight and just as fragile.

"Why not?" I asked, still manipulating her sex, not letting up for even a moment's reprieve, which went against everything I should have been doing, but I was too far gone. Gone for her.

And that's when it hit. I pressed my thumb on her hot button...hard. Her eyes went wide, and her mouth dropped open. A crimson blush washed over her cheeks. She locked her legs, pressing her groin hard down on mine over and over. Her body shook, trembled in my hands, as I continued to work her pussy over her clothes.

"Why, Amber. Tell me!" I growled into her mouth, biting down on her bottom lip as she reached her peak. Her body went tight, like a rubber band stretched in both directions to full capacity. I smashed my mouth over hers to muffle her response and kissed her through it all. I let her dig her nails into my back and gloried in the fact that I had made her feel this.

As she started to descend, coming off the high of her orgasm, three words I never expected to hear in a million years tumbled out of her kiss-swollen lips against my mouth.

"I'm a virgin."

CHAPTER ELEVEN

SACRAL
C H A K R A

The natural element for the second chakra is water. Those who are driven by this chakra may love to submerge their physical forms into large bodies of water to find peace and a sense of serenity. Simply taking a hot bath and burning a vanilla candle can activate your sacral chakra in a positive way.

DASH

Rushing out of class tonight was not one of my best moments. All I knew was that my love had thrown me for a loop. The woman that I'd fallen in love with, was balls-to-the-wall-crazy for, was a real-life virgin. I shook my head and tugged at my hair, pacing back and forth alongside the pool table. My best pal Atlas stood silently, pool stick to his chest, hands resting along the top, chin resting on his hands, waiting. I knew what he wanted, but I was loath to give it to him.

"Spill, Cosmo." He used the nickname Amber had given me. I should never have told him that she'd called me that. He'd never let me live it down.

I winced and slugged back a few swallows of the IPA. The stuff tasted like warm, wheat-flavored water. The beer sloshed over the edge of the glass as I slammed it onto the high-top table. "Warm piss."

Atlas's eyebrows rose, but he still didn't move. Such a cool demeanor. The guy had always been that way. Probably what drove the girls wild. They didn't get much out of him. Then again, people could say the same about me. Aside from Amber. I spent the last three weeks spilling my soul out to her. And for what? So she could lie to me? A lie by omission was still a lie.

"My girlfriend has been keeping something from me, and tonight, she laid it out. Among other things."

Atlas held the stick with one hand and then lined up his shot. "Well, I can see you're not angry, but you're definitely flustered. So she's not cheating."

I scowled at the mere mention of cheating. He knew a woman I thought I loved had cheated on me in the past. I'd never accept cheating from anyone I was dating, but I knew Amber. Even with the professor's son, Landen O'Brien, I trusted her.

And therein laid the crux of my problem. I trusted her. Trusted her to share her secrets. I'd shared mine. Maybe not *all* of them, but there was time for that. Years in fact. But this, when the hell was she going to share something so crucial to our relationship?

"Okay, not cheating." Atlas pulled back his stick and clocked the white into the orange one, sinking it into the corner pocket. "She lie about something?" He leaned against the pool table and tilted his head, assessing my sour expression. "Yep, lying. What'd she lie about?"

I scowled. "None of your damn business. I thought we were here to play pool and have a beer."

He chuckled and scoured the table, looking for his next best shot. "Technically, you called me and told me we needed to go out. You and I both know that's bro code for shit's going down personally. Dash, man, nobody knows you better than me. And here you are, pacing the floor, tossing away good beer. Not like you man." He shot another ball and missed this time.

Slowly, I sucked in a calming breath. I fisted my hands around the pool stick as if I was strangling it. I hadn't felt so betrayed in... Crap, I couldn't even remember when. Since I'd begun practicing the art of Tantra and yoga, I spent more time viewing the world in a positive light. Right then, however, I felt less like myself than I had in years. Maybe if I talked about it, I could work through it.

"Come on, Dash." Atlas clapped a hand on my shoulder. "You can tell me anything, man."

His eyes were focused on mine, and I stared into them. One brown, one blue, a feature that I'd pointed out to him the day we met freshman year. He'd been wearing one colored contact, and it was out of place, showing the blue eye through the brown ring. I'd never mentioned it again, nor did I punk him out to our friends. Kids in high school could be cruel, so I kept that bit of information to myself. He was in college before he ditched the contacts and went au natural with the fact that he had different-colored eyes. Now, it was almost a party trick and fun to use to pick up women. Of course, that was before I'd committed to my life's plan of finding *the One*.

I pressed my lips together hard.

Atlas's brows pushed together. "Shit, she did a number on you. Dammit! I thought Amber was one of the good ones. Sweet, you know. I'm..."

I growled. "She *is* sweet. Too frickin' sweet."

He frowned. "How you mean?"

I closed my eyes and reined in my concerns. This was Atlas. He'd keep anything I told him in the strictest confidence. "She's a virgin."

Atlas's eyes widened. "Excuse me? I don't think I heard you."

"You heard me." I pinched my lips together tight and let out a long breath through my nose. I felt like a fire-breathing dragon, not sure how to let out all my steam.

My friend leaned against the table and rubbed his chin. "Okay. I can see how this would pose a problem for you, being who you are."

I stepped forward and placed my hands on the front of the pool table, rolling my shoulders, working the knot that was building between my scapula. "What's that supposed to mean? *Being who you are*? Please, enlighten me, Atlas."

Atlas shook his head, uncrossed his arms, pressed both palms to my shoulders, and leaned in. He lowered his voice when he spoke. "I'm sorry. I didn't mean anything offensive. I just know that in your job, you've had a lot of experience with women. I'm not calling you out on that. I'm stating a fact. Hell, man, you're one of the state's top educators on the subject. I can see how this would rattle you."

I nodded and pursed my lips.

"Now, how's Amber?"

I raised my brows. "What do you mean, *how's Amber*?"

He ran a hand through his curly hair and sighed. "I mean, this had to be a hard confession for her, right? She okay? Did you two settle it up before you called me?" His eyes searched mine, moving left and then right a couple times. "You didn't, did you?"

My head was too heavy to hold up under the weight of my shame. I surveyed the ground and kicked at the busted peanut shells littering the wood floor.

"Ah shit, Dash...what the hell, man! You're so in the dog house."

"I'm in love with her, and she's in love with me," I said at random, needing to get it out. To tell someone, anyone.

He chuckled and rubbed at his bearded chin. "*Mazel tov.* So why the hell are you pacing like a caged animal and putting back beers with *me,* when you should be working through this with your woman?"

"I've never been with a virgin, okay?" I whispered under my breath.

Atlas rolled his eyes. "Are you kidding me? This, this is what you're fretting over?"

I gripped his bicep and tugged him so that his face was closer to mine.

"I'm not good enough for her." The words came out muddied and dragging along the filthy bar floor, my heart in tow.

Atlas slapped my other bicep and held on. "If she thinks that, she's not good enough for *you*. But, I've met Amber. And I see that dopey expression on your face when you talk about her. I'm here to tell you, Dash, this is not a big deal."

What did he know? I'm certain he wasn't the world's expert on taking a woman's most prized possession. "It is. If she's held on to it this long, there's a reason. Because you've seen her. She's gorgeous with a..."

"Bangable body." He nodded avidly. "Yeah, your girl has the athlete hottie thing going on with a rack that..."

I dug my fingers into his bicep, cutting him off.

"Shit. Ouch. Let up. I'm sorry. You started it."

"And I'll finish it if you disrespect my girlfriend."

That's when Atlas busted up laughing. A full on, hysterical laugh. I let him go, and he backed up until he was sitting on the edge of the pool table again.

"Do you hear yourself?" He sighed. "Dash, you're sitting here in a pissing contest with me when you should be making sure your woman is okay. That had to be hard for her to admit. It's definitely not something you hear every day, especially when you're dating a twenty-two-year-old college student."

"Dammit! I screwed up." I ran my fingers through my hair and tugged on the edges.

Atlas rubbed his chin. "Yep, you did. All that matters now is, how are you going to fix it?"

AMBER

Class was a joke today. I couldn't focus on anything. Not a single thing. I had pretty much shut down since the moment Dash left me standing in the yoga studio, my admission still caught in my throat. My body was still coming down from the highs of the best orgasm I'd ever received when he'd stood up suddenly, addressed the class, saying he had an appointment, and raced out. Away from me. And I haven't heard from him since.

I expected a call last night. Nothing. Instead, I spent the

evening crying in Vivvie's lap. Worst problem there—Trent was home. He and Dash had worked out their debacle over Genevieve months ago, right after he'd manned up to his responsibilities with her and his baby. The two of us had also worked out our differences. I'd hated the guy for hurting Vivvie back then. Still, even with our rocky past, Trent comforted me. Brought me hot tea and a blanket. Left his girl and me alone even though they only had a few precious days together at a time.

God, was I an idiot for falling in love with the wrong man?

Was he the wrong man? How could he be when every single solitary cell that combined to form my genetic makeup had fallen down the rabbit hole in love with him?

"Hey, you look like you could use a cup of coffee." Landen's green eyes swirled with concern. "Or maybe a shot of tequila?" He set a hand on my shoulder and patted my back. "Come on, I know just the place."

Completely numb, I stood, followed him out of class, and to his car. Throughout the ride, Landen didn't so much as ask me a question. Somehow he must have sensed that I needed the quiet. My mind had been racing for the last twenty-four hours, wondering what to do about Dash. What was he thinking about what I'd admitted? How did this information change the fact that we'd both said we were in love?

I cringed and stared blindly out the window. The streetlights flickered against the glass, causing a halo effect when I tried to focus on something. Reminded me of being blinded by a camera flash.

Finally, the car stopped in front of what looked to be a pub. The building was made completely of bricks, which was uncommon in California. Almost everything here was concrete, wood, or stucco, most often a combination of the three.

Landen jumped out of the car and ran around to open my door. Chivalry was alive and well in Mr. O'Brien. Speaking of O'Brien, the same last name was in a bold font text on a bright green sign with four leaf clovers acting as the apostrophes. The sign proudly identified the establishment as O'Brien's Pub and Grill.

"Does your dad own this pub?" I asked, watching the bright sign sway with the breeze.

"Nope. My uncle Cal owns the joint. Come on. You need to let your hair down." He grabbed my hand and pulled me toward the door.

"But my hair is down." I puffed out my lip.

He shook his head and dragged me inside. The moment we entered, a man behind the bar who looked shockingly like Professor O'Brien, waved us over.

"Landen, my boy. You look a wee bit thirsty." The man held up his fingers, showing an inch of air between them. He turned his head toward me while I sidled up to the bar. "And you look like you have a girl... Oh, sweet mother..."

The man's face went a pasty white. His mouth dropped open in a gasp as he stepped back and banged into the bar back behind him, one hand clutching his chest.

"It can't be. Either time's been perfect to you, darling, or you're a ghost." His uncle didn't move a muscle, holding his chest and staring at me as if I had a gun pointed at him.

"I'm sorry, I'm Amber."

"A-Amber." He said my name slowly.

"Yeah, Uncle Cal, what's the deal?" Landen looked at me and then back at his uncle, who kept staring. "You're making my friend uncomfortable."

Cal shook his head and then blinked a few times. "You look exactly like someone I know. Well, knew when I was a very young man. What did you say your name was again?"

"Amber. Who do you think I look like?" My throat went dry, and I gripped the bar so tight my fingers turned white. A sour knot churned in my stomach as I suspected he was going to react the same way Landen's father had.

Cal wiped the bar top with a dishtowel, lobbed it over his shoulder, and then leaned forward. His eyes pierced mine. "A woman I once knew named Kate St. James."

I closed my eyes, trying to stem the flow of emotions that seared through my chest and hit my eye sockets like a rushing river. After the night I'd had, this was the last thing I wanted to deal with. Apparently, that's just the way things went sometimes. Fate could be a coldhearted snake.

I quickly swiped at each eye, wiping the tears away. I couldn't keep up. They fell all the same as I spoke. "Kate St. James was my mother."

The bartender, who had the same curly hair as his brother and far kinder eyes, leaned forward, put his hands over mine where they still clenched the bar top, peeled them away, and brought his face close to mine. "Dear girl. I'm sorry. She's gone, isn't she? Your mom?"

I swallowed, forcing myself to breathe through the emotion clogging my thoughts. "Yeah, she is."

He squeezed my hands, and for some reason, it was beyond comforting. Not in a creepy older man way, but in a friendly manner. Even though I'd just met the gentleman, I knew instinctively he could be trusted.

"When, darling?" He tilted his head to the side, giving me

his full attention.

A full moment passed as I let his question sink in before I could mutter, "Childbirth."

His face crumbled, his eyebrows curling in, his lips turning down. Genuine sadness. "How old are you, darling? You couldn't be much younger or older than my boy Landen here." He cupped a hand on Landen's shoulder and gave him the male pat that guys did.

I chuckled, and Landen's worried expression finally lifted. "I just turned twenty-two."

Something about me saying my age struck a chord with Cal. He stood ramrod straight, turned around, grabbed a bottle of whiskey, and set it on the bar top with a wallop. He then laid out three shot glasses and filled each to the rim.

"Drink up, then, darling."

After the day I'd had and the fact that I'd just met another man who'd obviously known my mother, I grabbed the shot and tossed it back. "Another, please."

★ ★ ★

My phone buzzed in my back pocket, vibrating and tickling my bum. I leaned back, thrusting my chest out toward the bar, and twisted around, my noodle-like limbs not cooperating properly. Landen, who sat next to me, backed up the best he could where we were squished next to one another in a crowded bar. I swear it was like digging for gold to get to my phone. Eventually I pulled it out, but it stopped ringing the second I had a hold of it. I frowned as the display said, "Missed Call from Mr. Yoga."

I pouted and slapped the phone on the bar and picked up

my shot. While squinting one eye, I focused on not allowing the golden liquid to slosh out the sides this time. When I got it to my lips without losing a drop, I sucked it back with pride. The drink was liquid fire going down my throat, but I relished the burn.

Landen chuckled and was about to speak when my phone started buzzing on the tabletop. The screen showed, "Mr. Yoga" again, and I smiled huge. He'd called back.

"Whoa, now that's the first time I've seen you smile all night." Landen grinned.

I sloppily turned the phone on and put it to my ear. "H'lo." I meant to say the full hello. Apparently, I was far more inebriated then I thought. My mouth was not working at full capacity.

"Amber, thank God. Where are you? I've been waiting at your grandparents' all night."

"You spoke to my nana and papa...mmm...why you there? Y-you"—*hiccup*—"you...Cosey...Coshmo...should be with me. I'm fun!" I said into the phone.

"Who's dat?" Landen asked loudly in my ear, poking a finger at my phone.

I swatted his hand and laughed. Then I closed one eye and focused on Landen's pretty boy face. "That's m-my my um...boyfriend. Yes!" I cheered when I got the word correct. Then a heaping dose of sorrow poured over my good time, and sadness crept into my party because I remembered yesterday.

"Baby, why you sad now?" Landen asked.

His face was funny when he puffed his lip and squinted. Kind of all pinchy-faced. I patted his knee.

"Amber, who are you with and where are you?" Dash sounded so strange. His words were all growly and unhappy in my ear.

"You don't love me anymore," I slurred and then choked on a sob-slash-drunken hiccup.

"Where. Are. You?" His words brooked no argument.

I looked around. "Oh, yeah." Snapping my fingers was really hard all of a sudden. With effort, I watched as I attempted a couple times until I got a solid smack sound out of it. "I know this one!" I screamed and raised my hand in the air. "O'Brien's."

Dash groaned in my ear. "Amber, are you at the study buddy's house? I can hear music in the background."

Lowering my voice, I giggled. "No, silly." I twirled my chair from side to side and then spun it around lifting my knees into my chest. "Whee!" I laughed. "'Cause I'm at a bar, don'cha know!"

"That's down the street from me. I'll be there in five minutes."

Before I could say okay and that I loved him, he hung up. I pouted and looked for my drink, but everything was blurry with streaks of color.

Landen patted my arm a little harder than I would have liked so I shoved him back. "Hey! That hurts."

His eyes widened, and he rubbed at his face. "Sorry. Sorry. I think I'm drunk!"

"Me, too!" I laughed.

"I think you're both three sheets to the wind," Uncle Cal cut in and put two big glasses of water in front of us.

"Booo!" I brought the chilly glass close to me and sucked at the straw. "You no more fun." Then I turned to Landen. "Uncle Cal is no more fun."

Landen nodded, trying to get his tongue around the straw, and looped an arm over my shoulders. "See, you had a good time with me, right?"

"Boy...what are you doing?" Uncle Cal's eyes got hard, and his face was all wrinkly.

My buddy kissed my cheek. "Just trying to show a pretty girl a good time. That's all."

Uncle Cal glared. "Not this girl you're not." His tone was loud and mad like when my papa was scolding me for sneaking his cookies.

Landen pushed his water aside angrily. It tipped over and the rest of the ice and water sloshed out all over the bar top. "Why not?" he roared but then saw the water and his indignation ran out. "Oh shit." Landen tried to help by sopping up the water with his shirtsleeve. Puddles of icy water spilled in every direction and soaked both his arms, leaving giant water rings.

"Dammit, Landen. Boy, just leave it." Uncle Cal looked like he was gritting his teeth the same way one of the dogs did, the ones that always had the mean faces. What did they call those? Ugh. I couldn't think. My head was so dizzy.

"I'm not leaving anything. I like Amber and she likes me. Right?" He smacked a wet spot on the bar, and it sprayed out.

I piggy-laughed at his silliness. He turned to me, and his face was so cute and sad that I patted his cheek. "Yep!"

A voice I dreamed of nightly broke into our conversation. "Well, she's *in love* with me, so get your goddamned hands off my girlfriend."

Big fat meanie! "Hey! You, you can't speak about God like that. He gets pissed!" I swung around in my chair and knocked heads with Landen. "Owee!" I rubbed at the sore spot but knew that voice. The voice that could make angels sing. Dash. My Dash Alexander.

Dash stood with his arms crossed over his chest. "Little bird, you're drunk."

I nodded a bunch of times while trying to get out of my chair. I wanted to make a graceful jump into his arms, only my limbs would not comply. The second my foot hit the floor, I wobbled and fell forward. My body was jerked upright and slammed against the widest, warmest, most comfy chest I'd ever had the pleasure of snuggling.

"Are you drinking away our troubles, my love?" Dash asked and then kissed my forehead.

Our troubles. The simple fact that we even had troubles at only the three-week mark struck a chord with me, and the water faucet turned on. Tears filled my eyes and fell down my cheeks.

"Oh, little bird..." He kissed away as many tears as he could, but they kept coming. "I need to get her home. Can I settle up her tab?" Dash offered.

See? He was a good man. Even though we had a problem, he wanted to cover my tab. "I love you." I held his face as best I could. I needed to tell him what he meant to me, but the words were all garbled up in my brain, and I couldn't get any more of them out.

Dash locked an arm around my back and cupped my cheek. "I know. Relax. It will be okay."

"Promise?" I touched my thumb to his lips. I wanted to feel his response, not just hear it.

"On my love for you, I promise."

CHAPTER TWELVE

Crow Pose
(Sanskrit: Bakasana)

Crow pose is considered an intermediate to advanced pose that helps with balance, strengthening, determination, and pride. Standing at the top of your mat, bend your knees and lower into a squat. Drop your torso forward and bring your upper arms to the inside of your knees. Then lift one knee onto the back of your bicep. When you have your balance, repeat on the other side. Consult a yoga instructor on ways to work up to this asana prior to attempting the full pose.

DASH

A real-life angel lay snuggled against my chest. Her bare leg was thrown over my thigh, and one of her hands lay directly over my heart. I wondered if she could feel the contentment spilling out of my pores. This is what it felt like to hold your future. I'd never had that before now.

She sighed, her breath tickling the hair over my sternum. I curled a hand low on her back, and the other I planted firmly on her ass. I couldn't help tilting my pelvis against her, creating a bit of friction against my cock. Having this girl sprawled over me was the sweetest form of torture. Temptation dressed in white. Only she was barely dressed.

By the time I got ahold of my girl, it was past midnight, and she was three sheets to the wind. I didn't want to disrupt her grandparents any more than I already had. Hell, I'd had dinner with Sandra and Harold St. James waiting for my little bird to come back to her nest. When it was clear she wasn't coming home any time soon, I took my leave and paced my loft. I'd warned her grandparents that if it was late when I located her, she might not come home. Her grandfather warned me about his granddaughter being a good girl. Not the kind of woman a man took home for a wild ride, but the kind a man put a ring on.

While holding Amber, I stared at the ceiling and recalled the private little chat I had with her grandfather last night.

"Have a seat, son." Harold St. James ushered me into his den after Mrs. St. James had stuffed me full of her self-proclaimed world-class pork chops and peppers. She had not lied. They were by far the best chops I'd had, my own mother's included. Not that I'd ever admit that to Mom.

I sat stiffly in one of the lounge chairs, legs spread apart, elbows resting on my knees, hands locked together. I'd known it was a risk coming to her house, but after a full day of her ignoring my calls, I was desperate.

The older gentleman sat down in the chair across from me. "Now, you seem like a nice fellow and you are obviously concerned about my granddaughter, which leads me to believe you are smitten with her in a way that makes a man feel things deep. Her absence seems to have rattled you something fierce. So tell me, son, why are you so worried about her not being home? It's not uncommon for Amber to come home in the wee hours after studying or carrying on with Genevieve next door."

"Mr. St. James, sir. I've already contacted Genevieve. She's not talked to her all day, and I know she had class. I'll admit I wronged your granddaughter through my silence. She shared something with me, and I didn't handle it well. I want to make up for that, which is why I'm here."

Harold grinned, and one of his eyebrows rose up on his forehead. "Sounds to me like you're in the ol' doghouse. Is that right?"

I rubbed a hand through my hair, pushing the loose strands away from my forehead. "Yes, sir. That about sums it up."

The man chuckled and crossed his legs, resting his ankle on the opposite knee. He steepled his hands and rested his fingertips against his lips. He could have been sitting there solving the world's problems for all I knew. I, on the other hand? I was stewing in guilt.

Guilt for walking out on Amber.

An arrow of sadness ricocheted through my chest, bouncing off every rib until it pierced my heart. I stood up. I had to find Amber.

The old man's eyes rose, but he didn't move otherwise. "Son, Amber is special. She's not like other girls her age."

"I know that, sir. That's why I'm in love with her."

The man stood, his rounded belly leading the charge. He narrowed his brows and put a hand on my shoulder. "You say you're in love with my girl, eh?"

I nodded but noticed the intensity in his eyes. He wanted

to hear it and do so while looking me dead in the eyes. "Sir, I'm in love with your granddaughter. We've only been dating a few weeks, but that doesn't change how I feel. And I know she feels the same."

"You think so?"

With a hardened chin lift, I focused my gaze on his steely one. He was going to make me work for it. When it came to Amber, I'd do just about anything. Hell, I'd grovel at this man's feet if that's what it took to stay in her good graces.

"I know so. And now, I need to fix what I screwed up."

Harold tightened his fingers on my shoulder. "You hurt her?"

Hurt was a relative term. "Not physically. I'd never lay a hand to one hair on her head. I swear it."

He scowled and narrowed his eyes. "What'd you do?"

I swallowed the football-sized lump in my throat. "She shared something private, and frankly, sir, it scared me. So much that I walked away from your granddaughter without staying to hear her out."

The man nodded and squinted. "You going to do that again?"

I shook my head almost violently. Maybe having my brain bang around in there would knock some sense into me. "Never. Lesson learned. But now, I just want to make things right."

On that note, he turned around and sat back down in his chair, placing his hands over his burgeoning stomach. I could now attest to the fact that Sandra St. James was an excellent cook, and it was obvious that Harold partook handsomely in the results of that talent.

"All right, son. She told her grandmother earlier that she was going to have drinks with a friend from class."

A prickly heat started low in my back and crawled over my spine. The green monster inside me unfurled its evil body and wound its way up my chest to claw at my throat. She was with him. Landen. The professor's son. I hadn't even met the soon-to-be-doctor yet, and I already despised him. Now that response was one I'd never had with any other women I'd dated. With Amber, everything felt different. Better when I was with her, Hell when I wasn't. She was my personal double-edged sword.

I took a deep breath and held out my hand. "Sir, thank you for dinner and the chat. I promise from now on, I will treat your granddaughter with the utmost respect that she deserves."

He nodded. "You better, or you're gonna have me riding your ass, son."

Hearing this old-fashioned man curse struck a chord deep inside. He meant business. I had no doubt he'd hunt me down and cut me to size if I so much as spoke ill to his precious granddaughter. Knowing that they'd lost her mother after Amber's birth meant she was all they had left. Protective didn't quite cover the intensity of this man's gaze. It blinded me with a fire so bright it would shake the knees of a lesser man. But I was up for the challenge. Right then and there, I vowed internally that I'd soon make this man proud.

"You have my word." I held out a hand.

He shook mine, gripping me with firm intent.

Message received.

My sleeping angel shifted her leg, brushing against my erection. *Down boy.* I tried to rationalize with the more carnal side of my anatomy, but with the most beautiful woman sprawled on top of me, my greatest dream incarnate, I didn't have much hope it would relax any time soon.

Not being able to control myself, I rubbed a hand from her knee up her thigh. Silky smooth. She hummed sleepily against my chest and nuzzled in like a snoozing kitten. I glanced down when I felt a fluttering along my chest. She blinked her green-eyed gaze open, crinkled her nose, and then pressed her lips together. One of her delicate hands came up and pushed against her forehead as her brow furrowed.

"Oh, my, who are the little gremlins dancing around my brain, and why do they have jackhammers?" She groaned and nudged my nipple with her chin. I bit back a groan and fought the desire to rub my lower half against her heat for fear I'd scare off my little bird.

All of a sudden, her entire body went ramrod stiff. Her eyes fluttered open, and she tried to extract herself from my arms. Not happening in a million years. I was not ready for reality to break into my slice of sweet bliss just yet.

"Where do you think you're going?" I asked.

She swallowed and nudged her chin up, her teeth sinking into her bottom lip. "H-How...uh...did I get here?"

I smiled and wrapped my arms around her. "You were drunk. I saved you from the young doctor and brought you home."

Amber squinted. "This is not my home, and I'm lying half on you, and I think I'm naked." Her eyes widened and she gasped. "Oh no, did we..."

I tunneled my hand into her hair and held her head, ensuring she looked directly into my eyes when I spoke. "Amber, I'd never take advantage of you. You were in no state for anything more than crashing out. Unfortunately, you spent some time hovering over the porcelain throne prior to face planting on my comforter."

She frowned. "I got sick. Threw up on my shirt and pants. And you! Oh gross. I'm so sorry, Dash." Her lip trembled, and she glanced away almost as though she was afraid to make eye contact.

I hiked her up and over me with both arms so that she was lying completely on top of me. She attempted to escape by wiggling out of my hold, but I gripped her with just enough force that she wouldn't get far.

"Hey, hey, Amber, don't look away from me."

Her pretty green eyes focused on mine. "I'm sorry you had to take care of me. Honestly, I never drink like that. It's just I..."

I cupped her face and caressed the apple of her cheek with my thumb. "Stop. You have nothing to be sorry for. I'm the one that screwed up. You trusted me with something very private, and I didn't handle it well. I'm the one that's sorry."

She swallowed and her lip shook. "Does it bother you that I'm a virgin?"

I let all the air out of my lungs slowly. "No. I'm rather impressed. Surprised even. I've never been with a woman that's held onto her innocence so long, but it doesn't bother me."

Amber smiled and propped her chin on her hands where they rested on my bare chest. "Do you still want to be with me?"

Now that was an easy question to answer. I found it telling, however, that she was worried I wouldn't want to be with her over it. "Amber, this changes nothing. It means that, when the time is right, I'm going to be given something special. A piece of you that no man has ever had."

She glanced away and pursed her lips. I could tell there was something she wasn't saying, but right now was not the time to push it. Her psyche was fragile enough and besides, I had a hot brunette straddling my lap. There were far better things to do than to grill her for more information.

"Listen, when you're ready to take that next step in our relationship, it will be an honor, a gift that I will cherish." I focused my gaze so that she could see only the truth clearly showing through my eyes.

Instead of responding, she leaned forward and laid her lips over mine.

AMBER

Dash understood and didn't think I was a weirdo for having held onto my virginity this long. I should have known God wouldn't lead me to a man who wouldn't see my vow as something special. I flicked my tongue against his mouth wanting to taste him fully. Just because I was a virgin didn't mean I wasn't willing to test the boundaries of my chastity. And honestly, I wanted to feel him touch me, take me to places I'd never been before, as long as it didn't cross the line.

Dash ran his hands down my back, his fingertips tickling my spine as he skimmed over each bump before landing squarely on my panty-clad ass. He lifted his hips up and pressed my ass down, creating the perfect friction against my clit. My, my, it felt so good. Like heaven on earth. I nibbled on his lips and sucked his tongue. He moaned into my mouth, dipping his tongue flat against mine over and over. The man could kiss. He made a meal out of each kiss. A sweet nosh of rubbing lips against one another. Then a main course where he delved his hot tongue deep, repeatedly, until all I could taste was him. When he lacked air, he'd back off and suck the top then the bottom lip as if each bit of flesh was the most decadent of desserts.

Following his lead, I lifted my knees and rubbed my center down against the hard steel between his thighs. He wore only a pair of burgundy boxer briefs that clearly outlined the long shape and width of his male anatomy. I'd never touched or tasted an erect penis before, and in that moment, I wanted nothing more than to wrap my fingers around his length and tug, knowing it would make him lose control. In Dash's presence, I felt lost to his words, being, and everything in between. Sitting atop him, I had all the cards in my hand and could play whichever I chose.

"What are you looking at?" He jerked his hips and smirked.

I swallowed and pushed my hair out of my face. "Can I touch you?" I gestured to the general vicinity of his groin.

"Amber, I'd like nothing more than to have your hands all over me. Have you ever..."

Before he could ask, I shook my head. "Never."

He grabbed my hands and gestured for me to lift up off his thighs. He pushed his briefs down far enough that he could hook them with a foot and kicked them off. Then he clasped the meaty part of my hips and had me sit on his muscled quads once more.

He dug his fingertips into my thighs. "This okay? Me naked? I don't want you to feel pressured."

I nodded demurely and inspected every inch of him from his dirty blond hair, sticking up in every direction yet still ridiculously sexy, down his rock-hard chest, to where two perfectly flat disc-shaped nipples stood erect. I laid my hands over his taut pecs. His skin was so warm, far warmer than mine, especially when he was lying naked above the covers. I trailed my hands over the square bricks of his abdominals. They bunched and shifted when I ran my fingernails across each one, before moving to the hair at his navel. The brown-blond wisps formed an arrow pointing directly at the close-cropped thatch of curls surrounding the root of his penis. Every inch of Dash was beautiful, especially the well-formed, impressive length reaching up his pelvis. His penis was long, thick, and perfectly rounded at the crown.

The medical community seriously needed to work on better depictions of the male body. Compared to what I'd seen, the illustrations of a male's penis in the height of an erection were nothing compared to Dash and his magnificence. Worlds apart, in fact.

"Well..." His voice bordered on a low growl, barely tamed, and filled with a heavy dose of arousal.

"You're so hard. Everywhere." I really didn't know how to explain it. From his broad shoulders to the tapered in V of his waist and the erect penis, hard best fit the bill.

He chuckled and slid his hands up and down my thighs, wooing me without even trying. Or perhaps he was, but I was too inexperienced to know otherwise.

I focused my gaze on the thick root between his legs. With tentative fingers, I ran just a fingertip from top to bottom. Instantly, it jolted up and back down again. I chuckled and did it again.

"Little bird...you're making me crazy," he said through clenched teeth, but a smile still adorned his face, telling me he wasn't mad but eager.

Pulling together all my courage, I curled a hand around his erection. "Wow. It's softer than I thought it would be." I tugged it from bottom to top and gasped when a drop of precum appeared at the tiny slit at the crown. I knew about sex from my medical texts and personal study. I understood technically how the male anatomy worked, but experiencing it firsthand, with the man I loved, was so much better.

Dash moaned and arched his chest up when I repeated the stroking motion. His expression was strained, and his skin seemed stretched tight over his muscles as he rocked his hips up and down to my movements as I stroked him. The realization that I was giving my first hand job hit me like a hammer to the head. Once that reality sank in, I got into it, rubbing my thumb over the crown, smearing the liquid. I wished I had the courage to put my mouth on him to wet his penis even more. Instead, I licked the length of my hand several times.

"Jesus," he cried out when I put my hand over him and ran it up and down.

"Hey now, no bringing the big guy into this. I could very well be breaking some biblical rules."

His eyebrows furrowed, and he was about to speak when I decided to heck with it. I wanted to know what it was like, and who better than the man I loved to try it with? Shifting my hips back farther down his legs, I leaned forward and laid the flat of my tongue over the crown of his penis. I had to know what he tasted like. My mouth watered at the salty, rich flavor the second it hit my taste buds.

"Oh, fuck me." He put his hands in my hair but didn't press down. Thank goodness. Had he done that, I might have lost my nerve altogether.

"Do you like my mouth on you?" I licked up the length, tasting every inch. It made sense now why women did this for their men. They kind of went a little cuckoo. And honestly, having such power over his pleasure was heady, womanly, and downright intoxicating.

He gripped the back of my head and tugged on the roots of my hair. When the tiny prick of pain hit, I sucked him all the way into my mouth, taking him halfway down my throat. I kept my lips over my teeth to protect the velvety length as much as possible. Once I was graced with a litany of curse words followed by nonstop moaning, I doubled my efforts, picking up my pace.

"Amber, my love...so good having your mouth on me, but I'm gonna..." He lifted his hips, and his entire body went bowstring tight. "If you don't want me to come in your mouth, you have to stop now."

I thought about it for a moment while fluttering my tongue over the sensitive patch on the underside of his penis. Apparently, that tiny spot was a major erogenous zone on the male anatomy. I kept up a slow manual stimulation with my hand.

"Little bird, now is not the time to play," he ground out and breathed hard through his nose. Sweat dotted the skin of his golden chest. I wanted to taste those, too. I wanted to taste everything on this man. I loved him, and his essence was part of him.

"Amber, honey, lift up, I'm going to come," he warned again.

"So come." I wrapped my lips around his erection and took him as far down as I could go.

"Christ," he groaned and held me still. I crinkled up my nose and glared at him, but I didn't let up.

"Sorry, my love, oh baby, yyyeeesssss." The word left his lips on a hiss as hot spurts of semen filled my mouth. I swallowed it down, wondering if it would be nasty and I'd gag. Genevieve said she'd gagged on her ex-boyfriend's. With Dash, though, it seemed to happen so fast, and I swallowed it easily. I didn't really taste much of anything other than heat and salty essence hitting my tongue and going quickly down my throat. No harm, no foul. Didn't seem to be a big deal to me either way.

For long moments, Dash remained still, eyes closed tightly, hands cupping my shoulders and his breath coming in rapid pants that lifted and displayed his chest beautifully. I waited for him to catch his breath, feeling a bit self-conscious. Was it good for him? Did all guys go off like that no matter what? Medically, if the male sex organ was stimulated manually, the man would eventually ejaculate, but that didn't mean it felt as good as it sounded.

Eventually Dash opened his eyes, blinking slowly. His amber gaze settled on mine. Then he did an ab curl, lifting up and tugging me back on top of the length of his body. He kissed me hard and so deep I forgot the worry and focused on the heat of his kiss. Once he'd had his fill of my lips, he pecked each cheek and then ran his lips over my temple, forehead, and down the other side.

"Amber, my little bird. That was unbelievable." He threaded his fingers through my hair, petting me at the same time he caressed me. "Best I've had."

"Really?" I jerked my head back. Yeah, right. With all of his experience, I was certain he was just saying that.

He smirked, one side of his mouth lifting into a schoolboy grin. "The only woman I've ever loved gave me an experience unlike any other. Of course, it was the best I've ever had because it was from you."

Impeccable answer. I stared at him while running my

fingers over his face. "So my inexperience wasn't a turnoff?"

He chuckled. "Quite the opposite, if my coming in your mouth wasn't a hint. Besides, I wouldn't have known you were inexperienced. You seemed to know exactly what to do with your hands." He lifted one of my hands and kissed each fingertip, and then he repeated the process with the other one. "And your mouth." He ran his index finger over my swollen lips. "Absolute perfection. You could bring any man to his knees, little bird. I'm just the lucky bastard that gets to experience it for the rest of his life."

I rolled my eyes. "You're so sure of that?"

He squinted. "And you're not?"

I shrugged. "I don't know. A lot of people fall in love all the time. Genevieve was in love with her ex at the time. Gave him all of herself and, in return, got the shaft when life got too hard and her parents died. What's to say that wouldn't happen to us?"

"Simple. I'm not her ex. I'm the man who's in love with you. *You*, Amber St. James. And now it's my turn to show you."

Like a shot in the dark, I jerked up. "We can't have sex." I braced two hands on his chest, preventing him from getting too close.

He cocked one eyebrow. "We just had sex, little bird. I was there, and it was amazing. Now, it's my turn to feast on you."

"But I can't have intercourse!" I shivered and crossed my arms over my chest.

He sat up, uncrossed my arms methodically before shifting me closer. "My love, I told you, when the time was right, you'd give that gift freely. I'd never coerce it from of you. However, there are many things we can do that don't include intercourse. I promise to keep your virginity intact. Will you let me show you? Let me physically love you in return?"

"Just touch?" I asked, my voice shaking with anticipation. Visions of us in a variety of sexual scenarios flitted across my mind, taunting and mesmerizing me in equal parts.

"And taste." On that note, he locked an arm around my back and flipped us over so that he was lying between my legs.

Oh, Lord. I'm about to be bad. Very bad.

CHAPTER THIRTEEN

SACRAL
C H A K R A

This is quite literally the fountain from where life stems, direct from the womb. The sacral chakra is where we create life. In males, it is connected to where sperm are created in the testes, and an activated penis will respond with an erection, preparing to aid in the creation of new life.

DASH

Never in my life had I been gifted a more glorious sight. Amber, her dark hair fanned out on my pillow, her chest heaving in a ribbed tank, nipples erect and stretched against the fabric, her lower half only covered in a pair of low-cut cotton panties. The divine was shining down on me as I straddled her lengthy form. She squirmed around like a kitten swaddled in a blanket, but I knew my love well enough to calm her down. Sure, this would be a first for her, but I was determined to make it the best sexual experience of her life so far.

"Do you trust me, little bird?"

She stopped jittering around, stilling her body under mine. "I'm nervous but...excited, too."

I smirked. "Oh, my love, I know you're excited." I held onto her panties and slowly ran my hands down the length of her smooth thighs, removing them inch by delicate inch.

She swallowed and sucked in a harsh breath. Her skin prickled with gooseflesh.

"Remove your tank," I instructed, lust clearly evident in the gritty tone of my voice.

Her eyebrows scrunched together. "Shouldn't you do that?" She gripped the comforter between her fists.

This was an important moment. Now was not the time for me to push. "Amber, I want you to give yourself to me freely, of your own accord. Not because I've turned you on or used sexual powers of persuasion. I promised you I'd never take advantage. So if you want to proceed, then you're going to have to help me along." I tilted my head and waited, my hands running up and down her bare legs, sensual and soothing at the same time. She still had her knees smashed together, not giving even a hint of bare pussy.

I watched her face change from indecision to determination in a split second. "I want you." Bravely, she curled both hands around the edge of her tank, lifted it, and pulled it off, throwing it to the floor. Her breasts bounced free and the sandy color of her quarter-sized areolas hardened.

My mouth watered at the sight of those perfect breasts, but I had other plans. Namely the intoxicating, musky scent emanating from between her closed legs.

Amber lay back against the mattress and raised her hands

above her head where she clasped them together. I'd have bet anything she was holding them so they didn't shake. I knew my girl was incredibly nervous but was also ready to take our relationship to a more physical plane, a fact for which I couldn't begin to express my gratitude.

With a light caress, I slid my hands up to both knees. I quirked an eyebrow in invitation. She extended the tiny tip of her pink tongue and wet her bottom lip before she nodded. Watching only her eyes to make sure she saw the love and desire I had for her, I pushed her legs open wide, her knees splayed and touching the mattress.

Her sex flowered open, pink and glistening with her essence. "Amber, my love...thank you." I stared in awe at the most private part of her, watching in adoration as her legs twitched and her anus puckered and relaxed with anticipation of what I might do to her. More than anything, I wanted to fist my cock and take what was mine, but she hadn't offered her virginity. Not yet, and I respected her decision to go slow. Besides, today was about exploration, introducing her to the physical side of her sexuality so that when the time was right for me to claim her, she'd be ready, body, mind, and spirit.

"Thank you, for what?" Her voice shook when she spoke. The fear and nerves were likely getting the best of her.

"For giving me you." I cupped her bare, wet pussy with my hand, grinding the edge of my palm against the hard button of her clit. She gasped and arched her pretty tits up in invitation. Waiting was no longer an option. I had to taste those sweet tips for myself.

"Oh, sweet man," she moaned and buried her hands in my hair when I covered one erect tip with the heat of my mouth. I still held onto her pussy. Just held it in my hand, allowing her arousal to coat my palm and fingers. I wanted her to get used to me touching what would soon be mine for the rest of time.

Using one finger, I rimmed her slit, making sure to keep the edge of my palm pressing on her clit. Women could orgasm over and over through clitoral stimulation alone. I wanted a combination of the two and planned on using the sacred spot massage technique to achieve a multifaceted orgasm that would not only make love to her clit but her G-spot, and essentially her mind. I planned on having my little bird so far gone that she might even experience a female ejaculation, which would release her second chakra, allowing her a deeper sense of sexual freedom and intense pleasure.

I tugged on her nipple with my teeth until the areola was a dark raspberry hue and the tip a tight knot of need before shifting to its mate and proceeding with the same attention.

When Amber became so wet I could hear the sounds of my fingers moving in her arousal, I backed off. Jesus, she was responsive. I'd likely be able to make her come over and over just from stimulating her breasts. Sounded like loads of fun for another day, but today I was determined to awaken her kundalini.

The kundalini is the serpent-like energy that sleeps at the base of the spine. In the female, it's the energy source that needs to be awakened so that it can channel it through the rest of her chakras with the goal of reaching the path to enlightenment.

After both nipples were nice and red, I licked my way up her neck to her mouth. "I'm going to enter you now, my love."

Her eyes widened, and I used my free hand to cover her mouth.

"Only with my hand, although my cock"—I chuckled and rubbed my hardened shaft against her thigh—"would not be opposed to making a home in this juicy pussy." I slid my fingers through the wet curls and over her entire cleft.

"No, uh, penis yet." The words left her lips garbled and accompanied some mumbled praise to the Lord as I massaged her slit with two fingers simultaneously. "Dash!" she cried out when I worked one and then two digits up and found, deep within the core of the woman I loved, the bumpy wall in desperate need of attention.

"Shhh," I whispered against her lips, kissing, sucking, and fucking her mouth the same way I manipulated her pussy.

Amber's entire body moved with me, humping my hand and mouth like a wild woman. I had no idea I'd fallen in love with the most responsive and intensely sexual creature I'd ever known, and that she would be a God's honest virgin. What did I do in my past life to receive such a blessing? Whatever the reason, there would be no looking a gift horse in the mouth. I intended on partaking...liberally.

"Dash, oh my goodness! I'm gonna..."

At those words, I stopped adding pressure to her G-spot and, instead, pressed tiny kisses on every inch of her face. The apples of her cheeks, her temples, the sweet roundness of her chin. Each new spot seemed to bring with it clarity and relaxation of the high I'd worked her through.

She groaned under me and tried to jerk her hips and fuck herself on my hand. Tantric rookies might allow her to get off at the first sign of orgasm, but so far, I'd shut her down twice. Once with her perfect tits, and second with the vaginal massage.

"Dash...baby, I don't understand what's going on," she muttered and pressed a hand over her eyes. Her hips were still moving while I stirred my fingers inside her. Even stretching her with two fingers was not going to be enough for my cock to fit. I'd need to work her pussy and make sure she had a couple orgasms before taking her when the time came. I'd read enough about virgins to know that the first time didn't come pain-free. When we took that step, I intended to make it pleasurable and memorable. She would only get one chance to give this gift, and with my Amber, I wanted that to go both ways.

I smiled at my little bird, her feathers ruffling as I slowly worked her G-spot again. I wasn't giving her enough pressure to make her come or stimulating her in other ways. This process was deeply personal and meant to connect the couple in a more profound way. It took time to do it just right. I wanted Amber to know only my touch, to believe that I'd bring her to the greatest heights of pleasure...me. Her one and only.

When I could tell her breathing was back to a more even pace, I shifted my weight so that I was farther down the bed. I hovered over her sex and glanced up. Her lips were parted, her breath coming in shallow puffs as her eyes zeroed in on my location. Keeping my eyes on her, I flattened my tongue and put it on the tight little bundle of nerves at the apex of her thighs. She swallowed and her eyelids went to half-mast. Cue hard-core sucking. Like a freezing man in a snowstorm, I wrapped my mouth around her hot clit and relished in her heat.

"Oh God, oh God, oh my God!" she cried out, lost in her pleasure.

I loved having that effect on her. Knowing she'd lost all her inhibitions made me feel like a king. I picked up the pace with my fingers pressing into her, massaging deep inside with a petting motion. Her body thrashed around, and I had to use my left elbow and arm to hold her legs open. She rode my face like a jockey racing to the finish line. Unfortunately for her, I backed off again at the first sign of orgasm.

"No! No! No!" she screamed and tried to push my head back to her tasty center. Believe me, I wanted to suck her dry, but there was a method to the sacred spot massage, and she had at least three more rounds of this to go before she'd succumb to the kundalini, opening and allowing her the freedom she needed.

For another hour, I built her up and brought her down. Over and over, she responded like a goddess, her body so primed for Tantric sex, I couldn't get past it. With every sigh, every heated cry, each tear that fell down her cheeks as I worked her almost to the point of no return, and then back down, my heart filled with a love so intense I knew with everything within me this woman was my soul mate.

Finally, after a full eight times of bringing her to the brink, I knew she was ready. We both were. My cock burned with the intense desire to meet its mate, but on that, I held back. This experience was all for my love.

"Dash, baby, I can't take any more," Amber cried, tears rolling down her cheeks. Her head turned from side to side, utterly aimless. Her legs shook as I continued the endless manipulation of her G-spot. I had her so split apart she'd lost hope in receiving release. And now it was time to give it all back.

"Amber, my love, it's time." I kissed her mouth.

Even beyond exhaustion, she kissed me back, her tongue tangling with mine. Her lips were so swollen they might have hurt, but I didn't care. My greedy side sucked and bit down on them, bruising them further. I wanted everything she had to give and more. I'd settle for nothing less. Kiss by kiss, I made my way down her neck, my hand going to town against that magic spot. Her juices soaked my hand, coated her thighs, and dripped down between her ass cheeks.

As I moved down, I sucked on each nipple before biting down, ripening my berries once more. She sighed and arched into each touch. God, she was magnificent, lost to her passion, to my touch. Moving my head lower, I circled her belly button with my tongue, dipping into her navel, tasting her everywhere. There would be no inch of this woman untouched by my mouth, hands, and tongue. She was mine, and I'd brand her as such as soon as she'd let me. The first woman I wanted to come inside, to mark in the most carnal animalistic way possible. But not today. Soon, though.

Amber mewled and sighed when I tongued her clit. I sucked on the hard knot until her hips swirled and synchronized to my movements.

"Dash, Dash, oh God, please, please let me," she begged.

"I love you, Amber," I said while I wrapped my mouth around her clit, hooked my fingers inside and up, and pressed deep against her G-spot, applying pressure repeatedly.

She screamed through the power and intensity of her orgasm. She held my head to her pussy and bowed and rocked as if possessed. She wrapped her other hand around the edge of the bed. I locked my upper body over hers and kept going. One orgasm rolled into two, three, and four before I lost count. I was eating her like a man who hadn't had a taste of the sweetest pussy in ages.

My hand cramped, and I almost pulled out and switched, but my love was still coming, her body convulsing in ecstasy. Silent whispered growls left her mouth as tears rippled down her cheeks. I wanted to kiss them away, but I couldn't move my mouth away from her cunt. I'd never tire of eating my woman, especially if her responses were this fantastic. She was the epitome of every man's Tantric dream. My own personal Tantric goddess.

"I love you, I love you, I love you," she cried out.

That's when I sat up, one hand inside her pussy, the other wrapped around my rock-hard cock. Her eyes blazed, and she licked her lips as I coated my cock in her moisture and jerked myself off under the steady gaze of the woman I loved.

"So hot," she said, her eyes never leaving my cock.

I loved having her emerald gaze on me, urging me silently to show her how affected I was by our lovemaking. Feeling like I'd been transformed into Durga, the Indian goddess with eight arms, I continued manipulating her in the hope we would both orgasm at the same time. To experience shared orgasm was the most intense form of meditation and unity with your mate. In Tantra, this was usually done while having intercourse, but this was as close as I could get right now.

Eyes on her, fingers moving, hand tugging, I felt my orgasm coil tightly at the base of my spine, my own serpent working free. My balls tightened, and I held onto my cock, using her essence to coat my cock from root to tip. Her body jolted at the same time nirvana hit, cum firing up my length to land on her creamy pale belly. While I came, spurting hotly over her body, a gush of liquid sprayed out past my fingers still inside her, soaking me and her pussy.

She flopped flat as I removed my hand and fell on top of her, our breathing jagged and uneven, yet I could sense our hearts beating in synchronized rhythm with one another.

"Oh, no, what was that!" She hiccupped and clung to my back.

I pushed up to my forearms and grinned. "That was you... ejaculating."

AMBER

It took about five full seconds for me to comprehend what Dash had said before it resonated with a wall of acid churning inside my stomach and a sour taste hitting my tongue. I breathed through the disgusting thought. He had to be joking. I'd read about it in my medical texts of course, but it's a rather uncommon occurrence and not experienced by women generally, though studies do suggest every woman is capable of it.

I blinked a few times, letting what he said roll around in my head. My vagina did feel ridiculously wet, but he'd spent the last hour or so with his hands and mouth stimulating me. Maybe it just builds up? On a long groan, I sat up and pulled the sheet to my bare chest. The sheets below my bum felt wet, more so than I thought they probably should have. I knew female ejaculate wasn't urine, but I felt uncertain and uncomfortable about everything. Why did I have to fall for the Tantric guru instead of the bumbling fool who sticks his fingers in and maybe gets me off? Isn't that what the girls at school used to say about fooling around with their boyfriends? They rarely got off? And I'd gotten off so many times, I wet the bed.

A rush of embarrassment so hot it scalded my chest and burned against my cheeks rushed through me. I looked away and frowned. Was he grossed out? Of course he was. *I* was grossed out. I needed to shower and leave. And wash his sheets. No, buy him *new* sheets. Yeah, that's what I'd do. Forget ever doing that again. Even though he took me to places I'd never even thought possible, I'd forego it in the future to avoid the humiliation roaring through me.

Jeez, I'd connected with him so completely, there had been several moments where I'd forgotten we were two different people. When his hands were on me, it was just us. Dash and Amber. Love incarnate.

Dash placed his hand on my chin and tugged it toward him. "Hey, what's wrong?" His eyebrows were drawn together with concern, and I wanted to lift my hand and rub it away and make him smile again.

"Has that happened to you before? The female thing?" I gestured with a hand beyond my lap where the sheet was very obviously soaked through.

He smiled and shook his head. "Not like that, no. God, Amber, it was so—" He looked off into the distance.

With every scant millisecond that went by without him consoling me, I lost myself to despair.

"Gross. You can say it. It was gross!" Tears filled my eyes, and I jumped out of bed, pulling the sheet with me as I hobbled to the bathroom, the linens following behind like a bridal train.

I felt raw and exposed. I'd had the most intense experience of my life, and it had come with the most embarrassment. Talk about a double whammy. The sound of the door slamming shut echoed off the walls. I started up the shower, dropped the sheet, and jumped in.

A knock pierced the silence outside of the shower stall. "Amber, you have to talk to me. I'm coming in."

The door opened, and I faced the tiled wall. I left my hands on the shower wall in front of me, the cold squares chilling me straight to my toes even though the water was so hot it turned my skin a bright pink.

I chanced a glance through the glass door. Dash stood leaning against the vanity, his arms crossed over his chest, hair flopping into his eyes, which were blazing with fury. "Two questions, and I expect honest answers," he practically growled. "One, why did you leave the bed? Two, how can you see anything we did as gross? Please explain it to me, Amber, because I had the exact opposite experience."

His words were tight and restrained. He was angry, and I couldn't, for the life of me, imagine why. I was the one who'd had the embarrassing thing happen to her. What did he have to be irate about?

"Can we talk when I'm out of the shower? I'm having trouble hearing over the water," I fibbed.

He unfolded his arms, opened the sliding door, and entered the stall. With me. Naked.

It took a moment for my brain to come back into play when the hottest man in the universe stood in front of me in all his naked glory. I looked my fill until I got to his face and noticed his scowl and fire in his gaze.

"Now you can hear me. Shall I repeat the questions?" He tilted his head to the side and waited.

Giving myself a couple more seconds, I squirted shampoo on my hand and rubbed it into my hair. He watched, leaning lazily against the back of the shower, his muscled body getting just enough of the spray to glisten sensually. If we made it through this, and he still wanted to be with me, I knew I'd need to thank the Lord above for sending me this beautiful angel. His body was insane, cut in all the right places, toned all over, basically built for sin.

"I'm waiting, little bird. Speak. Do you regret what we shared?" He winced when he asked the question.

The word regret hit my heart like a jackhammer. "My goodness, no! Dash." I held out my arms, and he stepped into them, circled his around me, and buried his head against my neck the way an apologetic child might, though he didn't have anything to be sorry for.

"If I hurt you in some way, let me fix it. I know what we did was intense," he started.

"Dash, baby, no. I thought you'd think what happened... you know, the ejaculation thing...was nasty."

His eyes opened wide, and he sighed before pulling me hard against his chest, locking his arms around me. My wet breasts rubbed against his skin. The hot water pounded on our intertwined bodies and fogged the room with a steam.

"Amber, I was trying to make that happen. Honey, what we experienced, including the part at the end, when we ejaculated at the same time, was our bodies experiencing enlightenment together. I've never been blessed enough to share that with someone before. Probably because I wasn't in love with the person I attempted it with."

I closed my eyes and kissed his moist neck, rubbing my nose against the corded muscle there. "Really?"

He chuckled and cupped my cheeks. "That was the most beautiful Tantric experience of my life. The way you rolled into one orgasm after another was a testament to our love. I can't even express how much today meant to me. How your love and trust have shaped me as a man, Amber. It's unparalleled."

I reacted by locking my arms around his neck and kissing him with everything I had in me.

Dash responded instantly. Our tongues waltzed as our slick bodies rubbed against each other, starting a new fire of desire.

I was drunk on Dash. Every caress was a precursor to another drink, each kiss another shot to the system, dizzying and gratifying with each new swallow. I scaled his body, rubbing my softer, needier spots along his harder, more male ones.

"You want to come again, little bird? You haven't had enough for the day?"

Now that he mentioned it, I did want to come again. Flickering tingles and fluttering arousal rippled up and down my body where my skin made contact with his. Under duress, I'd have to admit that this was the first time I remember being, for lack of a better word, horny. It was as if he'd opened up something inside me and unlocked the door to where I'd stashed my inner sex kitten.

"Um, is that a problem?" I smiled and placed my hand over the satin-covered pole standing at attention between us.

He grinned, put his hand over mine where I held him, and together we manually stimulated his erection.

"Not at all. How do you want it, little bird? My fingers, my cock, or my mouth?"

A rush of adrenaline so intense shot down my spine and settled between my legs. All of them sounded magnificent but so far, nothing felt as good as his tongue.

"What do you want?" I quirked an eyebrow, trying to play along, even though I knew absolutely nothing about the game we were playing.

He shook his head and gripped my bum with both hands, grinding against my body while I jacked his shaft.

"You're going to have to ask me for what you want, my love." He rubbed his nose along my cheek and then whispered in my ear. "You saying the words turns me on." He groaned.

"Makes me *so* hard."

That I believed. His erection was huge beneath my fingers. I turned my head and kissed him, dragging my tongue along his while we ran our hands along one another. The water was getting cold, and I knew I needed to tell him what I wanted or he wouldn't give it to me. Knowing Dash, this was another way to open me up. Not that he hadn't already had me splayed wide open for his viewing, touching, and tasting pleasure.

My clit throbbed as I thought about what I wanted him to do. I shuffled my feet, firmed up my spine, and looked him straight in the eyes. Green to amber.

"Dash, I would like you to put your mouth on my vagina," I said with as much confidence as I could muster.

Instead of him melting down to his knees and doing what I asked in a fit of passion, which is what he implied he'd do, he stepped back two feet, threw his head back, and laughed like a hyena. Big, bursting cackles of laugher.

Mad as the dickens, I pursed my lips and held my hands in two tight fists. I barely stopped at tapping my foot. "What's so funny?"

He kept laughing, big heaping breaths of air leaving his chest one after the other. "Put my tongue on your va-va-vagina!" he said between bouts.

"I'm not seeing the humor in this. You asked me to say what I wanted!"

"Oh my love, we are so going to have to work on your sexy talk. My, my, you are just the cutest thing I've ever seen. Come here." He held out his arms.

I shook my head. "Nuh-uh. No way. You can go hug yourself! Laughing at my dirty request! You should be ashamed of yourself!" I harrumphed, pulled back the shower door, and stepped out soaking wet. At least my hair had been rinsed and the sticky mess from our earlier escapades washed away along with the shampoo.

Dash followed me as I pulled a towel off the rack, wrapped it around myself, and stormed into his room to find my clothes.

He grabbed me from behind. "Now where are you going, little bird, hmm?" His arms locked around me.

"Does it matter?"

Dash nuzzled into my neck. "I'm sorry I laughed, but you have to admit, asking a man to put his mouth on your 'vagina' using the most clinical word possible is kind of funny." I went to open my mouth, and he covered it with his hand. "I know, I know. And I'm sorry. Let's do this again. Only this time...how about I talk dirty to you?"

Now you're talking is what I wanted to say to Dash, coupled with a punch to his smug face. What I actually said was, "Bring it."

CHAPTER FOURTEEN

Plank Pose
(Sanskrit: Phalakasana)

This pose is the quintessential precursor pose for all beginners working on arm balance. It strengthens the arms, core, legs, and most importantly, the mind. When doing more difficult yoga poses, you must use the mind over matter theory. If you believe you can do it, you will. If you believe you won't, you'll never stand a chance.

DASH

"Glad to hear you worked things out with Amber, man." Atlas clapped me on the back as we entered Mila's heated Vinyasa Flow room.

Both Atlas and I decided that we needed a bit of cardio, and there was no better way than to take one of Mila's hard-core Vin Flow classes. Vinyasa Flow was a mixture of cardio-driven yoga poses that synchronized breath with movement. Typically, the transitions from one pose to another were faster than what you'd experience in an average gentle or hatha class and were oftentimes geared toward intermediate level yogis. The students got the benefit of awakening their strength and energy sources while working on flexibility and balance.

In this particular class, Mila, the pint-sized Mexican American hottie who taught it, turned the heater up to around eighty-five degrees so participants could sweat out any toxins and negative crap we were holding onto. I loved the class personally, but I was looking forward to finding out what Atlas thought of it. And by *it*, I meant Mila. She was just his type. Petite, firm body, and skin the color of toasted almonds. I'd had my eye on Mila for years now, but I'd tried not to date the women I worked with. Made that decision after a few rounds with the wrong women in previous positions. It wasn't easy to get away from an ex when you worked in the same place. Not that it mattered with Mila. Once we became friends, that was that. Didn't mean I was blind. The woman had that ethnic exotic beauty thing going on, and if I knew my best friend, and I sure as heck did, he'd notice her attributes right away. Now, if he could keep his mouth from spewing stupid shit, we'd have a match made in heaven.

"Yeah, thanks for setting me straight last week. Amber and I worked through it, and everything's good. Really good actually." I grinned.

He smirked. "Should I take that to mean that your girl's problem is nonexistent?" He rubbed his hands together before gripping his mat hanging over his shoulder, unhooking the buckles, and rolling it out on the wood floor.

I cringed. "No. I mean yes, but no." I shook my head. "It's not like that with Amber. She's not a piece of tail. I'm in love with her. She's it for me. Hands down, no regrets. This woman is the one I'm going to spend the rest of my life trying to prove my worth to."

Atlas ran his hands through his dark, curly chin-length hair. The curls went all over the place in the way that made women drool. The look screamed *lazy, I don't want to take the time to cut it*, but on him, it worked. Women loved it, so I didn't judge...much.

"That's a damn strong statement. You gonna follow that up with a ring on her finger sometime soon?" he asked.

Marriage. Even the thought sent a blade to my gut. "Marriage isn't a sure thing. It doesn't last and my family has proven that, repeatedly. My mom is on her fourth marriage, and my dad on his second. I don't want that for us. Besides, I think I could talk her into foregoing traditional vows of commitment for something a little bit more private. I was thinking maybe down the road we could do a light ceremony at a Buddhist monastery or say our vows to one another at the top of a mountain at Lake Tahoe. I'd love to have her consider a Pagan wedding, but she's Catholic."

Atlas sat down on his mat while I flopped mine out. "Wait, she's Catholic? As in, raised in the faith?"

I nodded and placed my yoga towel over my mat to catch the sweat that would inevitably drip down. Vinyasa Flow was great at cleansing, but the amount of sweat that poured off the body was abundant.

"Does she go to church regularly? Pray at dinner? Wear a cross around her neck?"

What the hell was he getting at? "What is this, twenty

questions? Yes, yes, and yes. My girlfriend is religious." I chuckled. "Actually, she gets really mad when I say Jesus Christ or goddammit. And she tells people all the time that she'll pray for them. Even says 'God bless you' to strangers when they sneeze. They can be half an aisle up in the grocery store, and she'll go out of her way to bless them." I shrugged. "It's cute and quirky."

Atlas pursed his lips, leaned into the space between us. "And you and your girl haven't sealed the deal yet, right?" He made a sliding into base type baseball gesture with his hand.

I rolled my eyes. "Not exactly, no. Like I said before. She's a virgin. Not that it's any of your business, but we're taking it slow."

"Have you talked about the future and marriage?" Atlas asked rather directly.

I focused my gaze on his one blue and one brown eye. Something in those eyes didn't sit right with me. "Man, what are you getting at? Why do you care?"

He sighed. "Okay, look. One time, I was dating this girl. We were around twenty or so. I'd been dating her for six months and we'd fooled around, pretty much everything but you know..." He lowered his voice and leaned closer. "Intercourse. And come to find out, she was a hard-core, devout Catholic."

Atlas made his statement as though it held an answer to some giant secret.

"So?"

He huffed. "Man, from what I understand, women who are deeply religious may not give it up. Well, they will..."

I cut him off. "Of course she will. We're taking it slow."

"Did she say that or did you assume that?" he asked.

That time I groaned and pressed back into child's pose.

My ass rested on my ankles, my knees were wide so I could lay my chest between my thighs, and my arms were stretched out in front of me flat on the mat. God, that felt good.

"What are you getting at, Atlas? You're talking yourself in circles."

"I'm saying, maybe she's saving herself for marriage like a good little Catholic girl would."

At that, I lifted up and glanced at him. "Shut the fuck up."

He rubbed a hand over his mouth to stanch the flow of his laughter. "The fact that it hadn't dawned on you why your hot, twenty-something-year-old girlfriend was untouched due to the possibility that her religion played a part in it is mind-boggling. You used to pick up on shit like this, man."

I rested my head in my hands and sucked in several slow breaths as the intensity of what he suggested slammed over my entire body. I focused on my *Ujjayi*, oceanic breathing, and let my mind go.

Was Amber saving herself for marriage?

What would I do if she said yes?

Would she take that next step in our physical relationship without it?

Is there a time limit on waiting?

How religious was the woman I loved?

Could she leave me over this?

I pressed on my scalp and tugged at my hair until the pain reached the surface, releasing me of the fears that were running rampant inside. I needed to talk to Amber. "Fuck me!" I groaned.

"Not in this lifetime, studly," came a rich, sultry voice from behind us.

I sat up and turned around. Mila Mercado, the feisty little

teacher that every man wanted but nobody got, stood a few feet from where we'd set up. She stood all of five foot two and maybe a hundred pounds, all muscle, tits, and a toned bubble butt.

"Hello, hotness," Atlas drawled while getting to his feet. He held out a hand. "Atlas Powers. I'm one of the other Vin Flow teachers."

Mila studied Atlas with her chocolate gaze. "Hotness?" She frowned and ignored Atlas's hand and looked at me. "Hey, you okay? You don't normally start with the profanities until at least midway through the class." She grinned.

I stood up, wrapped an arm around her shoulder, and kissed the side of her mouth. She returned the gesture, kissing me back. Ever since I'd gotten in trouble for kissing Genevieve on the mouth, I'd changed up the way I connected with the single women in my world. That day when Trent punched me, I thought about how I approached women, and though I'd not had complaints before that day, I could see his side of things. Kissing was a no-go zone for most men. Just the thought of my Amber putting her perfect lips on another man made the green-eyed monster within me shudder in agitation.

"Sorry, Mila." I glanced around to make sure there weren't too many people that had overheard me. It wasn't professional to blast out an F-bomb, especially within the walls of the Lotus House Center. People came there to find solace and serenity, not profanity and vulgarities.

She pinched her glossy lips together before tipping her head to Atlas. "Who's curly?"

I snickered. "Curly? Oh Mila, I'd kiss you again just for that if my girlfriend would approve."

"Curly? Curly? You've got to be kidding?" Atlas ran a

hand through his mop of hair.

"If the shoe fits," Mila said.

"I'd have you put it on and then wrap those legs around my waist," Atlas shot back.

Her eyes blazed white-hot fire and her perfectly shaped brows pointed down, much like devil forks. "How about I take it off and spike you with it?"

Atlas took two steps closer, and I backed up, ready to watch the fireworks.

"So it *will* be a stiletto." He grinned and licked his lips. "*Nice.* Your legs will look a mile long in a pair of sky-high heels." He leaned closer, his face only a few inches from Mila's.

I'm certain my eyes were the size of milk jugs, and I was afraid to take a breath for fear I'd screw up the animal sniffing or sparring these two were doing.

Mila put her hands on her small hips and started walking around Atlas. "You think so, eh?"

His eyes shifted, practically walking all over her tiny form. From her bare feet with red-painted toes, up her yoga pants to her bare midriff to her chest, where she wore only a sports bra to cover two healthy handfuls of fine womanly curves.

Her eyes turned into steely points of irritation. "Did you just check me out?"

"Hell yes, I did, wildcat. Your body is insane. You must work hard to look this good."

Mila's lips curled up into the smallest smile. I noticed the brief slip in her bravado, but more importantly, so did Atlas. "I do. Work hard. Speaking of...get ready to be worked over." Mila turned around swiftly, leaving Atlas off balance.

"You could work me over any day, wildcat."

"Simmer down, man. Damn. I thought the two of you

were going to catch fire circling around one another like that. Like oil and vinegar."

Atlas didn't take his eyes off Mila when he spoke hoarsely. "Yeah, put us together and we taste fantastic on a salad. Shit man. That girl just got my number but good. I think I'm in love."

I shook my head and clapped him on the back. "Easy, boy. Mila's a tough one."

"Challenge accepted. I'm all over that."

AMBER

The halls were rather quiet as I made my way through the medical building toward the auditorium we used for my course in the Joint Medical Program at the UCSF campus. My boot heels clicked and clacked against the off-white linoleum surface. Usually, I wore my Nikes, comfort being priority when I had the potential of having to do class followed by grand rounds. Tonight, however, Dash was picking me up from school to take my family and me to dinner. Dinner wasn't supposed to be a big deal, but it was to me. I didn't need to look dolled up, but I wanted to for him.

It had been two whole days since we'd had what I was calling our night of enlightenment. Still, the thought of what had occurred made my skin burn and gave me the giggles like a silly schoolgirl. Technically, I was still in school, even if it was to secure my MD.

I'd spent the better part of two days aching inside for him. Every piece of my existence seemed hyperfocused and on edge. Needless to say, my clitoral vibrator was getting more use than previously. Dash and I both agreed that we needed to connect with the other people in our lives. It was easy to lose ourselves in a new relationship and forget about all the coming and goings of the rest of the world, especially when we were chest deep in love with each other. I wanted to be with Dash all the time, and when I wasn't with him, I was thinking about him, wondering what he was doing, who he had in his classes, and how his day had gone.

He admitted he had the same clingy need I did. Which was why we'd agreed to take two days to connect with our friends and family. He'd mentioned that he wanted to go out with his buddy Atlas, take a couple classes at the center in his off time, and chat up his yoga buddies. I'd spent yesterday with Genevieve preparing the baby's room. Baseball-themed, of course. Trent wouldn't have it any other way. Then again, neither would her brother, Rowan, who was quickly following in his almost-brother-in-law's footsteps.

Genevieve was about ready to pop. We were now at the end of July, closing in on her August due date—if she made it a couple more weeks. The woman would not stop. She'd been teaching prenatal and gentle yoga classes all the way up until now. On top of that, she'd finished the rest of her coursework for cosmetology. What she didn't know was that Trent had already bought her a salon around the corner from the yoga studio. She was going to be happy and pissed at the same time. Vivvie did not like things handed to her, preferring to earn everything she had in life. Something about the law of karmic debt. When she started in on the spiritual stuff and started quoting Deepak Chopra, I usually lost interest. It wasn't that I didn't believe... well, I didn't really. What I did believe in was God. And I knew that God would make sure that Genevieve, Trent, and all the kids would live a happy and healthy life together.

Tugging my book bag up my shoulder, I turned the corner

to where the classroom was and found Landen leaning near the door, standing on one Converse-clad foot, the other perched against the wall. When he saw me, he smiled and pushed off the wall.

"Hey you, where have you been? I haven't seen you since we went to the pub."

"Oh, yeah. I had a conflict with class the other day and met with my advisor. Professor O'Brien approved it. Apparently, all the newbies have an advisor around this time to make sure they focus their goals and academics on the right area of study."

His eyes widened. "Did you pick one? A specialty?"

I grinned and nodded. It seemed stupid, but I kind of wanted to tell Dash first. Nevertheless, I really was bursting at the seams to share.

"Well, what did you choose?"

"Guess?" I quirked an eyebrow and shoved at his chest playfully. Landen and I were buds. I think.

He grinned and then tapped a finger on his lips. "Obstetrics and gynecology!"

I shook my head. "Nope. Peds!"

"Woo hoo!" he whooped, wrapped his arms around me, and spun me in a circle.

I giggled, and he set me back on my feet but didn't let me go. He held both of my biceps and ducked his head close to mine. "That is so fantastic. Are you happy?"

"Yes and no. I'm still nervous I may have chosen wrong, but I couldn't choose based on something that happened to my mother. I love kids. Want to have a gaggle of them."

He smiled. "You planning to have a big family with that man who picked you up? The giant who claimed to be your boyfriend?" His lips pinched together into a thin line.

"I'm sorry about Dash. Yes, he's my boyfriend. But that night, I don't know. I was worried that we'd lost something, and he wouldn't understand...ugh, I'm not explaining very well," I said, my shoulders dropping down heavily.

"It's okay. I mean, hey, we're friends, right?" He lowered his eyes to mine.

I brushed a strand of hair away from his forehead. "Yeah, we're friends. Totally."

"So then if you're not available, you'll just have to hook me up with someone as hot as you."

On that I laughed, hard, butting my forehead into his chest.

"I'm serious!" He patted me on the back up and down before curling a hand around my jaw.

I leaned back, looking into his eyes. They were lovely, like fresh-cut grass on a bright, sunny day.

"You're a hard one to beat, too, so you better find me a good one," he finished.

I tilted my head up, making sure he could see the sincerity in my face when I patted him over the heart. "Easy. You're perfect to me. Any woman would fall all over herself to go on a date with you."

A loud booming male voice interrupted us. "What do you think you're doing, Landen?" his father grated through a hardened jaw and clenched teeth.

Landed pulled me against his side, wrapping an arm around my shoulders. I locked an arm around his waist, as uncomfortable with the professor's tone as he was.

"Dad, what's your problem? Amber and I are just talking."

His eyes pinched together behind his thin-rimmed glasses. The curls in his dark brown hair had been cut close to his head, making his normally distinguished appearance more severe.

"Talking?" He huffed. "That's not what it looked like."

"Dad, it's not what you think. And even if it were, who are you to say who I can and can't date?"

"I'm your father!" he warned.

I could tell by the way his face had hardened and the blue vein that pulsed in his forehead that his father was beyond unhappy. Why, I didn't know. Still I felt the need to butt in and clear up the misunderstanding.

"Professor O'Brien, sir. I'm not sure what you think you saw, but your son and I are friends. Good friends. That is all. I have a boyfriend with whom I'm very much in love. Landen was just asking me to set him up. However, I wouldn't mind knowing why you think I'm wrong for your son. Have I done something that has made you think ill of me? Because if I have, please give me the opportunity to clear it up. We have several more years together, and I'd rather not have that time tainted with a misunderstanding."

The professor's shoulders curled in and slumped forward as he sighed. He pushed his glasses farther up his nose, centering them. "Amber, I'm sorry. It's not you. We need to talk. Privately. Are you available after class?"

"Is this about my mother?" I asked, deadpan. It was what I wanted to know most from him, and he'd steadily avoided it since the day he mentioned her name. I was pretty sure he'd gone out of his way to ensure we wouldn't discuss it.

His eyes widened, and his entire face paled the same way his brother's had the other night in the bar.

"Landen, go on in. I'd like a word with Ms. St. James."

"Are you going to be nice, Dad? Seriously. She deserves

better than the way you've acted around her."

He took a long breath. "Yes, son. She's safe with me, and you're right. She does deserve better. Hopefully, we can work some of that out. Go on in."

Landen tugged me to his side and laid a friendly kiss on my temple. I watched as his dad's nostrils flared. "I'll be just inside if he starts being a brute again. Okay?"

I chuckled and patted his arm. "I'm fine, buddy. See you in class." He left me alone with his dad, who did everything but speak to me for a full two minutes. He shuffled his feet, adjusted his collar, shook the coins in his pants, all while I waited, arms crossed over my chest, trying desperately not to scream or shake it out of him.

Eventually, I couldn't wait any longer. "Are you finally going to discuss your problem or whatever your issue is with my mother? She's dead, Professor. It's not like she's going to rise up and haunt you or anything."

He shook his head and coughed into his hand. "Just like her. Quick wit and so damn bright. You know you're probably the smartest student in the class?"

"Um, okay." That being a bit of information I'd fist pump to later, like when sitting down to dinner with Dash and my grandparents tonight. "I'm sorry, but what does this have to do with my mother and your reaction to me because of her?"

The professor rubbed at the back of his neck and looked off to the side. "Amber, it has everything to do with your mom. Because if what I suspect is true, a lot is about to change."

Right then, two of the girls from class scuttled up to us in a rush. "Sorry we're late, Professor. Won't happen again."

He sighed and opened the door. "Can we continue this after class?"

A little niggle of dread tap danced its way up my back and settled on my shoulder. "Yeah, that's fine, but my boyfriend will have to come. He's picking me up for dinner. I'll call my grandparents and change the time. Would an hour be fine?"

His lips pinched together. "Yeah, that should work fine. Thank you for waiting, Amber."

"I feel like I've been waiting my whole life." I wanted to add...*to learn about my mother* when the words he said under his breath, just loud enough for me to hear, sent a stone the size of my car crashing on top of my chest, cracking my ribs open, and flattening my heart to a gooey mess.

"Me too."

CHAPTER FIFTEEN

SACRAL
CHAKRA

Weak sacral chakras can be found in individuals who have sexual problems, lack desire or ability to experience pleasure, including orgasms or erectile dysfunction. Weaknesses may also present in a person through illness with the bladder, penis, uterus, and back. There are mental concerns to be cognizant of, as well such as irrational behavior, jealousy, and anger issues.

AMBER

Dash arrived right at the tail end of class, as planned. He was waiting for me in the hall. I could see him through the open lecture hall door, his tall, muscular frame in a pair of black dress slacks and a lavender button-down shirt, sexy as sin. He looked positively edible leaning against the wall opposite the door, as could be attested to by the gaggle of women copping a look-see, flirting, or attempting to make eye contact as they passed him in the hall.

The best part was, he didn't even give them a second glance. His eyes were on me and only me as I took each step slowly toward the top of the stairs to the exit.

"Hey, Cosmo." I smiled huge, unable to contain it. "You look handsome."

He winked and made a show of rolling up the arms of his dress shirt to display those golden forearms with the light smattering of dark blond hair. Yum.

"As do you, Dr. St. James." He lifted an eyebrow, ramping up his sex appeal times about a gazillion.

"Oh, I like the sound of that," I said, walking toward him. I didn't stop until my breasts bumped against his chest.

"Then I shall address you as such more often, Doc." He grinned.

I practically preened, looking up at him with a heaping dose of love and desire. How had this man so quickly become the center of my world?

Dash wrapped both arms around my waist and locked his wrists together over my bum. Then he did the ultimate. He leaned down, brushed his lips along mine, nuzzled my nose, and asked, "How's my girl?"

Swoon.

Lord, I cannot be held responsible for my actions. I was born a sinner, and sin I will.

"Perfect, now that you're here," I whispered before curling a hand around his neck, rising onto my tiptoes, and kissing the daylights out of him.

If he was surprised, he didn't act like it. No, my guy took over the kiss, hissing into my mouth like a snake ready to strike its unsuspecting prey.

I nibbled on Dash's lips, alternating between licking and sucking the top then bottom, adding just enough pressure to get the lower half of his body in the game.

I'd learned a fact pretty quickly about Dash. He had absolutely no qualms about PDAs or public indecency for that matter. When he got in the mood to show his affection, he went for it. And me? Well, I was incapable of stopping that train once it left the station. Not that I'd even try.

His lips devoured mine while his hands gripped my ass in a firm squeeze, rubbing my groin against his hardening shaft. I gasped into his mouth and attempted to pull away, knowing I was in the hall at school and lacking all common sense. Dash would have none of it. He chased my mouth, wrapped a hand around a section of my hair, and tugged my head back far enough so that it was immobile, and I had to take his kiss.

Secretly, I loved when he turned alpha Neanderthal male. I found it wickedly sexy. He wasn't demeaning me in the slightest. On the contrary. The man was so taken by our connection that he *worshipped* me wherever I stood. Public be damned. Now, if I could get him to keep these reactions to more private locations, we'd be set.

"Told you, Dad!" I heard Landen's voice behind us.

I ripped my mouth away, but Dash only allowed us to separate a few inches. "Dash, um, we have company." I hooked a thumb behind me.

He glanced over my shoulder. "I know. I'm deciding if I care."

Oh no, he didn't. "Seriously, rude!" I growled into his face, fisted his shirt, and pushed off. Finally, he let me go. By go, I mean he allowed me to shift to his side where he wrapped one hand around my shoulders and the other he splayed low on my belly. Very low. Too low to be considered just friendly.

Professor O'Brien smacked his hands together, the loud clap echoing off the mostly empty hallway. "Well, I guess I owe you an apology, son," he said.

Landen nodded and smiled smugly.

I did my best not to roll my eyes at his immaturity. However, I did think it was funny that I was the only one who noticed the professor didn't actually apologize, just said he owed Landen one. Point for Dr. O'Brien.

Whatever worked for them. I didn't want to get them going at it again, especially in front of Dash if it had anything to do with the concept of Landen and me in a romantic sense. Not that I understood why it would be an issue. I mean, I never thought I was much of a catch before, but I definitely wasn't a dog. Also, he had told me I had the highest intellect in class, so what was I lacking? Not that it mattered per se, other than the fact that it irked me not knowing.

"Ms. St. James, would you be so kind as to join me in my office?"

Landen blinked. "Why? I thought we were having dinner with Mom?" His tone was curious but lacked any knowledge of whatever his father had to say about my mother.

"Son, go on home and tell your mother I'll be there within the hour. I have a matter to discuss with Ms. St. James."

Landen tucked his hands into his pockets, looked at his dad, then me, and finally Dash. I don't know what he saw in Dash's eyes, but whatever it was got him to move along because the next thing he said was a grumbled, "Fine, see you in class on Wednesday, Amber."

"Yeah, see ya. Thanks for the help with the A and P today.

I owe you one." Anatomy and Physiology could be tricky when the sole focus was the nervous system.

"Score me a date with a girlfriend of yours and we're even!" He laughed, walking backward toward the turn in the hallway.

I shook my head and looked at Dash. "Professor O'Brien wants to talk to me about my mother. Would you, you know, like to sit in?"

Please say yes. Please say yes.

Dash cupped my cheek. "Amber, I told you whatever you need, I'm your guy. When you're uncomfortable, I'm uncomfortable. Yeah?"

"Yeah."

"You don't mind if I join you, do you?" Dash geared the question to my instructor.

Dr. O'Brien rubbed at the back of his neck and yanked at his collar again. Looking more closely, I noticed a layer of darkened strands at his hairline. Either he was nervous or sweating due to being overheated, and frankly, the temperature in the building felt just fine to me.

"If Amber is okay sharing very private information with you, then it's okay with me."

Dash threaded his fingers through mine and squeezed my hand so we were palm to palm. "Lead the way."

The professor walked in front of us and led us down two barren hallways to a row of offices. Each door had frosted glass with a different doctor's name on it. I recognized a couple of them from the program syllabus. They'd likely be one of my instructors for certain portions of the coursework. Dr. O'Brien couldn't teach every specialty. He had to bring in experts in the different fields beyond general medicine and emergency care.

He opened the door to his office and turned the light on. The room was chaotic, to put it mildly. Bookcases ran the length of both walls, making the room feel closed in and dark. A single window on the back wall was covered with shutters closed tight so you couldn't even gauge whether it was dark or light outside. On his desk were books, stacks of files, and bits of paper with words scrawled on them. Only a small eight-by-ten-inch space in front of him was bare for working. Even a chair in the corner was filled to the brim with a stack of books, a wayward plant that could have used a cup of water, or twelve, and a hat that was teetering on the edge of the seat just waiting for a strong wind to push it over.

"Nice digs," Dash commented dryly.

The doctor glanced at the two chairs sitting in front of his desk. Both of them held stacks of files and other odds and ends.

"Sorry, Landen's my TA, but I haven't let him into my office to organize me. The last time he came in here, I couldn't find anything for a month."

I chuckled. "What did he do? Toss your stuff?"

He shook his head while clearing the files off the chairs and stacking them on an already leaning pile at the edge of his solid wood desk.

"No, he put it in order."

"Blasphemy," Dash joked, and the doctor actually laughed.

"All joking aside, it's..."

"Organized chaos. Looks like my desk at home. Drives my grandparents insane. I'm meticulous with my room, clothes, study habits, but my desk is an utter nightmare to anybody..."

"But you." He pointed at me, a strange look crossing his eyes.

I tilted my head. "Yep."

"Birds of a feather," Dash said, grabbing my hand across the chair and pressing his lips together in a small air kiss.

Professor O'Brien sat down across from us and positioned his hands on top of the desk. He looked me straight in the eye and proceeded to blow my God-loving mind.

"Back when your mother was nineteen or twenty, she and I had an affair. For a year."

DASH

"Holy shit!" I said out loud. The plan was to stay quiet while Amber and the doc discussed his knowledge of her mother's past, but him stating he'd had an affair with her was not at all what I'd expected.

Amber opened her mouth, closed it, and then swallowed. "Excuse me?" she whispered.

He ran a hand through unruly hair that had bits of gray at the sides. "It was my first year teaching Anatomy and Physiology, just about mid 1990s. Kate, your mother, was in my class. She was a sophomore. As a second-year student in my program, Kate was my first choice to be my teacher's assistant."

Oh Christ. I knew where this was going before he even said it. The old "late one night...things got out of hand." I could already hear the excuses a mile away.

As it was, Amber was squeezing the life out of my hand. I would have pulled her into my lap to give her the extra touch I knew she needed right then to ground her, but she'd never approve. Definitely not in front of her instructor. Instead, I ran my thumb along her wrist to remind her I was there, listening, and ready to battle any demons that might surface with this new information.

"Go on." Amber's voice was raspy, emotion already starting to muddle her beautiful timbre.

"Kate was top of her class, like you. Bright, had the entire world ahead of her." He took a slow breath and sighed as if he'd been waiting years to let the weight of this secret fall from his shoulders. "My wife and I were at odds, separated. I was living in a hotel and running back and forth between teaching, spending time with my six-month-old son, and trying to give her space."

"You were married at the time? And you had Landen?" Amber closed her eyes and took several breaths.

Waves of painful energy banged against my psyche. My girl was not taking this information well, but she deserved to know the truth, and I was determined to help her through this until she got it all.

The doctor sighed. "I'm not proud of what we did. Not only was I ten years her senior, the breach of the teacher-student relationship unethical, I was cheating on my wife. Kate though, she had this way about her. She was convinced that we were meant to be and had I not already been married with an infant son, I'd have agreed with her. Hell, I *did* agree with her, in silence. I loved your mother deeply, Amber. Please know that. She was everything I'd ever wanted in a mate. She just came into my life too late."

"So you carried on a relationship with Amber's mother for a year, you said?"

He nodded. "Yes. My wife and I were separated almost immediately after having our son. She didn't take his birth and being a mother well. She wanted to be at work where she was confident, strong and, in her mind, needed. Ultimately, she was diagnosed with postpartum depression. Only it took over a year for her to even remotely return to the woman I'd married eight years prior."

Amber choked on a sob. "You'd been married eight years before you were with my mom?"

He licked his lips and looked away. "As I said, I'm not proud of the decisions I made. I can only say that your mother, there was something about her. I couldn't *not* be with her. It was like she was gold dipped in liquid sunshine. Her warmth and love shone so bright, it blinded everything else in my world so that all I saw *was* her. She got me through the most difficult time in my life."

If everything was all roses and rainbows between Kate and the professor, why'd she end up pregnant and alone? Oh no. Oh *hell* no. Dread so strong crawled up my throat and coated it with a thick slime. I could hardly breathe. There was just no way...

"Then why were you not together?" Amber sniffed, and he passed her a box of tissues. She wiped her eyes and licked her lips. "I'm okay. Go on."

He clasped his fingers together in front of him. "Well, throughout the time I was with Kate, my wife was seeking help. She was officially diagnosed and then given antianxiety meds and antidepressants to help with the depression. Within a couple months, she was a new woman. The woman I married. The very same woman I had a child with. Our son...Landen... needed both parents. I couldn't just give up on him."

A tear slipped down Amber's cheek. I wanted to kiss it away, pull her up and over my shoulder, and storm out of this vile room. This man had hurt her mother deeply, and in turn, he was hurting Amber. I'd about had it.

"So you broke it off," she said bluntly.

He nodded. "One night she came to me, had something important she wanted to tell me. God, if I knew then what I know now...needless to say, I wish I'd listened. But I didn't. I cut her off, told her that we had to end our affair and that I was going back to my wife to give it another shot." The professor rubbed at his face, removed his glasses, and that was when I saw it. His eyes. As familiar as my own because I spent hours looking into them when I looked at the woman I'd die for each and every day.

"H-how did s-she take it?" Amber asked.

He closed his eyes. "With grace. She hugged me, kissed me one last time, and told me that she'd always love me and would never speak of our affair."

Amber swallowed, tears flowing down her cheeks. "And what did you say to her?"

"That I'd never forget her. That there would always be a place in my heart she owned, and finally, I'd never love another the way I loved her. And I never have." Sorrow overflowed his tone, making me believe he meant it.

"Thank you for sharing your story with me. It means a lot and gives me more to go on. Definitely helps to understand why she left school when she did." Amber wiped at her runny nose, and I squeezed her hand.

Sometimes there's a moment in time when everything in the world as it's always been is about to change. Almost like experiencing a premonition about how certain life events are going to rip the world into bite-sized pieces. Right then, that feeling hit my heart like a tidal wave blasting the shore during a hurricane.

"May I ask you a question, Amber?"

She nodded.

"How old are you, and what day is your birthday?"

Her nose scrunched up in that cute way I adored. "I'm going to be twenty-three on November sixteenth. Why?"

He closed his eyes, and his hands shook as he pressed his fingers against his temples. "Valentine's Day."

"Huh?" Amber said.

"You would have been conceived around Valentine's Day."

Amber chuckled. "I imagine a lot of babies are. It's a romantic holiday. What are you getting at?"

"My wife and I didn't celebrate Valentine's Day, but that year, Kate and I did. I took her on a dinner cruise where we danced in the moonlight, shared our future desires. I wanted to be the department chair over the medical program. Kate wanted to be a pediatrician."

Amber jerked her hand from mine and leaned forward. "A pediatrician? I just chose that as my specialty. It's why I missed the last class."

He smiled solemnly. "You are your mother's daughter. It's why when I saw your face it was like looking into my past. You look so much like her, only with subtle differences."

"Yeah, green eyes for one."

"That and your chin is rounded here." He pointed to his own rounded chin.

My heart sank. He was going round and round the mulberry bush, and I still didn't know when he was going to stop and tell my girlfriend the obvious truth! If he didn't get on with it, I was a solid two point five seconds from laying it out in black, white, and glaring multicolors.

Amber blew her nose into the tissue, wiped up, and squirted some hand sanitizer into her hand that she'd magically seen on his desk. "That's really nice of you to share your experience, but why the questions about my birthday?"

Dr. O'Brien placed both of his elbows on his desk, took off his glasses, and left them dangling in one hand. "Because, Amber, the year your mom would have conceived you, we were together. The Valentine's holiday we spent together fits as well. A DNA test would prove it, but I'm almost a hundred percent certain that I was the only man Kate was in a relationship with at the time."

Amber's eyes widened, and her pupils dilated so much that the green had nearly disappeared. Her cheeks had taken on a deeply flushed appearance. Her expression looked surprised, anxious, and frightened all at once. "Are you suggesting..."

"That I'm your father? Yes, Amber. That's exactly what I'm suggesting."

"No," she whispered, her hand coming up to cover her mouth.

"I'd like to have a DNA test done to be sure but looking into your eyes, Amber, darling, it's like looking into my mother's eyes and mine. Even Landen's."

"Oh my God, Landen!" Amber stood up, tears flowing down her cheeks once more.

Bastard made her cry again. That was two for two, and I sure as hell was keeping track. I gripped both hands into tight fists. I'd never been a violent man, until another man made my woman shed a tear. A blast of anger sizzled along my nerves, and I had to grit my teeth in order not to go apeshit on him.

He stood up and brought his hands up in front of him. "He doesn't know anything, yet. I wanted to talk to you and be sure. Do you know who your father is?"

Amber shook her head, the long, dark waves I loved

running my fingers through falling in front of her face.

"Did your mother write a name on your birth certificate?"

Again, no words left her mouth, just a slight jerk of her head in the negative.

"Okay, perhaps your grandparents mentioned your biological father?"

Amber straightened her spine, pushing her shoulders back and down. "My mother died in childbirth. She took my paternity to her grave." Each word was a cold, lifeless utterance from a woman so far gone emotionally I wouldn't have recognized her had she not been standing in front of me.

"I think it's time to go, my love. Get you home."

"Home? Where's home?" Amber's eyes were flat, emotionless, her face deathly pale.

"Amber," he tried, but I slashed the air.

"No. You don't get to be concerned. Not now. Maybe not ever," I gritted through my teeth. "Amber, honey, your home is where I am."

She nodded, picked up her backpack as if on autopilot, and reached for the door handle. When she got there, she stopped and turned just her face. "I believe you loved her. And I believe that, even in death, she died protecting the ones she loved. She protected you, and her promise to not speak of your affair, with her very last breath."

"Amber, I'm sorry." The guy's voice was strained and broken.

She pursed her lips and nodded curtly.

"Wait," I said, and with the gentlest touch I could manage, I plucked a single stand of my little bird's long dark hair from her head. She didn't even wince. My girl was as numb as they come. I placed the strand of hair in a tissue I pulled out of the box sitting on a shelf. "Do your test." I handed him the tissue with her hair in it. Then I grabbed my wallet and took out my author business card. "Send the results to this address or call to discuss."

The professor glanced at the card and held the tissue within a white-knuckled fist.

"I did love her," he said one last time.

"Not enough," I deadpanned. It was the truth, and in this case, the truth hurt.

I opened the door and ushered Amber out of a room filled with sorrow and regret and into a life of possibilities and future happiness. We just needed to get past this landmine in time. I'd be there to help her through it.

On the way home, I called her grandparents and told them that she wasn't feeling well. I was going to watch over her tonight, and we'd do dinner later in the week. They agreed and sent their love. Now, those two people knew how to love someone.

CHAPTER SIXTEEN

Plough Pose
(Sanskrit: Halasana)

Plough pose invigorates and rejuvenates the entire body. As an inverted pose, it aids with asthma and high blood pressure. It's also great at building strength in the shoulders and loosening tension in the back and spine. As an intermediate level asana, consider working on shoulder stand prior to transitioning into full plow. A yogi needs a strong core and sense of flexibility to master this pose.

A M B E R

Dash took me to his warehouse loft and led me over to his bed. I stood silently, the tumultuous emotions spinning in an endless vortex of flashes of our conversation with Dr. O'Brien. No, possibly my biological father. A man who had supposedly loved my mother but not enough to keep her. Obligation...he claimed. What about his obligation to my mother and to me? How could he not know that she was pregnant with me when he broke it off?

You know why.

A little voice nagged inside my head.

She kept it from him, from everyone...even you.

I closed my eyes as Dash pushed me to a seated position on his bed. He leaned down and pulled off the sexy boots I'd worn for our first formal "meet the grandparents" dinner. Technically, it would have been the second for Dash since he'd admitted to worrying about me the night I went out with Landen, and he ate with my grandparents and sat through a third degree with my papa waiting for me to come home. Which I never did.

Socks removed, Dash lifted one foot and kissed the top and then proceeded to lift and kiss the other. He clasped my hands and tugged me to stand. He lifted my blouse and tossed it on the chair beside his bed. He kissed each shoulder and the space over my heart. I watched motionless and unfeeling as he unbuttoned my jeans and pulled them down my legs. He tapped each ankle so that I'd lift my foot so he could remove the pant leg. I did it all detached from the acts.

Leaving me standing, he turned around, went over to his dresser, and pulled out a plain white T-shirt. He lobbed the shirt over his shoulder the way a waiter would a towel in a restaurant. Then he reached around me, unclasped my bra, and set the girls free. A tiny prickle of relief filtered across the numbness. Dash ran his hands down my arms, leaned forward, and kissed the very tip of my right breast. His tongue then circled the tight nipple, sucking and nibbling until I gasped.

He then moved to its twin. I gripped his hair, closed my eyes, opened them again, and looked up at the ceiling, finally feeling something for the first time since we'd left the school.

Dash put both of his hands on my waist and set me on the bed. Once I'd lain down, he shifted me farther up. Without any words, with only the intense love pouring from him, he kissed my neck, running a trail of wet kisses down toward my breasts where he stopped and spent a long time, feasting, sucking, and nipping. I squirmed and shifted my legs restlessly as he worked on each nipple. He held them both together, glanced at me, and tongued both hardened tips simultaneously, ramping up my lust a hundredfold. He watched my every reaction while he plucked and pinched each peak into rock-hard points of need.

He settled his hips between my thighs where I could rub my lower half against his hard body while he played. Just when I was going to come from the nipple stimulation alone, he backed away.

I groaned and held his head as he moved down my body, licking a trail down my abdomen to my panties. In what felt like a second, he'd removed my underwear, opened my knees wide, and put his hot mouth exactly where I wanted it most. I cried out, his tongue fluttering against oversensitive tissue before sucking on my clit hard enough for stars to appear across my vision.

Without words or any other sound, Dash made love to me. He showed me that, when I thought all was lost, our love was something beautiful to hold on to. He was my light in this dark, the reason to move on, to take this information for what it was and let it go. Life with him would be beautiful. Heck, it was glorious now.

His tongue piercing my center forced a lungful of air out

of my mouth. He held my legs open as wide as he could. I felt split apart, fractured mentally, and through the expert way he mouthed me, I was about to lose it physically. This time, however, I wouldn't fall apart because Dash was there to keep me grounded when I wanted to fly away.

The sensation of his tongue flicking, his lips rubbing, and that magnificent mouth sucking deep at the heart of me sent a bolt of lightning through me so intense I arched and shook. He held me down, kept at my most vulnerable spot like he'd never tire of the taste and couldn't get enough.

"Dash," I moaned, pressing my hand to his head. I rode his face shamelessly. I couldn't stop. The sensations overpowered my will, leaving me a dangling ball of need and desire.

He growled, rubbed the flat of his tongue against my clit, and then bit down on the tiny bundle of nerves until I literally screamed as the orgasm washed over me, my body contracting, bowing up and down. I gripped his hair in both hands and held on as the tremors washed through me, over and over, until he moved his mouth to my opening and forced his tongue deep. Another jolt rocked my body at the intimacy of the act. His tongue moved against the spasming walls of my sex as if he was licking up every drop of my release.

My mouth watered, thinking about doing the same to him.

"Your cock, give it to me," I whispered hoarsely. I wanted him in my mouth, wanted him all around me so that I'd drown in him and not the past.

He shook his head, kissed my wet center until every last pulse from my orgasm gradually diminished.

"Not about me."

Dash sat up and grabbed the clean shirt for me that had fallen somewhere. Once he had the cotton stretched just right, he pulled it over my thoroughly relaxed head, helped me put my spaghetti arms into each hole, pulled the covers back, and tucked me in. He went around the house and turned off the lights before he stripped down to his boxer briefs. My eyelids were so heavy, feeling more weighted with every blink. He turned off the light next to the bed, pulled the covers back, and slid in.

His body was hot as a bonfire and just as magnificent when he spooned up behind me. He lifted one of my thighs, held it up, and inserted his knee and thigh to drape over my other leg. Then he grabbed my hand, plastered his back against mine, and put his lips to the back of my neck.

"Go to sleep, my love. We'll talk in the morning."

I circled my hips to where his very impressive erection was still standing at attention. "What about you?"

He kissed the skin below my hairline. "What about me?" He yawned.

"Don't you want me to return the favor?"

He chuckled softly against my neck. Shivers rippled down my spine from the proximity.

"This is not a tit-for-tat situation. You needed to be loved, and it's my job to show that to you."

For a couple minutes, I thought about those words. His breathing deepened, but I could tell from the grip on my body he wasn't yet asleep.

"But what if I want to show you love?"

He snorted into my neck. "Tomorrow. Wake me up with a blow job, and I'll love the hell out of you."

I giggled at the thought of waking him up with my mouth on him. The idea had a whole lot of merit. Kind of like a sneak attack. Maybe I would.

"I love you. Go to sleep." His words were mumbled and slathered in slumber.

"Dash, I love you, too." I gripped his hand, brought it up to my mouth, and kissed the fingers I could feel. Then I closed my eyes, holding his hand against my lips. If I could smell and feel him all the time, maybe I could get through this screwed-up situation.

I started with the *Our Father* prayer before going into what I really needed to discuss with the man upstairs.

God, today was hard. I can't even process what happened yet. Regardless, I want to thank you for bringing me Dash and giving me the strength to hold onto him. I need him now more than I ever needed anyone. Aside from You, of course. Please, please keep him safe, and don't take him away from me. Ever.

Amen.

DASH

Amber had been a zombie all week. If I had a nickel for every time she sighed in defeat, I'd be a very rich man. And that pissed me off. I'd always been known as the easygoing, spiritual guy, more interested in loving than fighting, but after a week of seeing the woman I'd die for lose a bit of herself every day, I was ready to rage.

We hadn't heard anything about the DNA testing. It stood to reason that these things took some time even if some rich guy paid an insane amount of money to rush the results. Which I imagine he'd have the resources to do.

After that night almost a week ago, Amber had spent almost every night sleeping by my side. Each night, she allowed me to make love to her with my mouth and fingers but hadn't even hinted at taking things further.

She'd become a master at giving head. I swear, the second her silky lips would wrap around my cock and she would look up at me with those emerald eyes, I'd lose it in mere seconds. Maybe not *that* fast but it was definitely embarrassing, stamina-wise. I'd prided myself on the ability to go long hours without ever orgasming. My little bird took off her clothes, wrapped her hand or mouth on my cock, and all thoughts of holding out went right out the window along with my cries of pleasure.

I guessed my affinity for her sexually further proved she was my one and only. I hadn't doubted that since the day I had her under me in class. Speaking of class, she should be here any minute. I instructed the last Tantra class alone to give her time to deal with school and this new information about her prospective father. Tonight, I intended to bring my little bird back to the nest where she belonged. I wanted to immerse her in love and sensual delights and the unity of other couples' energies to purge the negative energy that had plagued her this past week.

Once I'd adjusted the music to a dull lilt, I glanced up and saw her coming my way. She wore tiny, dark blue yoga briefs that were more like underwear or a pair of hot pants. I was almost certain a bit of ass cheek winked into view with each step, but I'd have had to see her from behind to confirm. On top, she had on a zip-up matching sports bra that barely contained her bountiful tits. God, I loved her breasts. Those sandy nipples were like butterscotch candies in size and shape, and just as buttery. Overall, I wholeheartedly approved.

"New clothes?" I scanned her body from top to toe and back again.

She smirked. "Borrowed from Genevieve. She can't fit in anything anymore, and the odds of her bouncing back anytime soon after the baby are slim. Besides, she said they were ruining her life sitting in her drawer taunting her."

When she made it to where I sat, I got up on my knees, wrapped both arms around her, and planted my forehead to her chest before kissing her belly in greeting.

Amber threaded her fingers through my hair a few times. "What's the matter?" she asked, noticing my melancholy mood. Since we'd been together, she'd been in tune with my temperament shifts. Another testament to our unity.

I rubbed my chin along her abdomen, relishing in her strawberry scent. "Just worried about you."

Her eyebrows came together, and her lips flattened. "Me? I'm fine."

I shook my head and squeezed her waist. "But you're not. You're going through the motions, but you're not truly here. Today, that changes. Tonight's class we're going to focus on us, on being present in the moment."

Her lips curved up into a soft smile. "Whatever you need, Cosmo. I'm here for you." Secretly, I loved that she'd given me such a playful nickname. It had taken a bit of getting used to, but she could call me Shirley, and I'd jump for her.

"And I you. Now get your sweet ass set up. The couples are starting to arrive." I smacked her ass hard when she turned around. Definitely a sexy slice of ass cheek present. My dick stirred from its sleep, yawning and blinking, coming to attention.

Down boy. Not just yet.

The couples in the class flopped out their yoga mats and got settled. When everyone was seated, I addressed the class.

"Today, we're going to start with thirty minutes of hatha yoga. Then we're going to focus on being present in the moment. Part of that will be fun with Tantric sexual positions. I'm sure this is the part of the class that many of you were waiting for."

Several of the men and women laughed. I scanned each face. They were all smiling and ready to start.

"First, let's start seated in lotus pose with our seat bones directly on the mat, hands at heart center. Close your eyes and still the mind through your breathing.

"I want you to focus your gaze inward. What do you want to get out of class today? Set your intention for connecting with your mate in a positive, giving light. Be thankful for the relationship you have. Without both of you working toward enlightenment through Tantra, you wouldn't be here."

I watched as the couples simultaneously breathed in and out. What they couldn't see from my vantage point at the riser in front of the class was that the entire room was breathing in synchronization. Every chest expanded with the inhale and each couple exhaled as one strong unit. The energy in the room charged and filled with strings of togetherness, solidarity, and connection. Absolutely magical. The entire room breathed together as one entity. Most yoga instructors spent their entire lives waiting to have this experience, and here it was happening in my class. By all things holy, it was beyond beautiful. It was divine.

For twenty minutes, I took the class through a series of hatha yoga poses to loosen up their muscles and work their flexibility. The average person had the ability to become as flexible as any yogi. They just needed to work on it regularly. Sitting in office chairs, cars, on the couch were mini death knells for the body. Our skeletal structure and muscles needed movement in order to survive. Hence the reason people who sat all day had back and hip problems, stiff necks, tight shoulders, and rock-hard hammies. The body stiffened to stone, slowly losing its mobility and flexibility with every hour a person sat.

"Now one yoga pose that all of you could try is plough pose. The female moves into the position like so." I turned around and instructed Amber to get into the plough position with her bum up in the air and her hands to her lower back. I held her steady while both of her legs fell over her upper body and head, and her toes touched the floor behind her head.

Shit. Her tiny shorts crawling up the crack of her ass gave me a mouthwateringly good view of her barely covered, dainty pussy. It was all I could do to keep my dick soft. If we were alone, I'd simply shift her tiny pants to the side and force my tongue deep into the heart of her core. Since we were very much on display, I had to think of the most boring crap in the world to not get a semi. Taxes. Yes. Taxes. I submitted those, right? Yeah, I think I did.

I slowly put both of my hands on her hips and helped hold her balance. Then I pressed my groin right into the crack of her ass. "Now, if your mate is comfortable, and flexible enough to stay in this position, start slow and build up the power of each thrust until you both are ready to orgasm. The position may be too much with her bent over. Most of the time it will be, because when a person gets sexually excited, blood rushes to their head, and in this position, they're already inverted. Talk to one another. Make sure both of you are comfortable in the pose."

"Lift your legs to me, my love."

Amber smiled prettily and moved her legs up to the sky where she was in a full shoulder stand, the weight of her body resting on her shoulders. I held onto each ankle and then curved them toward my chest where her feet could rest. Then I wrapped my hands around each thigh and mimicked thrusting.

"Now this position takes a lot of the pressure off your mate and puts the male in full control. Ladies, I know you like to participate, but in this pose, you will get deep G-spot penetration, which as you experienced with the sacred spot massage"—I winked at Amber and her face flushed a bright crimson—"the orgasm will be intense. Just focus on attempting to have your orgasms at the same time so that both of you can reach combined meditation through sexual pleasure. It's a cornerstone of Tantric yoga and something I want all of you to attempt in your homework."

After plough, I reminded them of the yab-yum position where the two partners sit in one another's lap, facing each other. Then I explained the Butterfly position where the female lies on a table or the bed longways and the male enters the woman either standing or kneeling.

"For the next Tantric position, I'm going to have you both lie on your sides."

I cuddled in front of Amber, her back to the class. She giggled into my neck, the sound so sweet and innocent, that I kissed her cheek and then her mouth briefly. "Can't keep my hands and mouth off her." I chuckled and received several nods, smiles, and laughter in return. "Okay, now we're going to focus on the Sidewinder. This position is designed for face-to-face interaction where the two of you can kiss, caress, and look into one another's eyes while you stimulate the other. It's meant to be a gradual buildup of your arousal and ultimately your release."

I held onto Amber's knee and lifted it up and out so that

my groin would have direct access to penetrate her. "Now, lift your partner's leg. Once opened wide, you'd penetrate and then seal the connection by laying her leg over yours." I placed my hand firmly on Amber's tight ass and squeezed. "As you can see this position gives your hands freedom to play." I grinned when she buried her head against my neck, her chest pounding along mine with her silent laughter.

I watched as the class did the move, each couple following my instructions explicitly.

"Lift the leg even higher if your mate is more flexible to achieve a more intense connection and deeper penetration. You can grind against one another, your pelvic bone stimulating her clitoris with each movement. Now move sensually against your partner in whatever way feels best. Kiss, talk, tell your mate what you love about them, how much you love them. Share the intimacy of the moment now, privately."

When the class lost themselves to their own gyrations and sensual explorations, I took that time to lay my head down and look at my lover eye to eye. "You're enchanting, you know that."

Her corresponding smile lit me from the inside out. "You're not so bad yourself."

She gasped when I hooked her leg higher and rubbed my groin against her, making sure my erection grated along her tender nub through those barely there booty shorts. I held her ass firmly, moving my hips in a tandem to her much smaller ones.

"I like this position," she said breathily.

"You do?" I caressed her face, running my hand down her long form, waiting for the telltale sign that she always graced me with when she was languid and exultant.

She half sighed, half moaned, her eagerness presenting itself in waves of desire pouring out her lithe body into mine.

"Be careful, little bird, I could so easily work you over and have you silently screaming in orgasm if you push me too far. Your body rubbing against mine in that scrap of fabric is my weakness, and you know it." I ran a hand down to her breast and tweaked her nipple through the Lycra.

"Oh Dash, I want you all the time," she whispered into my neck before licking along the tendon there.

I groaned and pressed harder against her pelvis. "You ready for all of me, my love? To physically join...*all* the way?" I punctuated my questions with a circling of my hips.

She ran her tongue up to my ear. Soft puffs of air tickled and tingled against the small erogenous zone. "You're changing me, Dash."

Something in her tone warned me not to push, but I couldn't help myself.

"I don't want you to change. You're perfect the way you are." Using one hand, I caressed her from her knee to her hip wanting her to feel the truth in my words as much as hear them.

"Don't." She shook her head as if trying to dispel the compliment.

"Amber, to me, you're simple beauty. That's all any man could ever want. It's everything *I* want. *Need* in my life. Just you."

Her face seemed to crumble before me, like loose rocks falling over a cliff into the ocean below. We were losing the tight connection, and the melancholy from earlier poured into our blissful bubble, tainting our position with its negative energy.

Amber's body stiffened suddenly. "Dash, I love you with my whole heart, but I'm not sure I can give you what you deserve." Her voice shook.

I steadied my hips, tunneled my hands into her hair, and held her face so that nothing else could be a distraction. "What is it that you think I deserve?" I asked.

Her chin wobbled and her lips trembled as if saying the very words were breaking her into tiny shards of glass. "All of me."

I smiled softly and leaned my head closer to hers, gravity pulling me toward the one I adored. "Ah, but that's a gift I aim to receive when you are ready to give it."

"Dash." It was a breathy sound, a whisper on the wind. "I'm saving myself."

"I know. Soon, my sweet Amber, it will be I who is saving you."

"God, I hope so," she said and then cut off all conversation by sealing her lips over mine.

Once again, the issue of her virginity was not yet resolved. More than ever before, confusion sat thick and heavy on my shoulders. She said she was saving herself, holding herself back from making that physical leap with me, but I had no confirmation of what that thing officially was. Could Atlas have been right? Was it a religious decision?

Before I could find out, Amber pushed up and looked at the clock. "Class is over, and your students are practically turning the room into an orgy."

I glanced at the class and found couples in various arrays of copulation. No one was penetrating the other...well, I didn't think they were. "Damn. Class, settle down. Time to close up shop."

At that point, Amber stood, walked over to her bag, pulled out a pair of sweat pants and tugged them on. Then she zipped up a hoodie over her sports bra. Thank God, she was covering her body before heading out. My green-eyed beast would have had a fit if she'd tried to leave the building dressed in the outfit she'd worn in class.

"Where are you going?" I asked, concern coating my tone.

"I need to be home tonight. Alone." She pressed her lips together, and her hands formed two fists.

Using every reserve of courage within me, layered in the confidence I had in our bond, I nodded. "Okay. I love you, Amber."

She looked down at the floor and then back up. "I love you, too."

Even though she said the words, she didn't show them. In fact, her entire body language screamed discontent. I'd give her the night, and tomorrow, we'd talk. God willing, we'd settle this newfound wedge that had wormed its way into our relationship.

CHAPTER SEVENTEEN

SACRAL
C H A K R A

Individually, a person driven by the second chakra can be selfish, materialistic, and overconfident. However, if a couple is driven by the sacral chakra, they have the power to be stable and capable of having a long, healthy relationship. Communication and commitment to individual desires must be respected. Both parties must believe with their whole heart that the other is their soulmate and commit to being together forever in order for the relationship to last.

AMBER

A shrill ring blasted me from a dead sleep. I grappled for my phone and read the display. "Trent calling," was on the screen.

"Hello, hello? Is it time?" I pushed the hair away from my face, trying to get my bearings at the same time my heart was pounding a mile a minute.

"It's time. I'm getting the car ready. She wants you there, Amber. Ask your grandma if she can watch the kids. They're still asleep."

I glanced at the clock and noted it said two in the morning. "Okay, sure. I'll be right out. And Trent..."

"Yeah?" His voice was a hard growl.

"Yay! Baby time!" I squeaked.

He groaned. "Just get here. You have five minutes before I'm loading up the car with the kids."

In addition to being Vivvie's boyfriend and father of her baby, Trent Fox was also an alpha male, hotshot baseball player that was all kinds of protective and possessive of his new family. A lot of that had to do with the fact that my bestie had not yet agreed to marry the man—much to my dismay as well as his—even though she was carrying his progeny.

Moving as fast as my feet could carry me, I tugged on a pair of yoga pants, socks and tennis shoes, a tank, and a hoodie before wrapping my hair into a ponytail.

God, please take care of Genevieve. She needs Your strength, love, and guidance today to bring one of Your children into the world. I can't wait to see Your miracle come to life. Amen.

I tiptoed through the hall and to my grandparents' bedroom. I opened the door to the sound of my papa snoring away. Nana really needed to get him to agree to get his adenoids removed. Unfortunately, for my grandmother, my grandfather didn't believe in unnecessary medical treatments. If it wasn't killing him, he'd just as soon leave well enough alone.

When I reached my grandmother's side of the bed, I laid a soft touch to her bicep and whispered, "Nana."

She blinked her eyes open immediately. My grandmother was a light sleeper, always had been. Her weathered hand came out from under the covers, and she grabbed my wrist. I helped her sit up.

"What's the matter, poppet?"

"Vivvie is having the baby. She wants me there with her."

Her eyes widened, and she pushed her hair behind her ear. "Okay then, she needs me to watch the children. I'll throw my robe and slippers on and meet you there. God bless her heart. We've got a baby coming."

I grinned and shuffled out of the room, down the stairs, and out the door.

"'Bout fuckin' time!" Trent roared when I arrived. He looked over my shoulder. "Where's Sandy?" His jaw was tight as stone and his volume just below a holler.

"She'll be here in a few minutes. She has a key. Let's go."

He looked at Genevieve, who was already in the front seat, her eyes closed, teeth clenched, and her hands holding tight to her basketball-sized belly.

I ran around the side of the car and jumped in the back. I placed my hands on her shoulders. She jerked and then sighed. "Amber. Thank God. It hurts so bad," she moaned.

Trent got in the car and waited a minute. Then he saw our front door open and Nana coming down the stairs in her robe and slippers waving. "Now we can go."

I smiled but kept quiet. Trent had really proven himself worthy of my best friend and those kids. He loved them like they were his own siblings. It filled my heart with joy to see his protective side come out regarding their safety as much as that of the woman he loved and his unborn child.

Trent streaked out of the driveway and zoomed off into the dead of night. There was little traffic all the way to the hospital. He dropped Genevieve and me at the doors to Labor and Delivery and sped off to park the car.

Viv sat in the wheelchair an orderly provided. "You doing okay?" I asked her.

She nodded and blew out a long breath. The contraction must have passed because her face went from contorted in pain to simple elegance in a second flat. I never understood it when laboring patients said they were only in pain during the contractions. The rest of the time they were anticipating the next round, which had to be exhausting.

"Thank you for coming. I wasn't sure I wanted anyone else in the room, but you have this direct line to God, and I feel like I need that."

Now that made me cheesy smile. I leaned down and gripped both of her hands then closed my eyes, holding her hands against my lips. "God, please help Genevieve bring baby Will into this world safe and sound. We trust You to protect and surround this child in Your love. Amen."

"Amen," Genevieve said and then crunched up her entire face and placed her hands on her tightening belly.

I laid my hand over the places she hadn't covered. Whoa! The entire thing contracted and firmed so much her skin felt stretched to capacity against the tension. Incredible.

Just as an orderly was leading us down the hall to an open room, Landen turned the corner, clad in a pair of pale blue scrubs. Our combined shock was laughable.

"Hey you, what are you doing here?" he asked, glancing down at Genevieve.

"My best friend is having a baby! What are you doing here?"

He walked alongside us as we made it to our room. "All-nighter for labor and delivery. I think you're up for it in a couple weeks."

I nodded. "Cool. Are you going to be assisting us today?"

"Yep. I'm with Dr. Lee."

"Awesome."

Right then, a massive six-foot-something, wall of anxiety skidded around the corner. "Where is she!" he roared, probably waking up half the ward at this time of night. Then again, most of the people in this area were having babies or awaiting their C-sections. A man hollering probably wasn't that uncommon.

Landen approached Trent with his arms out. "Calm down, sir."

"Don't tell me to call down. My entire fucking world is somewhere on this floor, in pain, and about to have my baby!"

"Trent!" Genevieve called from behind the curtain not far from where we stood. The orderly had set her up in a cloth gown and a fetal monitor.

"Gumdrop, thank Christ!"

"Friend of yours?" Landen hooked a thumb over his shoulder toward Trent, who was fawning all over Genevieve.

I chuckled. "Yes. Dad-to-be. Very nervous dad-to-be, as you can see."

"Dude's built like a brick house."

I held my hand over my mouth to cover my chortles. "That's Trent Fox, star hitter for the Oakland Ports. They breed 'em big."

Landen's eyebrows rose up on his forehead. "That's... Trent Fox. *The* Trent Fox. The best flippin' hitter since, well... in forever?" He gasped and tried to get a better view.

I nodded and grinned huge. "So you better give him and his lady some seriously special treatment or he's liable to take you out."

Landen pushed both hands through his hair and bit down on his bottom lip. "Trent Fox...I'll be damned," he whispered. "Today just got insanely cool."

My soon to-be-nephew coming into the world...yes, it did.

DASH

The phone was my nemesis. I picked it up and put it down all damn day. The desire to call Amber was so strong I had to physically turn the damn thing off. That was when Murphy's Law came into play. Whatever could go wrong would. By the time I turned the sucker on, Amber had texted me that she was at the hospital with Genevieve and Trent. They were having the baby. Several hours after the text was a rambling voice message stating that the baby was coming and to notify the yogis. At least at the end of that message I got a rushed love you. Those two little words were enough to Band-Aid the fear crackling against my rib cage with every breath I'd taken.

Now, I was walking the white linoleum halls of the hospital, looking for Labor and Delivery to surprise my girl. From what I gathered, she'd been at the hospital since around two or so in the morning. It was now four in the afternoon, a solid fourteen hours later.

As I stared at the directory, a voice I recognized echoed behind me. I turned around and came face-to-face with Landen O'Brien, the boy wonder who wanted a piece of my girl. Of course, now it looked like the guy would likely end up being her half-brother. Talk about twisted situations.

A look of recognition swept across Landen's face. "You're Amber's boyfriend."

"That's right. Do you happen to know where she is?" I

asked.

"Sure do. Her friend just had her baby. I assisted," he announced with a dose of pride. His chest puffed up, giving him an extra inch or two of height.

"Oh yeah. What did you think?" I figured it couldn't hurt to make conversation with the guy. If he was going to be in Amber's life as a friend or a brother, and especially as her study buddy, I needed to get a handle on the guy. Feel him out.

He shook his head. "You know, I thought it was going to be awful and disgusting."

"And it wasn't?"

Landen chuckled. "Oh, it was disgusting. What comes out of a woman when she's birthing a baby is not for the faint of heart, but I don't know." He shrugged. "The second the baby's head made an appearance and he took his first breath of life on Earth, something just clicked, man. You know?"

He'd experienced a miracle. A unique spiritual occurrence that, when seen through the right eyes, can change a person forever.

"Believe it or not, I do know. Had a couple of those myself. One very recently with my girl." I thought back to the sacred spot massage. Heck, almost every sexual experience Amber and I'd had so far seemed like a spiritual blessing.

"She's really amazing. The way she helped her friend breathe and then helped her friend's husband not hyperventilate." He laughed and led me to a closed door. "Well, there you go. They had the baby a couple hours ago, so they should be settled."

I held out my hand. "Hey, it was good seeing you. I'm sure we'll be seeing more of each other in the future."

"If you stay with Amber, for sure." He waved and then

headed off to some unknown location within the bowels of the hospital.

If I stayed with Amber. Why the hell wouldn't I stay with her? He probably didn't mean anything by it, but even the mention of not being with her sent an uncomfortable spike to my gut. I breathed through the discomfort and then knocked on the door.

"Come in." A male's voice came through the door.

I opened the door and entered. The room was small, perhaps ten by ten. Genevieve lay resting with her hands over her now considerably smaller stomach, Trent by her side. He was caressing her face and making her smile. Amber was seated in the chair next to the bed, completely enchanted by the small bundle in her arms.

She looked up as I entered. "Hi," she whispered. "Glad you could come."

"Wouldn't miss it," I said and walked over to Trent with my hand out.

Trent skipped the hand and went right for the hug, clapping me on the back, hard. The big guy was full of smiles and unfettered joy seeped out of every pore. He reached into his pocket and pulled out a cigar. It had a blue seal around it labeled, *It's a boy.*

"Congrats, man. A son."

Trent inhaled and spread his arms out wide. "Best day of my fuckin' life."

I grinned and rubbed a hand over my scratchy jaw. "How you doin', pretty lady?" I said to Genevieve. "You holding up?"

Her smile of contentment was all I needed to see. "So happy. He's perfect, our William." She sighed and looked over at Amber.

AUDREY CARLAN

I walked over to Amber and looked down at the baby swaddled in a blue-and-white blanket, a pale blue knitted cap covering his head. His face was pink and round. As I was checking him out, he opened his puckered mouth and yawned as if he'd had a very long day, which I guess he had. Birthing was just as hard on the baby as it was on the mother I'd imagine.

"He's handsome," I offered.

Trent came over to me and clapped a hand on my shoulder while we both looked down at his son. "He looks like his mother, that's why."

Genevieve huffed from her spot on the bed. "Don't believe anything he says. If you pull that cap off his sweet head, you'll see tons of sandy-brown hair, and I'm almost positive his eyes will be green like his dad's, since they're blue now."

"That is true," Amber added. "Most babies are born with blue eyes that change color. Will's are so light that they could either stay blue or transition to green."

"Well, I'm sure you and Amber will be down this road before too long. After you get married that is." He gripped my shoulder tight.

Before I could filter my words, I laid it out there. "Oh, we're never getting married."

Amber's head jolted up, and the baby snuffled and blinked his tired eyes. "Excuse me?"

The entire room got surprisingly quiet. "Yeah, uh. I don't believe in marriage. Not in the traditional sense. I think the two of you got it right. Having a baby is a far stronger commitment than a piece of paper."

Still, not one sound left any of the three people in the room until the baby started to cry. Trent leaned down in front of Amber. "I've got him. I think my boy needs his mom. Don't

247

you, sweetness?" He cooed to the boy.

I will admit, seeing a huge man like Trent Fox cooing at a baby does put life into a different perspective.

Amber stood up and put her hands in her pockets. "Can I talk to you out in the hall?" Her voice was tight and no longer held the effervescence of a few minutes ago when she'd held the newborn.

"Sure. I'll give you guys some time together and come back tomorrow or catch up with you at the house in a few days," I told Trent and Genevieve.

"Thanks for stopping by, Dash," Genevieve said, now focused on undoing her top to nurse. Trent was so focused on the wiggling bundle in his arms, he wasn't even aware I was leaving. Definitely my cue to bolt.

Amber exited the room in front of me. The second I closed the door, she jumped on me. Not physically, but verbally.

"What do you mean you don't believe in marriage?" Her words were rushed and frantic.

I tilted my head and assessed her stance. She was wired for sound. Her body was ramrod straight, hands to her hips, and her face a wild mask of determination.

"What's the big deal? A lot of couples commit to one another in other ways. I don't need a piece of paper to know you're mine forever."

She clenched her jaw. "Well, I do. Dash, I made a vow to myself and to God."

Finally, we were getting somewhere.

"And what did you vow?"

Her face contorted into one of pain and frustration as her eyes glassed over. "I'm giving myself...*everything* to my husband."

I leaned against the wall more to hold myself up at the blast her words carried. "Are you telling me that you will not"—I lowered my voice, grabbed her wrists, and slammed her to my chest where I could see every nuance of her emotions cross her face up close and personal—"give up your virginity to me without traditionally becoming my wife?"

It sounded so utterly ridiculous to my ears, the question left me coupled with an ungentlemanly snort of laughter. I mean, the woman had let me touch every inch of her body, put my mouth all over her, but was holding this one thing back? For some ridiculous symbol of unity to a man she may or may not find?

Amber fisted my shirt and glared at me. "I want the man I commit to physically to be the only man to ever have that part of me."

"Why?" I shook my head.

Her gaze turned white-hot. "Because it means something to me."

"What you really should be saying is that you're following some archaic religious belief that is based on a book written by twelve men who may or may not have written the word of the Son of God. None of that has been proven to be fact anyway."

She closed her eyes and pushed off me so hard I lost my footing and had to catch myself against the rail on the wall.

"It's called faith, Dash. Apparently, you've never heard of it." Her words were scathing and dipped in poison and meant to harm.

Bull's-eye.

"I have faith, Amber. I have faith in you. I have faith in me. And I sure as hell have faith in our love. What more do you need?"

Amber licked her lips and turned her head to the side. She was so unearthly beautiful, I wanted to pull her back into my arms, hold her close, and shake some sense into her.

"I need the piece of paper."

Slow breath in, fast exhale out. "Amber, my mother was married four times. I don't want that for us. We're not a statistic. We can have our own private ceremony to symbolize our love. Tattoo rings on our fingers. A tattoo is far more binding than a piece of paper."

"Not to the Church, and not to me." Her voice shook with the power of her faith.

I closed my eyes and pressed both fists against my eyes. "Seventy-five percent of the marriages that originate in California end in divorce."

She uncrossed her arms, stepped over to me, and put her hands on my shoulders. Then she lifted up on her tiptoes and kissed me. Tears spilled from her eyes and wet her lips. I tunneled my hands into her hair, tilted her head, and slid my tongue along the seam of her lips until she opened. I delved into her mouth, the salty tears adding an element of pain and sorrow I didn't want to taste when I kissed the woman I loved. But the tears didn't stop. I thought I could kiss them away. Dry them with the power of my love. Goddamn, but I was so wrong.

Eventually, we both needed air. Together we breathed, like all things but this, in sync. "Amber, I love you. I'm fully committed to you, to us."

She rubbed her forehead against mine and sighed, tears still running like a river down her cheeks. "If that were true, I'd be worth the risk."

Those words pierced my heart and bled me dry. "Amber..." I whispered, feeling her slip away. Feeling our love dissipate in a white room that smelled of antiseptic and death.

"I have to be worth the risk," she said before turning and walking solemnly down the hall to disappear through the exit.

CHAPTER EIGHTEEN

Mountain Pose
(Sanskrit: Tadasana)

In this pose, the yogi stands with the feet hip distance apart. Tighten the legs and core, stand with the spine as straight as you can, leveling your chin with the floor. You can lift your arms up to the sky, point with intention, or place your hands at heart center to keep the energy flow circling. Mountain pose helps the individual feel strong, stretches the spine, and lengthens the body. Perfect for a morning stretch.

AMBER

Today, I turned on my phone. A week had gone by since I left Dash standing in the hospital. I couldn't forget the slump of his shoulders, as if his body was bowed in from the knife I'd placed in his heart. All week I'd chastised myself for not telling him about my vow, about the commitment I'd made to myself and to the Lord. Looking back, all the physical steps we'd taken in the past three months had led up to an inevitable ending of our coming together in the last possible way a man and a woman could...as true lovers. Only I wasn't ready to give up that piece of myself without the promise of forever.

Anyone could say they love someone and mean it. But it was when a person was willing to back it with everything that they were—physically, mentally, emotionally, and last but definitely not least, legally—that was when forever began.

I looked down at the myriad messages that popped up on my phone. None of them were from Dash. My heart squeezed, and all the air in my lungs left me on a choked sob. Nope. I would not cry. I stiffened my spine, cleared my throat, and sucked in a new bout of air.

Phone. Focus on getting back to the real world. A message from Landen popped up, sent only an hour ago.

From: Landen O'Brien
To: Amber St. James
Dad needs to speak with you. Said it's really important. He'll be in his office all day. See you at class tomorrow. :)

Smiley face. Oh good Lord, let whatever he has to tell me be worth smiling about, although I knew in my heart it wouldn't. My best guess was that he'd received the paternity results. My mind briefly went back to Dash giving him his card. Did he contact him first? Wouldn't Dash have told me Dr. O'Brien had called? Then again, he seemed like the type of man to go to the best resource, and that would be his own son. Did Landen know? Did he tell him? Did he tell his wife?

So many questions with absolutely no answers. As much as I wanted to call Dash and ask him to go with me to see the professor, I didn't feel as though I had any right to. We'd left things on a sour note. I didn't know if that technically was us breaking up or taking a break or just spending time thinking about what the other had revealed? God, things were so screwed up. Up was no longer up. Down was no longer down. I felt stuck in some type of quasi-center that had no high or low, pros or cons.

Limbo.

A shiver raced down my spine. Limbo in the Catholic faith was often referred to as purgatory, a state of suffering where the souls of sinners went when they were attempting to atone and cleanse their souls of sin before entering heaven.

Was that where my relationship with Dash was? In a place of suffering? It sure as heck felt like it. And did that mean that one or both of us had something to atone for?

I closed my eyes and pressed my fingertips to my temples. There was only one person I could talk to about this. Father McDowell. If anything, he'd help me see the light of God's will and what I had to do for me. First, I had to go meet with a man about a paternity test. Not that my life needed any more shaking up.

★ ★ ★

The lecture building was mostly empty. It seemed as though it was like this more often than not. Strange. I guess most of the students spent their time in the libraries or doing rounds in the hospital. I made the appropriate turns following the path I'd taken a couple weeks ago when the professor had admitted his affair with my mother.

When I got to his office, the door was open. Dr. O'Brien's head was down, his glasses dangling from two fingers, and his head rested in his hands.

I knocked on the frosted glass of his office door. "You wanted to see me?"

He looked up and smiled softly. He gestured to the surprisingly empty chair in front of him. The office still had clutter over every available surface, no cleaner or more organized than it was two weeks ago when Dash and I sat here, and he had dropped a bomb on me I hadn't expected.

"Close the door behind you, please."

I did as he asked and took the chair opposite him.

"How are you?" he asked.

Fine was on the tip of my tongue, but lying had never been something I undertook regularly, regardless of societal niceties.

"It's been a long week." I chose my words wisely.

He nodded, picked up a yellow business envelope, and handed it to me.

I pinched the envelope between thumb and forefinger as though the sucker might burn me. "What is it?"

"The results of your paternity test."

I quirked an eyebrow. "And?"

"Wouldn't you rather read the results for yourself?"

I shook my head. "No. Frankly, I'd rather hear the words come directly from your lips."

He swallowed, and a hint of a smile flickered across his lips. "It's confirmed. You are my daughter."

I closed my eyes and let the information sweep across my heart. After twenty-two years, I could now look my biological father in the eyes and put a face to the ghost my mother had left me with.

"And you're sure?" I asked.

He grinned. "Well, ninety-nine point nine percent positive are some pretty stellar odds."

"Why didn't you know my mother was pregnant with your child?" I asked bluntly, getting right to the heart of why I was sitting here after twenty-two years, meeting my father for the first time.

Liam, my *father*, not just the professor or Dr. O'Brien to me anymore, leaned back in his chair and rubbed both hands down his face.

"For the past two weeks I've asked myself the same question. How could I not know you existed and the simple answer, my dear, the *only* answer...your mother didn't want me to."

I scoffed. "But she went to the same school, took your class!"

He shook his head emphatically. "No. I broke things off two weeks before the end of the semester. She didn't return in the fall. I distinctly recall asking her academic counselor about her status."

I focused my gaze on his tightly fisted hands on top of the desk. "Why would you do that?"

"Because I loved her, dammit!" He pounded on the desk. "Even after I'd made the decision to try to make it work with my wife and son, I still couldn't get over Kate. I missed her like an amputee misses a lost limb. The ghost of our relationship haunted me for years. Hell, it still does!" he admitted, tears in his eyes.

Seeing a grown man break down was not at all what I

expected. In this situation, the regret washed over the both of us, made worse by the fact we had no one to blame. The one person who could have solved all of this had been dead for twenty-two years and wasn't coming back.

"What do we do now?" My voice was shaking, and a tear slipped down my cheek.

He closed his eyes, took a breath, and focused his gaze on mine. Green to green. I had his eyes. Plain as day now that the veil of truth had been lifted.

"We get to know each other. I can't even imagine not knowing you all these years. My own daughter." His voice cracked. "And you're beautiful. Just like her. Like my Kate." His eyes became glassy, filled with unshed tears. "And smart. So smart. I'll bet you were a joy growing up."

I swallowed the giant lump of anxiety and fear clogging my throat. "You'd have to ask my grandparents."

"I'd like to. And to thank them for raising such a lovely young woman."

A bubble of laughter worked its way up and out. "Oh my, I'm not sure you want to interact with them. They are very protective. Nana will want to hear all the sordid details of your love affair with her daughter, mostly because she's a ridiculous romantic, and Papa will want to tan your hide for hurting his daughter and knocking her up unwed."

He smiled. "If that's the only penance I have to take, I'd be happy to. I mean it, Amber. I want to know you and have you know me, become part of my family."

Family.

My family had always consisted of the grandparents, Genevieve, Rowan, and Mary. Now it included Trent and William, and God willing, Dash.

"That sounds wonderful, but what about Landen and your wife?"

"Susan? She knew about Kate."

I'm pretty sure my mouth dropped open so far it hit the desk, kind of like in a cartoon.

"I'm not all bad. When Susan and I agreed to give our marriage a shot, we admitted our infidelities. She had been seeing a guy at her firm. I was seeing Kate. Together, with years of marriage counseling, we worked through all of our issues." He sighed. "I never stopped loving your mother, but at the time, I thought what I was doing was right for all involved. Had I known about you..." He gasped. "My God, how different things would be."

"Not really. Mom died in childbirth, so technically, your relationship ending wouldn't have changed a single thing. Perhaps that's the way God intended for it to happen."

"Maybe you're right."

I sucked in a big breath, let it out, and steadied my shoulders. "Back to my earlier question. Where do we go from here?"

"How about dinner with your family?" he suggested.

"Well, I don't know about my grandparents, and Genevieve just had the baby so she's busy with that..."

Liam reached across the table and grabbed my hand. "No, Amber. Your new family." He squeezed my hand. His was warm and soothing, much like you'd expect from a fatherly type.

"Oh, yeah. Okay. That makes sense."

"I want to hear all about this Genevieve and her baby and your grandparents. How about I call you to set something up this weekend? You can bring your fellow, Dash, I believe."

The mention of Dash prickled against the nape of my

neck.

"Yeah, okay."

He stood, came around the desk, and opened his arms.

I walked into them, receiving a hug from one of my parents for the first time ever. A simmering warmth fluttered against the edges of my cheeks and shoulders as he held me tight. I wrapped my arms around him and soaked myself in it.

"I'll call you," he said and then kissed my temple the way I'd always imagined a father would.

"I'll answer."

DASH

A whole week. Seven days. A hundred sixty-eight hours. Ten thousand eight minutes. Six hundred four thousand, eight hundred seconds since I let Amber walk away from me. I hadn't talked to, texted, or seen my little bird since she flew the coop. To put it mildly. I was a fucking mess. A complete mess of contradictions.

I'd spent nothing but time going over the pros and cons of granting the simple condition she needed. Why couldn't I let it go? Just because ninety percent of the people I knew were divorced or came from divorced families didn't mean that would happen to us if we made that vow.

A vow.

The love of my life had made a vow to herself, to God, and to the man she'd spend her life with, even though she didn't know that man was supposed to be me. She spent twenty-two years saving a piece of herself that she only ever intended to give to me. The man she wanted to spend her life with. So why the hell couldn't I get over this one prickly point?

Because everyone I've ever known had made a mockery of marriage. My mother. My father. Hell, even their parents had all been married and divorced, and that was unheard of back in the day. The Alexander clan and the sanctity of a legal union did not equate to a happily ever after. More like a happily never after.

I groaned and pulled at my hair while standing in an empty yoga room. All the clients had already left. It was just me, my psyche, and the battering ram that was my heart.

"Knock, knock."

Crystal and Jewel stood at the entrance to the room. "Hey, thought you might care to grab a cup of coffee and a pastry with us," Crystal suggested.

I sighed. The pit in my stomach had not been agreeing with the concept of food as of late, though I knew I needed to stay nourished. I'd been working out and teaching nonstop all week. Part of a useless attempt to cool the savage beast that wanted to storm Amber's house, throw her over my shoulder, plop her on my bed and make her mine, once and for all.

"Sure." The only thing waiting for me at home was an empty loft. I shrugged on my zip-up hoodie, slipped into my yoga shoes, and closed down the room.

"Sunflower okay?" Jewel asked as we exited the building, her fiery red hair flowing in the breeze.

Crystal had her golden locks pulled up into a twist. Soft wisps of hair cascaded down her cheeks making her look far younger than her sixty years.

"Yeah, fine."

When we entered the bakery, my friend Dara was serving customers as usual. The resident meditation teacher at Lotus House moonlighted behind the counter of her adoptive parents' bakery. My theory was that the Jacksons had a great deal of business sense. They put a stunning dark-skinned woman with a great body, thick, wavy hair down to her ass, and Caribbean blue eyes, up front to greet customers. Yeah, pretty much every single guy within a twenty-mile radius was getting his treats at the bakery in the hopes they'd score a date with their daughter.

"Dash! Long time no see. You haven't come to any classes this week. You okay?" Dara asked, handing the customers in front of the three of us their order.

"Been a rough week is all." I pinched my lips together and assessed what they had in the cases.

"He's full of it. He's nursing a sore heart and a blocked third eye chakra," Jewel stated rather matter-of-factly.

I swallowed down the quick retort mostly because she was right. Instead, I went with self-incrimination. "Really?"

She pushed her red curls out of her eyes and pushed the black-rimmed glasses she wore up the bridge of her nose. "Uh, obviously. You think I was born yesterday? Pfft."

Crystal smirked and pointed at a vegan Danish.

Jewel held up two fingers.

"Soy vanilla bean lattes with organic sugar?" Dara asked.

"Yes, ma'am," Jewel said. "And when you're done with the lonely heart here, send him our way. Oh, and he's paying."

"Of course I am," I grumbled, not because I didn't want to, but because I was a gentleman. "Like I wouldn't pay?" I addressed Dara.

She grinned. "What's going on with you and the doc?"

"Nothing," I snarled.

Her eyebrows rose up on her head. "That's a whole lotta something, if I do say so myself."

"Who asked you?"

She placed a hand on her hip and ignored the entire line of people building behind me. Dara truly did not care who was in line. Her philosophy was that if they wanted the goods, they'd wait the amount of time necessary to get them, no matter if that time included her gabbing to each customer until they were blue in the face or agreed to name their firstborn after her.

"The universe. Hello, your aura is pink. Means your love life is tainted somehow. What's going on, sugar pie?" she prompted in her classic urban spunky tone.

I groaned and tossed out a twenty. "Will that cover it?"

She glanced at the money and nodded. "That will not, however, cover your remorse."

I balanced myself against the counter. "Remorse?"

"It's written all over you. Who do you need to apologize to?" Her blue eyes were filled with concern.

Taking a breath, I smacked the counter top. "Don't worry about it." I turned and headed for the table where Yoga Thing 1 and Yoga Thing 2, aka Jewel and Crystal, sat primly sipping their lattes and picking at their unsweetened treat. Vegan. I shook my head. I didn't get it.

"You know I'll worry until the color changes!" Dara called out and then proceeded to assist her next customer.

I sighed and fell into the chair like an elephant lying down. Did elephants lie down or sleep standing up? Hell if I knew.

"Dash, what's going on with you and Amber?" Crystal asked directly. "It's hurting your heart."

"And whatever it is, is blocking your third eye chakra, making you unable to find reason," Jewel added unhelpfully.

I slumped down and put my head in my hands. "She wants

AUDREY CARLAN

to get married." Through heavy lashes, I looked up. They were smiling at each other.

"And that's a problem because you don't want to be with her long-term?" Jewel asked in that painstaking tone of a mother treading through her son's love life over hot coals in bare feet.

I cringed.

"Hmm. I think it's the opposite, Jewel. I think he does want to be with her," Crystal surmised.

"Of course I do! I just don't believe in traditional marriage. They all end in nasty, vile divorces that wreck more lives than the two people in them."

Crystal laid her hand on my shoulder. "Now we're getting somewhere."

CHAPTER NINETEEN

SACRAL
CHAKRA

When the sacral chakra is balanced, people tend to be happy, energetic, sexually fulfilled, resilient, and connecting well in all their outside relationships. Most importantly, they are intimately sound with their mate and show it enthusiastically.

AMBER

The black wrought iron gate creaked as I entered the sanctuary garden. This place had been a haven for me over the years. It was where I went when I had to make a difficult decision or deal with something I had no control over. Being surrounded by God's earthly beauty helped calm and soothe the jagged edges of my tortured mind. Today was no different.

I sat on the bench that faced a small hill. Tall pine trees surrounded my little refuge. Circular bushes dotted the landscape and purple-and-white daisies were sprinkled throughout like a topping on a cupcake. The Blessed Mother sat on top of this cupcake. She was carved from white marble. Her hands in prayer position at her chest, and her head focused downward. Surrounding her were other statues, a woman, a child, a young boy, a lamb. All looking to her for guidance and wisdom the same way I was now.

With clammy fingers, I clutched the rosary my grandmother gave me when I was five years old. She'd given the same one to my mother when *she* was five years old. Today, I held it not only to connect with the Mother of Christ, who often intercedes for God's children, but to connect with my own mother, too. I bowed my head and started with the Lord's Prayer, followed by the Hail Mary out of respect for her grace.

Blessed Mother, maybe you can help me work through the discontent swallowing my soul and faith.

I looked up at the statue and waited, but she never replied. Usually, I just sat here long enough to obtain an answer. Whether it was one she helped me achieve, or God granted me in His mercy, or maybe even Jesus decided to give a sinner a break. Whatever happened, I'd never left the church without a clear path toward fixing the problem I'd presented once I sat on this bench.

"Amber, lamb, is that you?" a soft voice spoke from the gate behind me.

I smiled and turned. "Yes, Father, it's me."

Father McDowell opened the gate and approached, both of his hands clasped in front of him.

"What are you doing here, in Mary's garden, on this fine August day?"

I clutched the rosary in my hand so hard the crystal beads sank into the tender flesh of my palm. Not quite hard enough to draw blood but definitely enough to leave marks. I wished those beads would imbed so far into my skin that all the answers I needed would just bleed out of me.

"I'm lost, Father," I admitted to my priest, the only man aside from my grandfather I'd had any type of fatherly connection to.

Father McDowell came around and sat on the bench next to me.

He put his hand out, and I clutched onto it like a lifeline. "Lamb, what can our Heavenly Father help you with? You look tortured, and none of God's children should feel that when they have Him to give their problems to."

I slumped down and let out a breath I'd been holding so long, the power of it leaving curved my spine in. "I'm stuck between the man I love and want to spend the rest of my life with and the vow I made to the Lord and myself."

He patted my hand with his other one and held mine between his two. "Are you being pressured to give of yourself in a manner with which you are not comfortable?" he asked.

I shook my head quickly. "No, not at all. But...erm...I took a vow of chastity and I've held onto that vow my entire life. I know the man I'm with is the only man for me. I will die loving him. God wouldn't have put him in my path if I wasn't meant to be with him, right?"

He tilted his head. "God does work in mysterious ways. However, if this man is worthy of you and your chastity, would he not agree to commit to you in the Church before God?"

There it was. Black and white. If Dash loved me, truly loved me, he would understand the importance of my faith and be willing to commit to me in the eyes of the Lord.

"I don't know."

He squeezed my hands. "Yet you are still uncertain of your path."

I nodded. "I love him."

"And God loves all his children, even the misguided ones. Is it possible for you to expose this young man to the Church, to your beliefs?"

Mary's gaze was focused on those who knelt at her feet because she was free of sin. As an adult, I understood that we were born sinners. God sent his only son to die on the cross for our sins. We were taught that from a very early age. The Church taught that the way to absolution and reconciliation was to confess, ask for forgiveness, perform penance, and promise to sin no more. Our Fathers, Hail Marys, confessional, prayer— we could always find a rational way to explain it, the same as me, sitting here in front of this statue, in Mary's garden, talking to my priest. When all I really wanted was for God to tell me it was okay to commit a sin. To live in sin with a man I couldn't imagine my life without. How in the world could I justify that urge?

"He said he doesn't believe in marriage. That they end in divorce. I think his family wasn't a very good example of a healthy pairing," I admitted.

"I see. Then how do you propose to change his mind?"

"That's just it. I don't think it's fair to try. He doesn't believe what I do."

"Child, not every person on this earth will believe the same things. Just because you and I believe in the Father, the Son, and the Holy Spirit does not mean every person that we interact with or come to love will, too. I believe that all God's children will eventually have that 'ah-ha' moment. It's just a matter of time."

I smiled, let go of his hand, and stood up facing the Blessed Mother. "Then what do I do?"

"Do you love this man, child?"

"With my whole heart," I whispered as tears prickled in my eyes.

"Do you believe that God sent him to you to love and cherish your whole life long?"

"I've been telling myself that God wouldn't allow me to fall so completely in love if he wasn't meant to be my mate."

He stood and crossed his hands in front of him. "Then you must show him God's love. It may take a year, it may take twenty, but never give up."

"Then what do I do in the meantime? About my chastity and marriage?"

He took a slow breath. "Only you know the answer to that, lamb. And I believe you've already come to terms with it, but haven't been able to voice it."

Father McDowell gestured to me to come closer. He held both hands out for me to hold. I did and he closed his eyes.

Together, we recited the Our Father and then he shared his own prayer.

"Lord, let Your child find peace and solace in Your love. Guide her in her effort to fulfill Your will. Ease her mind through her path to enlightenment. Through the Father, the Son, and the Holy Spirit. Amen."

We both made the sign of the cross, touching our fingertips to our foreheads, hearts, and shoulders, in the practiced way Catholics close their prayers. "Amen."

Father McDowell cupped my cheek the same way a parent would. "Go with God, my child." And then he turned and left me alone in the garden. Alone with my sins, or the huge one I was about to commit.

The Father knew what I'd not been able to admit to myself. For Dash, for our love, to sustain our lifelong bond...I was going to break my vow.

Lord, be with me.

DASH

Yoga Thing 1 and Yoga Thing 2 had my balls in a vise. literally but figuratively. They'd bombarded me with question after question about my relationship with Amber until I had no choice but to give up the golden goose and tell them the truth.

Crystal's clear blue eyes pierced mine. "Dash, do you believe in love?"

I swallowed down the lump in my throat with a mouthful of hot coffee. "In my twenty-eight years on this Earth, I've never seen true love. Hoped for it. Wished for it. But I never experienced it myself. Not until Amber. She's love. Everyone before her pales in comparison."

Jewel and Crystal shared a look.

Crystal grabbed one of my hands and brought it close to her chest. "Dash, is she worth letting this stigma go? Can you truly say that letting her go instead of taking a risk on love is the better option?"

I closed my eyes. The last three months played through my mind.

★ ★ ★

Amber sitting in my lap instructing the class. Her strawberry scent clouding all reason.

The two of us snuggled up on my couch, watching an

movie. ...e agreed to watch any movie. Said her goal
only to b...ith me. The film didn't matter.

My li...e bird, crying out in release under my hand, my
...gue, ...love.

"...ve you, Dash. I'll always love you." Her private words
...whispered against my ear after we'd pleasured one
to ...er.

★ ★ ★

"I can't do this." I stood up.

Crystal tugged me back into my chair. "You can't do what?
Lose her and everything the two of you stand for or continue to
be bullheaded about something you can easily control?"

Usually, I wouldn't say a cross word to either of these two
women, but right now, I had a handful of them. "I can't control
what the future holds."

"Hallelujah, can I get an amen? Thank the goddess!"
Jewel said, rolling her eyes. "Finally, you realize that."

"And what's that supposed to mean?"

Crystal gripped my other hand and looked me straight
in the eye. Her clear blue gaze was like looking at a cloudless
sky over the ocean. "You can't control your future. But you
and Amber have the power to control your relationship. If you
need to make that legally binding to please her, then you do
so with the knowledge that you are never ever breaking that
contract. The only reason the statistics are so high is because
people are getting married for the wrong reasons. But the only
right one is because you cannot imagine living your life each
day without her in it. Now can you?"

"Live my life without her?"

She nodded.

The past week had been devastating. Not having Amber had been like walking through perpetual night. Happy things didn't seem so pleasant. A clear day didn't hold its beauty. The sun didn't seem as bright. Food didn't taste as good and sleeping? Pssshhh...sleeping's been a total joke. All I did was dream of her. Miss her. Want her by my side, today and always.

"Not happily, no."

A slow, easy smile slipped across her face. "Then I think you have your answer. There's only one thing left to decide."

"And that is?"

"How are you going to get your girl back?"

I pushed my hand through my hair and gripped the roots. The prick of pain centered and grounded me. "God, Crystal, I don't know."

AMBER

O'Brien's Pub was booming with the dinner crowd when I entered. Families and couples milled about enjoying the food, drink, and environment. But there was only one man I came here to see.

He tossed back the last dregs of whatever was in the pint glass in front of him. Uncle Cal, who I guessed, technically, was really my uncle now, winked at me from across the other end of the bar. I offered a small wave in greeting.

"So, can I buy you a drink?" I asked, hanging my purse on the hook under the bar.

Landen turned and propped his head in his hand, elbow on the bar. "Fancy seeing you here...sis."

I couldn't discern whether his tone was angry, hurt, or

otherwise. All I knew was that for the last three months, we'd been friends. Good friends, and I didn't want to lose that. Especially since I'd found out we were actually related. More than ever, I wanted to know him as my brother. The question now was whether he'd allow that relationship.

"Your father told you," I said softly, knotting my fingers together.

"Yeah." He sighed.

"Are you mad?"

"At him? Fuck, yes!"

Pretty sure that was the first time I'd heard him drop an F-bomb. He didn't seem the type to use profanity. Maybe because I'd always viewed him as too preppy.

"And me?"

His head jerked back, and he turned fully toward me. "You? What would I have to be mad at you for? You're not the one that cheated on my mother and got your aide pregnant."

He had a point. A huge one. One that could be on top of a billboard in bright flashing lights.

I laid my hand on his bicep. "I'm sorry, for whatever it's worth."

Landen huffed. "You're sorry. Hell, Amber, I'm sorry, for you. You're the one who was raised without parents and your brother. Fuck me. I've had a sister my entire life." He shook his head. "All I ever wanted was someone to share the crazy that is being the son of a doctor and a rich ad executive, and this whole time, there you were, being raised by your grandparents. He should have known, and I'm pissed that I missed out on having a sister growing up."

A weight the size of Texas lifted off my heart. He wanted me in his life. This new information didn't change our relationship. Well, it did, but for the better.

"And worse," he continued, "I perved out on my own fucking sister. How disgusting is that?" His entire body shook with an exaggerated tremor.

I laughed hard. Full on piggy-snort-style laugh. "You thought I was hot."

"Did I say that?" He cringed.

"You so think I'm pretty!" I cackled.

He looped an arm around my shoulder and mashed his temple against mine. "Well, yeah. We come from the same tree. Obviously, we're smoking hot. Duh!" He grinned.

I placed a tentative arm around him. "I'm glad we met and became friends before the truth came out. Ever since the day I met you, I was comfortable in your presence, and it's not normally like that for me. I've always been a bit of a loner, but you pressed on and made me come out of my shell. Thank you for that."

He kissed my temple and then pushed me away. "Girls are so dumb." He winked. "Always trying to make something more out of nothing. Uncle Cal, get over here and give your nephew and niece a drink. We're parched!"

Looks like Landen wasn't the only one that knew the truth. "Your father told Cal?"

He nodded. "And Mom."

A trickle of dread wormed its way through my body, raising gooseflesh down my limbs. How did his wife take the information that he had a twenty-two-year-old daughter he never knew about? From the affair he'd had when they were separated all those years ago.

I bit down on my bottom lip. "Is everything uh...okay?"

Cal took that moment to come over and place two fresh

pints in front of us. He leaned over the bar and kissed me on my cheek. "Glad to have you in the family, Amber. Looking forward to introducing you to your four cousins."

"I have four cousins!" I yipped and gripped the bar to keep my balance. Hearing that I had a brother and father, as well as an Uncle Cal, was enough to make my year, maybe even the next five, all filled with glee. I had real-life extended family. Cousins. "Oh my Lord, I want to know everything!"

Uncle Cal slammed the bar, pointed a finger, and winked while giving me a thumbs-up. "We'll barbecue. It will be awesome."

"Mom took it really great, actually. She'd always been worried about the fact that she was unwilling to give Dad more children. He'd wanted a house full of them."

"So did my mom, according to what Nana says anyway."

He sucked down a large gulp of beer. I followed suit. "She wants to meet you. Have you over for dinner. Start the process of bringing you into our lives. If you're, uh, willing." The skin around his eyes tightened, and he curved his lips to the side. "You are willing? Right?"

"Yes, of course. I mean, it will be strange, but if I could maybe bring my grandparents to dinner, that would go a long way toward helping me."

Landen placed his hand on my shoulder. "Of course. They're a part of you. And now, you're a part of us."

"Well, okay then. We'll set something up." *After I tell them*, I wanted to add, but didn't.

I'd just found out today that I now had this huge family. Telling my grandparents, the people who'd raised me since birth, was not going to be easy. More like I expected tears and mass quantities of praying. Possibly even a church run to see

Father McDowell again. For them this time, not me. Eh, maybe me. I could never get too much God on my side, especially knowing what I planned on doing when I confronted Dash.

I smiled at Landen and then watched as he glanced at something over my shoulder.

Speak of the devil.

Dash stood behind me, arms crossed, head tilted. He had the same expression that night he found Landen and me in these seats drunk as skunks. This time, however, we weren't drunk. I'd barely sipped my first beer. Also relevant was the fact that his jealous beast could take a hike, because now I had a really good reason to be hanging on Landen.

Curling an arm around Landen's shoulders, I watched as Dash's face twisted from shock to jealous rage in a mere second.

"Dash Alexander, I'd like you to meet my brother, Landen O'Brien. Landen, this is the man I'm going to spend the rest of my life with."

CHAPTER TWENTY

Child's Pose

(Sanskrit: Balasana)

Child's pose in yoga is the primary resting pose. Kneel with your knees wide. Lay your chest down between your bent legs, resting your forehead on the mat. Stretch your arms out wide or tuck them in. Breathe. Find your center. Become in touch with your subconscious mind. Let everything around you, melt away...relax.

DASH

I stopped breathing when she said the word "brother," and almost fell to the floor to worship her feet at the revelation she was going to spend forever with me. It was exactly what I needed to hear. Sans the brother part. That was a mind-bender all on its own, and although I suspected it was eating at her, dealing with our issue was paramount. I would not go another week without this woman in my life. Not even another day. Ever.

After tonight, she'd be living with me and planning a wedding. Period. She just didn't know it yet. Once lunch with the ladies of Lotus House finished and we'd said our goodbyes, I spent some time going over what I wanted in life. Truly thinking about each day, year, my future overall. Nothing seemed to exist without her.

I now had my head screwed on straight and my life plan set. Amber St. James, soon-to-be Alexander, was at the top of every one of those plans.

1. Get Amber to forgive me for being a jackass.

2. Admit undying love and commitment to her.

3. Apologize for trying to make her choose between her faith and her future.

4. Ask her to marry me.

5. Get married.

6. Live happily ever after.

Okay, so I admit the list was weak, but it held all the important parts that mattered.

"Your brother?" I quirked an eyebrow and waited for her to work out what she wanted to say.

"Yep. Paternity test confirmed that Liam O'Brien is my biological father." Her eyes were sad and tired.

I'd change that when I could get her out of here and back to my place. I nodded and stood my ground. As much as I wanted to run to her, wrap her up in the blanket of my warmth for all of eternity, she owned this show.

With a natural grace, she exited the bar stool, pulled her purse over her shoulder, and kissed Landen on the cheek. "Dinner soon?" Her tone was hopeful yet still guarded.

My gut tightened. My little bird was hurting, I could see it all over her tired expression, puffy eyes, and rose-dotted cheeks. Knowing I contributed to that hurt ate at me.

Landen smiled and nodded. "Soon."

I'd hoped she'd walk right into my chest the way I envisioned, but she didn't. Instead, she walked around me to the door. Her hair fell thick over one shoulder as she looked back. "Your place or mine?"

"Mine. If that's okay with you."

"I'll meet you there," she said, the exhaustion in her voice breaking me down to confetti-sized pieces.

Get your shit together, Dash. Your girl needs you. Be a man and follow through with your plan. Make her yours.

I'd spent the better part of the last two hours figuring out how I was going to solve this rift between us. The only thing that I came up with was to grovel. And grovel I would. She deserved that much.

The ride to my loft went by in a haze of streetlights and stop signs. All black and white. The only color the blue of her car as I followed close behind, never letting her out of my sights.

We both parked, got out of our cars, and I led the way into the elevator and up to my part of the building. There were ten lofts in total in the old warehouse, and I'd bought my place for a steal of a deal. Renovated it myself. In the future, Amber and I could put up some walls up if we needed to for children's rooms.

Children. Christ. I was already planning my heirs, and I hadn't even gotten her to agree to marry me yet. But I would. I'd die trying. Besides, less than an hour ago she introduced me as the man she was going to spend her life with. All I had to do now was be worthy of it.

When she set her bag down, her back was to me. I couldn't hold myself away from her any longer. I stormed over, turned her around by the shoulders, pulled her against my chest, and buried my hands in her hair.

Body-racking sobs left her as if the act of releasing them tortured her entire being. Tears flooded my own eyes, and I let them fall. She deserved to see them.

"I'm sorry. Amber, my love, I'm so damned sorry."

She shook her head against my chest and rubbed her nose against my shirt. "I can't be without you. I need you, Dash." Her choked sobs came with a price. A lock around my heart so tight I never wanted to be released.

"You never have to. I don't want to change you."

"But you have." She sniffed and laid her hands against my chest.

The touch burned like white-hot fire, warming me. For the past week I'd been cold, frozen to anything around me due to the icy chill of my heart.

I curled my hands around her cheeks, threading my fingers into the thick strands of her hair. Strawberries assaulted my nose, and my cock stirred. God, I couldn't imagine not having that scent surround me day in and day out.

Her eyes were a watery mess of tears. I felt my own sadness leak down my cheeks. "I love you just the way you are. And I'm going to prove it to you."

She shook her head. "No. I've made my decision. I'm breaking my vow. I want to be with you no matter the cost. God is merciful. He'll forgive me. I'll forgive me." She laid her mouth over mine and kissed me. Hard.

Her kiss turned feral instantly. "I want you. Make me yours forever. Take all of me."

More tears fell down my cheeks to mingle with hers as our tongues did a feisty tango. She tasted of sadness and hope. I wanted to drown in her essence, fill her with light and love again.

Amber shifted her weight and tugged me backward until her knees hit the edge of my bed. With all her strength, she pulled at me, letting her body fall onto the bed in a tangle of blankets. I lost my footing, as I suspected was her plan, and fell on top of her. My cock hardened, and I jerked my hips against her, taking her mouth more fiercely.

She moaned and slipped her hands up the back of my shirt. Her fingers were cold but quickly warmed when she ran them up and down my spine.

I ripped my mouth away from hers but just barely. She attempted to follow, but I needed to gauge her intent.

"What are you doing, little bird?" I smiled and traced her face with one hand, wiping away the drying tears.

"I want you to make love to me, Dash. Let me prove that I'm yours forever."

"But the vow..." The words left my throat on a hoarse whisper.

Her hands clasped my wrists where they lay on each side of her head. Her hair was fanned out like a dark halo. Her green eyes sparkled and moistened, opening up her soul for my viewing. Her normally pale pink lips were now swollen and bruised a darker rose from our kisses. She'd never been more beautiful than she was in that moment.

"I've changed it."

I pursed my lips and took in her entire face. Her eyes weren't their normal brilliant green, and dark smudges marred the skin beneath them. "Changed how?"

She swallowed and inhaled, her lips parting on an uneven breath. "I'm vowing to you, Dash Alexander, that I will love and cherish you for the rest of my days. I will be your wife in spirit and give you all that I am in exchange for your vow of love and commitment."

My entire body tightened. The blood rushing through my veins roared, sending sprinkles of light to cast across my vision.

"Amber."

"Take me. Make love to me. I'm giving myself to you. I don't want to live my life without you in it."

For a moment, I closed my eyes and let the power of her words bathe my soul in a sacred serenity.

When I opened them, I saw my future. Amber. Nothing but happiness and solace for the rest of my days. She'd chosen me. Her faith was now in me, and I'd spend my days attempting to be worthy of her sacrifice.

I stood up and walked over to my coat. I pulled out the tiny box that held the item I'd purchased earlier in the day. Her expression was one of curiosity until I came back over and grabbed her hand, pulling her to a seated position on the bed.

"Dash..." Her voice cracked when I got down on one knee in front of her.

"Amber St. James, you have shown me true love exists. Before you, I didn't believe it was possible. I swore I'd never succumb to the propaganda. You have proven to me that with the right person, your soul mate, the individual God intended as your partner comes along, you hold on with everything you have. This is me, holding onto you, forever."

More tears fell down her cheeks. I held out the small box and opened it. Inside was a single thin platinum band. No diamonds. Our love was not flashy or for others to gush over. This was for us. Amber and Dash. A commitment beyond tradition. She gasped into her hand.

I pulled the ring out of its velvet mooring and held it up to her. "On the inside I've had an inscription added."

With a shaky hand she took the ring between two of her delicate fingers. She swallowed, read the inside, and closed her eyes. Inscribed on the inside of the ring was my truth.

My path to enlightenment.

I watched in awe as her cheeks pinked and a rosy blush stole across her face. A serene smile slipped across her lips before she blinked the remaining tears from her eyes.

"You're my path to enlightenment, too," Amber whispered as if the room alone could listen in, but this, these words were just for me to hear.

"Marry me, Amber."

Her nose scrunched in that cute way I adored. "But, you don't believe in marriage."

I slipped the ring on her thin finger. "I believe in us, and more than that, you're worth the risk. Our love is worth the risk."

AMBER

Our wedding day was the most incredible day of my life. To my grandparents' dismay, it was not held in our Catholic church nor presided over by Father McDowell because Dash was not Catholic. However, Father did attend and granted us his blessings for a long and happy life together. That alone was enough for me. Not for my papa, but he'd get over it. He didn't like that I was getting married at twenty-three to a man I'd known for less than a year. Technically, we'd met and married within nine months.

Our wedding was held at Grace Cathedral, a church that allowed nondenominational ceremonies, in San Francisco. We held ours on the outdoor paved labyrinth on St. Patrick's Day, in the middle of the week. I wore a simple sparkling white lace and satin tea-length gown. The sweetheart neckline accentuated my feminine attributes along with the middle that nipped in perfectly at the waist. Simple satin ballet flats adorned my feet, and my hair was pulled back on one side with a diamond-encrusted comb. It was an heirloom that my grandmother gave me. It had been passed down throughout generations in the St. James family, and I couldn't have been more honored to wear it, knowing that one day I would pass it down to my future daughter or daughter-in-law.

The outdoor space was rich with nature, so we did very little to add decoration to what God had already provided with His organic touch. Chairs had been set around the labyrinth in a circular shape so that all witnesses could have an unobstructed view of the ceremony. An interfaith pastor stood at the center of the labyrinth. A very small number of witnesses including my grandparents, Genevieve's family, Dash's parents, the O'Briens, a handful of the yoga instructors at Lotus House, and of course, the owners Crystal and Jewel, were all present to witness our union.

Instead of walking down the aisle, I met Dash at the start

of the paved maze. He was stunning in a simple khaki suit, pristine white dress shirt, and a cream-colored tie. His hair was styled enough that the top was tamed but not so much that I didn't want to run my fingers through it and hang on while I kissed him.

In true Dash style, when we met at the entrance to the labyrinth, he gave me an out.

"Now's the time to fly away, little bird." He smiled. A hint of fear was etched across his amber gaze.

I gripped onto his hands, puffed my chest with pride, and nestled to his side. "Flying is easy. Staying grounded is more challenging. Are you ready to walk our path?"

"To enlightenment?" His grin was everything I would remember about this day and then some. Being looked at with complete and total love and adoration is not something I would easily forget.

"Every day I'm enlightened by you," he said and lifted my hand, kissed the top, and together, we took the path.

The journey of walking the labyrinth symbolized three stages.

The first phase was a releasing. Simultaneously, we shed our tumultuous thoughts, quieted the mind, and let go of the details of our lives.

At the center, we reached the illumination or receiving phase. That is where we stopped, met our pastor, and said our vows officially, in front of God and our witnesses. Afterward, Dash kissed the daylights out of me, sealing our union as husband and wife.

We finished the last half of the maze hand in hand where we joined with our higher power, in our case God above, so that His love would heal, bless, and empower our union.

At the end of our ceremony, we were greeted with hugs and kisses from our friends and family. We took some pictures in the gardens and promised to meet at our favorite little restaurant in the hills where Dash's parents had secured the entire small French restaurant for our reception.

Before we left the cathedral, Dash tugged me over to a quiet indoor walkway that also included a labyrinth. The light streamed through myriad intricate stained glass windows. Stone walls and vaulted ceilings gave the space a heightened, cavernous intensity. Dash toed off his shoes, and I followed suit, wiggling my bare feet and pink-painted toes against the cold stone floor.

"This path is for us. It's mirrored. You walk from that side, and I'll walk from this side. We meet in the middle."

"Okay." I took the strides needed to start on my side.

With our eyes focused on one another we slowly made our first steps. The symbolism of watching where I was going, following the path's curving lanes but knowing at the middle it would lead to my greatest desire, was soul defining. I wanted to run to him, but something in his eyes prevented me from doing so. This was important to him. To us. And while I weaved through each lane, keeping a steady pace, it dawned on me. Dash and I were individuals. Two people with a mirrored path. And at the center, we would always meet, coming back to one another. No matter where we started or ended, we could backtrack and follow the other, or walk ahead, but throughout the path, it would always lead us to the center of our universe.

Our love.

When we got to the middle, I went into his arms, placed my chin on his chest, and looked up at the man I'd spend my forever with. "I understand."

His smile stole my breath.

"Even when we're working toward our own goals, individual desires, our paths mirror one another so that our happiness is in the center where we come together as one," he whispered and then kissed me. It was our second kiss as husband and wife but here, alone, we fully committed to one another privately, without the hoopla of a ceremony or witnesses. Aside from the good Lord above, this would only ever be ours.

"I love you, Dash Alexander."

"I love you, Amber Alexander."

EPILOGUE

AMBER

Cool air swept up my legs as Dash lifted me over the threshold of our loft home. Tomorrow, we'd leave for our honeymoon in Cancun, but tonight would be our first night as husband and wife in our home. I'd already moved in a few months ago. Dash was unwilling for us to be separated after the day he proposed. I gave him that compromise because I knew he needed the reassurance. And in turn, he gave me my vow. Tonight, I would give him all of me.

The entire loft was lit up with vanilla-scented candles. Speckled lights flickered from various places throughout the space. Dark red rose petals lay in a heart shape on what would now be our marital bed. Champagne sat in an ice bucket on the dresser next to the bed, alongside fresh fruit and the top tier of our small wedding cake. I'm certain Genevieve was to thank for the set up. And as a wedding present, Genevieve and Trent announced that they were engaged and planned on marrying in the fall after the next baseball season. Two best friends, married and living happily ever after with our mates. The stuff of fairy tales, for sure.

Dash walked all the way to the area we considered our bedroom, even if there weren't any walls. He let my legs go, and I slid down his muscled frame. My husband was something to behold in a suit on a normal day, and on this day, I basked in it.

"Did I tell you today how handsome you are?" I ran my hands from his shoulders to his cuffs.

He grinned and looped his arms low on my waist. "No, but I kind of got the hint with how many times you trailed your fingers down the arm and back of my suit. Once, you even copped a feel of my ass."

I huffed. "I did not!"

"You so did! In front of my mom and Father McDowell and everything. Frankly, I was surprised myself."

"You are lying!" I smacked at his chest, but he caught me and pulled me into a kiss. It started sweet and simple but turned ravenous, his hands roaming my body, hot with intent.

"Okay, I was kidding," he admitted when he pulled back.

I giggled. "You're forgiven."

He glanced over at the champagne and treats. "How about a drink?"

"That would be lovely. I'm just going to go inside the bathroom and hang up my wedding dress."

One of his eyebrows rose into a point. "Please, Mrs. Alexander, by all means." He lifted a hand toward the bathroom, the only space in the entire loft that had official walls.

I swayed my hips, allowing my tea-length wedding gown to sweep from side to side like the ringing of a bell.

Once in the bathroom, I unzipped the bag I'd hung earlier that held my wedding night lingerie. A full-length white satin slip nightgown gleamed under the track lighting above. The front had the same sweetheart neckline my wedding gown did, but the back had a severe V that highlighted the dimples above my bum. A prickle of excitement whispered across my skin as I slipped it on, thinking about how Dash loved to kiss those two indents. There were slits up each side that went almost to the hip. Under the lingerie, I wore nothing. Panties would just get in the way.

My heart pounded like a base drum against my chest. Tonight was the night we'd finally make love as man and wife. Waiting to give Dash my virginity as his wife had been the hardest decision of my life. Especially after I moved into the loft and we'd planned our wedding. I had offered him entry, in light of the platinum band I wore on my finger, but he wouldn't have it. In truth, it made me love him more because not only was he worried about my faith, he didn't want me to have any regrets. I'd spent hours over the past few months promising him "no regrets." In fact, it had become my motto for the better part of those same few months, but to no avail. His response was always the same.

"When you're my wife legally, I'll accept that gift."

Well, tonight I would lie down with my husband. Shivers rippled down my spine, and my gut twisted into knots. I wasn't sure if it was anticipation or anxiety controlling my movements as I removed my grandmother's heirloom from my hair and set it on the vanity with shaky fingers.

"Come on, Amber. This is Dash. Your husband. You have

nothing to fear. You've wanted this for months. Go out there in your sexy nightie and make love to your husband," I said to my reflection in the mirror.

Get on with it.

I pinched my cheeks and licked my lips. My hair flowed in long, dark waves over my shoulders and my eyes were still a startling green from Genevieve's makeup job. This would have to do. Shifting to the side, I checked out the nightgown. It framed my breasts perfectly. The nipped-in waist gave me the hourglass shape I didn't normally have with my athletic build, but the slits up the legs did wonders for my body. Dash liked my long legs. Thank God my husband was tall because at five ten, I needed a man like Dash to make me feel petite. And he did. But then again, that could have been because his personality and energy were so large and in charge that things in the general vicinity around him seemed to get smaller.

A soft knock broke the silence of the room. "Hey, you okay in there?"

I chuckled, gripped the handle, and pulled the door open in a whoosh.

"Oh, shoot." Dash stepped back, surprised at my action. He balanced himself against the doorjamb and stopped moving. Nothing but his chest rose and fell with his labored breathing. Then his gaze took in my nightgown from top to toe and back up. Then he did it again. I could almost feel his eyes caressing each dip of the satin over a delicate angle as he looked his fill.

"Amber, my God...you're...I'm..." He continued to stare, his eyes never staying on one spot for long. "I'm the luckiest man in the world. Your beauty...your soul, my love, it captivates me."

I smiled and walked toward him. I removed the champagne glass from his hand. "Does that mean you like the gown?"

He nodded, and his voice rumbled when he spoke. "I like the gown. I like what's in the gown. I'd like to have what's in the gown."

Ah, there was my possessive Dash making an appearance. I chuckled, reached for the other filled glass on the dresser, and handed it to him. "A toast."

Dash raised his glass next to mine hovering within the two-foot space separating us. "What should we toast to? I've already gotten everything I've ever wanted standing right in front of me. You."

"You haven't had *all* of me." I smirked.

"Yes. That ends tonight." His eyes were ablaze with desire and lust. He didn't even try to hide it. I glowed under his scrutiny, feeling like a goddess.

"God willing," I whispered.

"Oh, God gave me express permission the second I made you my wife." He bit down on his bottom lip, and his gaze roved over me once more. My nipples puckered under his inspection.

"Screw the toast. Drink. Now." He tipped his head back and swallowed the entire drink.

I sipped mine, but the glass and its contents magically disappeared. Dash's hands appeared around my form, and my back hit the bathroom door.

"Ooomph," I muttered right before his lips descended. He was gluttonous, voracious in his need to control the kiss.

His tongue explored my mouth, licking feverishly. One of his hands cupped my cheek and restrained all my movements. He had me pinned against the door, his body a wall of flames. I gripped the broad muscles of his back and took his kiss, relishing in the connection and allowing the fire to consume me.

Dash ran a hand from my waist to my breast, squeezing and molding the weighted globe in his hand. I sighed and mewled when his thumb rubbed circles over the furled tip. My husband ripped his mouth away from mine on a rough intake of air, before running his mouth down my neck. He licked a long line from my clavicle, up to my ear, where he nibbled on the edge.

"There will be no part of you untouched or untasted. I'm going to consume you, little bird, until there is no more you and me. Only us."

I moaned and then I begged. "Please."

DASH

Hearing Amber's plea broke every ounce of restraint I had left. I wanted in my wife, but I also wanted it to be the single most explosive experience of her life. A woman only lost her virginity once. I cherished and honored Amber for choosing to give it to me.

I still couldn't believe I was somebody's husband. The idea had been so archaic and unnecessary to me nine months ago. Now, with my whole world plastered against the wall, begging me to make love to her, I realized how insane I'd been. Getting married legally wasn't a death knell. It was a new beginning. The start of Mr. and Mrs. Dash Alexander. I'd forever thank my wife for showing me the possibilities, and I planned to start by giving her a night she'd never forget.

Sliding my hands over her heaving breasts, I tweaked each succulent tip through the satin, adding to the sensations. Her eyes closed, and her mouth opened on a quick intake of air. "These are only for me now," I said, allowing my dominating side to play in the night's activities.

She sighed. "Yes."

I leaned forward and pushed both breasts up until they were bulging and stretching the fabric to its limits. With a flick of the thumbs, the fabric slid down and two sandy-colored nipples popped out. Beautiful. I tongued both tips mercilessly, enjoying how Amber's body twitched against the door. Her elbows knocked against the wood, and her head turned from side to side. Her breath caught, the telltale sign that my love was going to come.

"Dash..." Her pelvis moved restlessly against mine.

"Your orgasms are only for me now, too."

"Oh God, yes." Her body stiffened when I bit down on one tight pcak. "Dash!" shc cried out as the spasms took her.

I hummed against her tips, letting her come down from her small high. That one was only the first of many I'd planned on giving her tonight.

Amber gripped my suit jacket and shoved it to the floor. Her eyes opened and the pupils were so dark, I could barely see the stunning green they normally were. She was so far gone with lust, I only needed to finger her, and she'd go off again like a rocket. Thank the Lord my love was so responsive. Her sacral chakra was primed and ready for me all the time. Driven by love.

Her fingers grappled with the tie, and in a far more forceful move than I expected, she ripped it up and over my head to the floor. The shirt came off my body so fast I wasn't sure if she had magical powers. Then again, I was lost in her eyes. The hungry gaze owned me, and I never wanted to be free.

Helping her along, I tugged off my belt, undid my pants, and let them fall to the floor. Amber dropped to her knees, curled her fingers around the waistband of my boxer briefs, and lifted them down and over my straining erection.

"So if I'm all yours, does this mean this is for only me now?" Her sensual smirk made my dick twitch.

"Absolutely." I cupped her cheek, running my thumb over her sexy-as-sin lips. I dipped my finger into her mouth. She responded, never blinking, just sucking the digit before biting down just enough to spark a minimal amount of pain.

Continuing her effort to get me completely naked, she removed my pants the rest of the way and pulled off my socks. Then her delicate hands curled around the back of my legs and slid up to cup and knead my ass. She licked her lips and then flattened her tongue. Starting at the root, she licked the entire length of my cock, wetting every inch until she flicked the tip and took my length down her hot little throat.

I gripped her hair and fucked her mouth. She loved it when I took her mouth hard. Proved to me that my little bird would take my cock in her pussy the same way. Tonight, I'd find out.

"Enough." I gripped the roots of her hair and pulled her up far enough so that my dick slipped wetly out of her mouth. She kissed just the tip and blinked up at me. My own personal celestial being. Amber could turn a Buddhist monk a decade into a vow of celibacy, into a begging, pleading, sex-driven fool.

I leaned forward and helped my wife up from her kneeling position. Then I lifted her up in a princess hold that made her giggle like a schoolgirl. Treating her as if she were a porcelain doll, I laid my precious bounty on top of the bed. The rose petals scattered around her, their flowery scent not even coming close to masking the scent of her musky arousal.

I slid both of my hands up her silky, bare legs. Her satin gown parted beautifully. My surprise came when I got to her pussy and found it bare and glistening. "No panties, wife?"

"Did you want panties?" Her eyebrow quirked up.

"No, I want to taste my wife's wet pussy."

She grinned. "Consider it a wedding gift then."

"Oh I do, consider this..." I pressed her legs open wide so that I could fully view the most vulnerable part of her. A part that no man other than me has seen or will ever see. I ran my finger over her slit and twirled it around her hot little button of need. "This is my favorite gift."

She hummed and arched her hips when I inserted a finger into her heat. Christ, she was so tight. Just my finger felt hugged in her viselike grip. I'd planned on taking her now, especially after she'd sucked me so good, I could have easily come in her mouth. Now, seeing the heart of her so wet and greedy, my dick throbbed at the desire to pound home.

Taking my time, I inserted a second finger, scissoring inside her to make room for what I knew was going to be an intense joining. Her arousal coated my fingers when I lifted up and found her sacred spot.

"Oh, oh, God. Dash, come in me." She widened her legs and fucked my hand.

I almost lost it when her hands moved to her breasts and she cupped and lifted each one. Her nightgown strings had fallen delicately down her shoulders allowing her breasts freedom. Each sandy tip had turned an almost raspberry hue as she plucked and pulled at them.

Wanting her too far gone to even know her new name, I moved to her wet center, licked around her clit, and then sucked her dry.

She cried out, her hands going to my hair, her hips jerking against my face. I massaged her G-spot repeatedly, until her second orgasm rolled into a third and finally a fourth. She was so wet, there was no way my entry would be too painful.

Removing my hands, I allowed myself a minute of licking up her honey. When my woman came, it tasted like the purest nectar. I could so easily stay between her legs and spend the evening gorging on her sopping essence. Something to look forward to on the honeymoon. She sighed as I kissed and sucked, making sure to run my tongue deep into her slit, soothing the walls I could reach within her.

Tasting her, eating her, feeling her around me made my cock hard as steel. Copious amounts of precum leaked from the tip. I straddled her and rubbed the liquid around the crown.

She watched in fascination as I slid my hand up and down the length. "Are you ready for all of me?" I asked, needing her to give me permission this one last time to seal all that had crossed our paths and our lives before us. This was the single final hurdle between us becoming husband and wife. She had to choose to give it freely.

Her fingers bunched at her waist around the white satin. She shimmied it up and over her body and let it fall behind her. We were lying sideways on the bed completely bare to the other.

"Make love to me, Dash," she requested.

That single phrase broke any further resistance I had. Shifting her up the bed, I placed one forearm next to her head and took her mouth. Her fingers threaded through my hair and held on while I used my legs to spread her. My hips aligned with hers, our most private parts kissing hotly in greeting.

Adjusting my pelvis, I ran one hand down her body, over her heart, breast, and rib cage and down to her hip. I squeezed her lightly and then let go to take hold of my cock. I notched it at her slippery center.

"I love you, Amber. My little bird. My love. My life," I said before wrapping my hand around her ass and plunging home.

She cried out, her entire body arching at the intrusion. I covered her cry with a kiss, muffling it while I shifted my hips back and thrust home again, seating fully inside her. Lights and stars streamed across my vision. Our bodies were finally merged in every way. I had to grit my teeth not to come inside her heat the second she took all of me. Embedded completely, I stilled, kissed her, taking long sips of her mouth. Rubbing my hands all over her body until the tension loosened.

"Are you okay?" I asked between kisses.

"Yeah. I'll be really good when you move. I need to feel you move." She ran her hands over my back and to my ass where she clenched not only her groin but also my ass, forcing me deeper.

"Amber, holy hell," I grated into her mouth.

She laughed, swiveled her hips, and lifted them up and down, almost as if she was liquefying and softening around me. The tightness loosened just barely, which meant to me my wife was more comfortable and ready for more.

Curling a hand around her breast, I lifted my hips up, pinched her nipple, and thrust harder.

"Yes," she hissed.

With every stroke, I took her a bit farther until her hips were moving in tandem with mine, and I lost all sense of time and space. I was balls deep in my wife, and it was the happiest place in the world.

"More, please more," she pleaded.

Who was I to deny such a perfect creature? I stirred my cock inside of her, pushed up on my knees, and lifted her ass into the air. I pulled back and sank home. I pushed her knees high and back so that I could watch my cock drive into her over and over again. The most beautiful sight, second only to my wife's smile.

"Dash, baby, I'm going to come," she warned.

Fuck yes, she was going to come. And more than once. I used my thumbs to open her pussy lips farther and sank so deep I ground my teeth against the viselike draw.

She screamed. Actually screamed through her orgasm. When it started to wane, I took my thumb and massaged her clit. The little hood that covered it was all the way pulled back. My nostrils flared in male carnal pride. My wife was lost to the pleasure only I could give her.

"Dash, Dash, Dash, Dash," Amber said my name like a prayer.

I couldn't take any more. My balls lifted high, a tingle set deep in my groin, and my spine jackknifed straight. I fell over my wife, curled one hand under her back to lock down around her shoulder, and the other on her firm ass.

"Hold on, baby. This one's for me."

"Yes...please. Give me all of you," she begged.

Something in me split apart. I slid my rock-hard cock out of my wife, firmed up my grip, and slammed home. Her legs locked around my waist, and she moved with me. Like an animal, she clamped around my body and took everything I could possibly give her, and I wasn't gentle. She demanded more and more, and I gave it to her.

My entire body cramped with the desire to let go, but I

kept holding on. Not wanting this moment to end. I'd never had anything like it before. I was fucking my wife. Making love to her in every way possible. Mind, body, spirit. Our souls were intertwining for eternity.

"I love you," she whispered as her body fastened around mine and convulsed.

I had no choice but to follow her into nirvana. Hell, I'd follow Amber anywhere.

"I love you." I took her mouth and tasted enlightenment.

At the height of our orgasm, we fell together. My essence shot up my cock and into her heat. Her center received and welcomed me in all things. The room disappeared, our foreheads touched, and all of our seven chakras fell into alignment. Rainbow colors drifted across my mind. Time ceased to exist. Amber and Dash were gone, only our souls danced as one in a divine state of combined Tantric meditation.

Together we floated on gossamer wings in heavenly bliss. The perfect ending to our wedding night.

AMBER

Sometime early morning I woke, Dash still embedded inside me, my leg slung up and over his hip. Our bodies were a sticky mess, but I didn't care. I'd dreamed of him, in between the times he woke me to take me to new heights. My body was deliciously sore, everywhere. After we'd made love the first time and the two of us passed out, he awakened me again and took me from behind. Then again later, he introduced me to riding him. I loved that. Being in control sexually was new to me, and I looked forward to experimenting with my husband in the future. Dash was well versed in the act of lovemaking, but in every position, he seemed just as taken as I was with our connection, with the intensity that the added layer of true love gave the physical act.

I stretched my toes and relished each twinge of pain. I'm certain if I looked at my body under the sheet, it would be marred with small reminders of our intensity. I glanced down at Dash, noted the purple bite mark on his shoulder. There was a matching one on the shallow dip near his hip that led to his penis. That spot on his body made me stupid with lust. And now that I could freely touch, kiss, lick, nip...I was ravenous. And intertwined in our marital bed, with my husband still wrapped around me, I was free to do so. Any time I wanted.

Briefly, I thought back to last night when he'd pushed into me that very first time. The pinch of pain was nothing compared to the intensity of being filled to the brim with the man I loved. It made me so glad I had never given that to any other man. Dash would always be my one and only in all things. Even though he'd experienced the act of coitus before, I don't know that he'd ever truly made love to a woman. So in that way, our marriage, our first time together, was a first for him, too.

Did not waiting make it less important for other couples who experienced sex earlier in their youth, tasted the fruits of other mates, but came together on their wedding night? I didn't know that it did. Because of all the physical things we'd done together, knowing our souls had committed in every way possible was the true testament to our sacred beginning. Together, as man and wife, we found our forever, and I believed no matter what experiences a person's had, sexually or otherwise, each individual will know when they've found forever with their mate. I thought that was God's way of officially blessing a couple. A sensation so acute would come over that person, and an impression of complete peace would encompass the union.

That was when a sacred serenity was found.

THE END

Want more of the Lotus House clan?
Continue on with Mila Mercado and Atlas Powers's story in:

Divine Desire
Book Three in the *Lotus House Series.*
Coming December 27th 2016

EXCERPT FROM *DIVINE DESIRE*
A LOTUS HOUSE NOVEL (BOOK #3)

I felt her presence before I saw her. Somehow the candlelit room brightened just a hair, as if the crackling light followed her essence through the rustle of air as she moved. Her eyes didn't meet mine as she laid out a mat in the front right corner of the class. A few other patrons laid out their mats and continued to the back of the room. I'd closed the thick curtains that separated the hallway and the class. Usually the owners wanted the curtains open unless it was a private session or one of Dash's Tantric couples workshops. However, for today's class, privacy was of the utmost importance.

The entire room came alive with new clients. Most of them women. I had to admit, going with Dash to walk the Berkeley campus and promote the class in person, worked like a charm. We'd secured so many phone numbers through winks and smiles, I felt like I was carrying around a pocketful of confetti when the night was over and I'd tossed them all into the circular waste bin. Amber, Dash's wife, had frowned when he'd told her about our day. Then she offered to take the class in support of her husband's friend.

At her suggestion, I'd laughed my ass off. I'd known Dash Alexander since high school and the only time he lost his cool was when Amber had told him she was a virgin about six months ago when they were dating. That was the only time I'd seen him react like a lovesick fool. This time was different. He was worse. Positively rife with anger he didn't know how to handle. In the end, he'd straight forbidden his wife from taking my class.

I tried to act affronted, but I got it. Before him, his wife had been untouched. He owned her body, mind, and soul. Men like me could only dream of being so lucky. But with my daytime schedule and trying to make the music thing work at night, I'd barely had time for a quick roll in the hay with a willing groupie I'd met at the local bar, let alone a lifelong commitment. Amber though, she'd been pissed. So upset I had to leave in order for him to grovel in peace.

Walking around the room, I made sure that everything was set up just so. I'd met most of the clients outside so that they could sign the required forms not holding the yoga center liable for anything they deemed inappropriate. From what I understood, none of the paperwork would hold up in court, but I liked to have something to deter legal action. Not that I expected anything to happen. At first, everyone would look down, up at the ceiling, or only at themselves and avoid all eye contact. Then they'd get into the poses, focus their attention within, and it would just be a regular yoga class.

Unfortunately for me, there was a divine cinnamon-colored, pint-sized goddess that currently held all my focus. I couldn't wait to drop the bomb on her. I wondered how long it would take her to roll up her mat and walk out of the class. That sass was hard to contain. My guess, two point five seconds. Testing the theory was going to be a blast.

Out of the corner of my eye, I noticed people were starting to disrobe. I checked the clock, went over to the door, made sure there weren't any stragglers chatting outside that needed to get in, and then shut and locked the door. Mila narrowed her eyelids and tilted her head, her gaze disapproving of the action.

I walked over to her and was about to welcome her when her scathing tone stopped me short.

"What are you doing locking the door? That's against the rules."

"Not when it locks from the inside. Any patron can easily unlock it and leave, not to mention the push doors for the fire exits. I don't want anyone else coming in mid-class. It would be inappropriate and incredibly disruptive."

She jerked her head back. "How so? You get paid for any additional late comers."

I smiled. "You'll see."

Mila's caramel-colored eyes blazed a yellowish burst of color and a rosy hue flushed across her high, wide cheekbones. I'd have very much liked to feel that warmth against my fingertips while caressing face.

Wow. Irritation looked damn fine on her.

"Class, we're about to begin. You know what to do," I said loud enough for the room to hear.

She tapped her foot and squinted. "Is that how you start a class? You really should welcome them, introduce yourself."

Know-it-all.

I chuckled behind my hand. Boy, was she going to eat crow. "Oh, I have. Outside when I was having them sign their waivers." I watched in anticipation as her mouth opened and her eyes widened in alarm.

"Waiver for what?"

"So we don't get sued for sexual harassment, public indecency, or any of the other mumbo jumbo things people have against anything remotely profane."

She pursed her lips. "I'm sorry, I'm not following."

I grinned, hooked my hands into my loose tank top, and pulled it over my head.

Mila gasped and licked her lips when my chest came into full view. Oh yeah. My heart started thumping, and I clenched my hands into fists. Seeing her sweet lips form an O-shape... God! I wanted so badly to bite into her, but the timing had to be just right.

"Mila, take off your clothes." My voice was thick with a desire I couldn't bear to hide. Not from her. Not with her standing in front of me looking like God's gift to mankind.

"Excuse me?" Even straining with the question, her own tone was low and sultry.

"Look around." I held out my arms as if I was displaying a Thanksgiving feast, not a class full of yogis.

"Oh my God." She lifted her hand over her mouth while her eyes seemed to take in each body in the room. "What are you teaching?"

I looked into her pretty brown eyes, grinned, and then pushed down my yoga pants and boxer briefs in one shove.

Mila didn't check me out by starting at my feet while casually taking in my form. Oh, no, she went straight for the gusto, pretty browns zeroing in on my bare cock. I could almost feel the heat of her searing through me. Sweat built along my skin and pooled at the dip in my lower back. I clenched my jaw and stood silent, allowing her the time to look her fill, hoping I was affecting her the same way she was me.

The gasp that came from her pretty mouth that time sounded more like a choked gurgle.

"Naked yoga."

Continue reading in:

Divine Desire
A Lotus House Novel: Book Three
Coming December 27th 2016

ALSO BY AUDREY CARLAN

The Calendar Girl Series

January (Book 1) July (Book 7)
February (Book 2) August (Book 8)
March (Book 3) September (Book 9)
April (Book 4) October (Book 10)
May (Book 5) November (Book 11)
June (Book 6) December (Book 12)

The Calendar Girl Anthologies

Volume One (Jan-Mar) Volume Three (Jul-Sep)
Volume Two (Apr-Jun) Volume Four (Oct Dec)

The Falling Series

Angel Falling
London Falling
Justice Falling

The Trinity Trilogy

Body (Book 1)
Mind (Book 2)
Soul (Book 3)

The Lotus House Series

Resisting Roots (Book 1)
Sacred Serenity (Book 2)
Divine Desire (Book 3)
Coming December 27th 2016

ACKNOWLEDGMENTS

To **Debbie Wolski** my yoga guru for teaching me everything I know about the art of yoga. I can only dream that this book will help give my readers a positive connection to the practice so that they seek out their own experience. Thank you for always opening your doors and inviting me into your world. I adore you.

To my husband, **Eric**, for sticking by my side through fifteen months of yoga instructor school, months of lost weekends writing and learning more about my connection to the beauty that is yoga, and loving this new facet of me as you have for the last nineteen years. I feel like every day I love you more than I did the day before and go to bed with the knowledge that I will again wake with even more love filling my life.

To my editor, **Ekatarina Sayanova** with **Red Quill Editing, LLC**...your knowledge knows no boundaries. Even in this world, your contributions are priceless and you are the yin to my yang, always.

Roxie Sofia, thank you for adding your brand of sparkle to the editing process and shining up Amber and Dash's story so that the world would see them as they should be. Beautiful.

To my extraordinarily talented personal assistant **Heather White (aka PA Goddess),** you will forever be a sexy new wedge heel, a shocking statement piece from Kate Spade, a rolled up skinny jean, and the woman that helps me present who I am to the world. Thank you for your unending support and love.

Jeananna Goodall, Ginelle Blanch, Anita Shofner: Thank you for being incredible betas but more than that, even better friends.

To the Audrey Carlan Street Team of wicked hot Angels: Together we change the world. One book at a time. BESOS-4-LIFE, lovely ladies.

ABOUT AUDREY CARLAN

Audrey Carlan is a #1 *New York Times, USA Today,* and *Wall Street Journal* bestselling author. She writes wicked hot love stories that are designed to give the reader a romantic experience that's sexy, sweet, and so hot your ereader might melt. Some of her works include the wildly successful Calendar Girl Serial, Falling Series, and the Trinity Trilogy.

She lives in the California Valley where she enjoys her two children and the love of her life. When she's not writing, you can find her teaching yoga, sipping wine with her "soul sisters" or with her nose stuck in a wicked hot romance novel.

Any and all feedback is greatly appreciated and feeds the soul. You can contact Audrey below:

E-mail: carlan.audrey@gmail.com
Facebook: facebook.com/AudreyCarlan
Website: www.audreycarlan.com

ALSO BY AUDREY CARLAN

The Calendar Girl Series

ALSO BY AUDREY CARLAN

The Trinity Trilogy

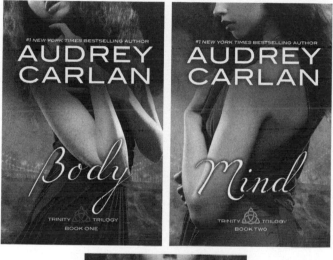

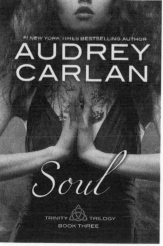

ALSO BY AUDREY CARLAN

The Falling Series

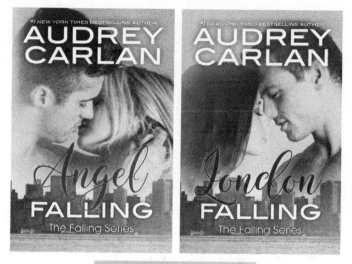

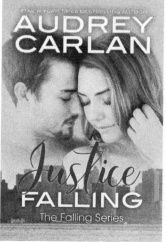